THE COMPLETE SERIES

ALIEN ADORATION
ALIEN ADMIRER
ALIEN ATTRACTION
PLUS TWO BONUS SHORT STORIES

JESSICA E. SUBJECT

DEDICATION

To everyone who believes we are not alone in the universe.

CONTENTS

ACKNOWLEDGMENTS

There are so many people involved in taking any story from a blank page to a published book. Though writing the first draft may be a solitary endeavor, the process after that is not.

To begin, I want to thank my local peeps, Deb, Liz, Mel, Holly, Arlene, Zoe, Stacy, and all the rest, for their friendship encouragement, and advice.

And a HUGE thank you to my former and current critique partners, Layna Pimentel, DL Jackson, Zee Monodee, and Rebecca Royce, for taking the time to read over my stories to tell me what works, and especially what doesn't work. I have learned so much from all of them, and they are great friends.

My editors, Valerie Mann and Kate Richards.... I can't say enough how much I love working with them. Every set of edits is a learning experience, and a pleasure.

Fantasia Frog Designs creates fabulous covers that I can stare at for hours. She always seems to capture the essence of my stories perfectly.

Shout outs and thanks go to my Reader Group members; Kacey, Tawania, Layna, Diane, Bj, Taryn, Shiela, Linda, Beckey, Carly, Tina, Olivia, Nancy, Winter, Giedre, Iris, Ameliah, Kathleen, Kelsey, Susan, Arc, Jo Carol, Lisa, Zee, Heather, Kim, JoAnna, Sharon, Alice, Sheri, Nancy, Shelly, Shannon, Valoria, Shan, Bonnie, Michelle, Christina, Jeanette, Ilona, Michelle, Joan, Tori, Elizabeth, and Marian. Their support means the world to me.

I can't forget my family in all of this. Without their support I wouldn't be able to do what I do. Thank you to my daughter who has her own cover collection, and keeps my son occupied while I'm trying to work. And thank you to my son who knows me by my author name and by "Mom", and for just being a kid.

Words cannot express how grateful I am to my husband for allowing me to live out this dream. He is my biggest supporter, my inspiration, and also a promoter of my books even though I don't ask him to. I'm sure he gets some strange looks when people see my covers on his toolbox.

ALIEN ADORATION

CHAPTER ONE

A car door slammed. Rachel flicked her eyes open, a flush of adrenaline racing through her body. *Not again.*

Even though common sense told her to go back to sleep, she slid off the bed and peered out the window. The driver of the red Camaro squealed the tires, tearing off down the street.

Rachel cursed the woman with long, bleached-blonde hair, tiny waist, and the biggest breasts she'd ever seen. Why did her neighbor go for women like that?

Stilettos and sports cars? They were all the same, reminding her she didn't stand a chance with her neighbor.

Luke Jones.

Whether he wore his work clothes of jeans and a T-shirt that clung tight against his muscular body, or leather pants and a jacket when riding his motorcycle, he defined sexy, making every other guy seem drab. She licked her lips, thinking of him, the hero in every single one of her fantasies since moving in two years earlier, and obviously as the leading man for so many other women, bringing home several each month. Though not one of them ever returned for a second visit. They all left with a commotion, waking her in the middle of the night.

What she wouldn't give to experience an evening with him. She rolled her eyes. *No, never going to happen.* Putting out on the first date led to one night stands. And sex on the second night didn't hold much promise for a long-term relationship, based on her past experiences. One month of seeing Dirk Chambers, the grocery store manager, and she still hadn't slept with him. Maybe if he didn't wind up drunk on every single date, she might consider it. Though his suggestions of making out in the bathroom of the local pub, and in the back seat of his car did not appeal to her. So not how she wanted their first time together to be. Those places were fine for the second round of sex and beyond. But, for the first time, she wanted romance, to be swept off her feet.

She studied the water stain on her ceiling, visible by the light of the street lamp. Yet another thing she couldn't afford to fix. If a man offered to fix her roof for her, she'd find that romantic, and break her first date rule. But did any guy know the meaning of romance anymore? Surely no one from Hanton. The small town boasted the highest rate of divorce in the province due to extramarital affairs. No one in town got married anymore, expecting all vows to be broken within the first year. Those of her classmates who'd been lucky enough to move away bragged of their success in both their marriages and their careers.

Rachel hadn't had the chance to move away. Thankfully, the view next door didn't hurt. Though he would never be more than a fantasy. She wanted a relationship, not a one-night stand.

Ready to return to her bed, she squinted at the glow of moonlight reflecting off her neighbor's front screen door. She sucked in a breath, hoping to catch a glimpse of him to use as a happy thought before going to sleep.

He walked out to his *LJ Construction* truck in only flannel pants hanging low on his hips. Opening the door, he ducked inside, grabbing…something. Then he slammed the door behind him. The view provided plenty of inspiration for her fantasies, his back muscles just as appealing as his washboard abs. Her pussy clenched, and she craved the toy she hid in her nightstand drawer.

Luke reached for the handle, but turned around before he opened it. Something above her house caught his attention. An airplane? The moon? No, his focus was on her. *Shit.*

He lifted his hand and waved and without so much as a smile, he returned inside.

Her cheeks burned. God, he'd caught her gawking. Did he think she was spying on him? It's not as if she gaped *into* his home. No one could with every window covered in heavy drapery at all times. It only added to his mysterious appeal.

She yanked her curtains closed and slipped back into bed, pulling the blankets over her head. The first time he noticed her, and she wore battered pajamas, her hair likely looking like a rat's nest. Groaning, she turned onto her side, trying to ignore the queasiness in her stomach. In a couple hours for work, she had to get up for work. And the late night interruption meant an extra large black coffee in the morning, just to stay awake. Closing her eyes, she locked away the images of her neighbor's bare chest for another night.

Luke rubbed the back of his neck. Rachel had seen him, glaring wide-eyed like she expected him to attack. Why did she keep her distance, never say hello? Did she remember him from years ago, or had she woken, disgusted with him because of the loud departure of another of the women he used to try and forget about her?

But he never could get her out of his head. From the moment he'd first met her, she'd implanted herself in his heart. She'd been so kind, so accepting. Now she stared at him from her bedroom, wouldn't even talk to him. Over the years, she must have become afraid of him, of what he was. An alien.

He trudged up the stairs to his room where the red glow from the orb—his only connection to the world he came from—had finally faded. After dinner, he and Marnie had moved to the couch to get more comfortable. Then the light had appeared. And it grew brighter while she tried to seduce him. Even though he imagined his neighbor in her place, he could never give any woman what she wanted. A brick wall always stood between him and his dates. His neighbor. The unattainable woman. And he refused to stop his female companions as they stormed from his house, calling him a tease, among other names.

He flopped onto his bed. They were right. No one could ever replace Rachel in his heart, and he refused to try anymore. Until she told him outright she didn't want him, he would never invite another woman over. But if she decided to accept an invitation to dinner, spend some time with him....

Smiling, he closed his eyes and visualized the possibilities.

Rachel covered her mouth, trying to hide her umpteenth yawn since arriving at work.

"I heard that," her best friend, Christine Shaw, called from the cubicle next to hers. She appeared in front of her desk only seconds later. "Late night?" Her smile seemed to hold some hope. She probably waited for some juicy details to spread around the bank.

"No, the usual twilight awakening." Though she wouldn't tell her friend about the recurring dream that followed. No one needed to know about her delusions of extraterrestrials.

Christine's smile faded. "Oh, another conquest leaving the home of your sexy neighbor. I don't know why you don't grab a piece of that action. I would if I had the chance."

Her cheeks warmed. "I have a boyfriend." But he didn't compare to the man next door. No one could.

"Dirk?" Christine raised her eyebrows. "Yeah, like that's going anywhere. I saw him talking to skanky Jenny Marshall, at the coffee shop this morning."

Rachel clenched her jaw. As if he didn't wait for her. "Jenny works there."

"No." Christine shook her head. "She had today off, and she went up to your boyfriend in her oh-so-flirty way, giggling, and running her hands all over him."

Her stomach clenched and the green-eyed monster took hold. "What did he do?"

"Besides grinning like a friggin' teenager and walking out with a hard-on? Nothing. But it's only a matter of time. This is Hanton. I say dump him before he dumps you, or you find out he's cheating."

She shook with anger, her blood boiling. How could he do this to her? And with Jenny Marshall?

Sure, the relationship wouldn't last forever, but being single again would lead to the entire town trying to set her up with someone else. Far worse than having a boyfriend with a wandering eye.

⁘❦⁘

Luke fumbled with his collar then ran a hand through his damp hair. He felt naked without a ball cap or his helmet. But he remained determined. Tonight was the night he asked Rachel to dinner. And hopefully in a few hours, he would have her in his bed. Waltzing out the door, he caught a flash of red across the ceiling. *Shit.* He was a grown man. Why couldn't he think about sex without the orb freaking out?

He shook it off, anxious to find out how his neighbor felt about him. Stepping off his porch, he glanced over at her house. A little run down, but nothing he couldn't fix. If only she'd talk to him.

Out the door she flew, wearing a white frilly blouse and a super short black skirt. Into the arms of another man. Dirk Chambers, of all people.

Fuck! His resolve deflated. He hadn't seen Dirk at her place in weeks. He thought they'd broken up afte seeing Jenny Marshall go down on him in the grocery store parking lot the other day.

His stomach twisted. He hated living in Hanton, needed to take her away from the town with no morals. Dirk traded groceries for sexual favors. How could Rachel have any interest in a skuzzy guy like him?

The image of her staring at him last night when Marnie left flashed through his mind. Did she think the same of him? How would she know he thought only of her during his dates? His actions were no better. Why had he waited so long? He should have dropped by the first day he moved in, instead of waiting two long years.

He stormed back inside to find the red light flashing around like an angry disco ball. The reaction of the orb fueled his frustration. Like he needed a reminder of his failure. The light grew even brighter. He cracked his knuckles. He had to get out of there. He shucked the button-down shirt and dropped it at the top of the stairs on the way to his room. Grabbing a sleeveless shirt and his reinforced riding jeans, he changed and bounded back down the stairs. He shrugged on his leather jacket and stumbled out the door.

Time to ride. Grasping a key from his pocket, he shoved it into the ignition of his Harley and started the engine. The rumbling underneath him that usually brought him peace only stirred his anger at himself and Dirk. He'd let the slimeball walk into Rachel's life by not acting sooner.

Helmet on, he shuffled the bike backward to turn it around. With one last look next door, he tore out of his driveway and down the street. He had no destination, only the need to vanquish the image of his neighbor with another man from his mind.

He rode on, unable to stop wondering what she was up to with her date. Would he ever have a chance with her? When the first raindrops hit his visor, he checked his watch.

Fuck. Two hours had passed, and he'd failed to rid himself of his frustration. He turned into the nearest parking lot to double back when his head burst with pain. He braked then closed his eyes, willing an end to the agony. With such pressure pounding on his skull, he couldn't drive any farther. But he had to return. Something was wrong with Rachel.

Rachel stepped out of the pub, one hand on Dirk's waist and the other holding his arm around her shoulders. Weaving right then left, he dragged her with him across the rain-slicked parking lot. Why did she think the night would end any different than any other date?

He'd phoned her at the bank earlier in the day to ask her to dinner, helping to rein in her jealousy and get Christine off her back. Seeing him dressed in slacks and a button-down shirt, she hoped she might finally experience the romantic night she longed for. But by the time they'd finished eating, he slurred his words and couldn't focus on anything. And she'd been left with the bill. Just like every other night. Now, she had to drive him home.

As they neared his car, he wobbled away from her, toward the back door. He grasped her hand and yanked her in behind him.

I don't think so. Twisting and jerking away, she slipped on the pavement, falling in the vehicle with him.

"C'mon, baby. It's about time we got down to business."

About time she ditched him was more like it. Hands on his chest, she propped herself up. "Dirk, it's not going to happen tonight. You're drunk. I'll drive you home and walk from your place."

"I don't think so." He grabbed her wrists, spinning over top of her, holding her arms behind her back.

He ran his mouth along her neck, drooling more than kissing.

A shudder ran down her spine. Her dinner threatened to come up, but she swallowed it back down.

"You owe me, Rach. What's it been? Like two weeks?"

Over a month, but who was counting?

"It's about time you put out. I've been patient long enough."

She struggled in his grasp, aiming to free at least an arm to punch him in the face. "I don't owe you anything." And when he sobered up, she would dump his sorry ass. "Now, let me go."

He tightened his grip. How did he have so much strength after knocking back three pitchers of beer?

"I'm going to fuck you tonight whether you agree to it or not."

Um, no. She wiggled even harder, managing to move her knee up enough to slam it into his balls.

"You bitch." He shoved her back, tearing her blouse and yanking it off. "I'm so glad I've been fucking Jenny on the side. I was going to give her up once you put out, but now I don't have to. We're through."

His admission stung like a slap to the face, but not enough to bring tears. Thank goodness all he got off was her shirt. She shimmied out of the back seat, anxious to get away. Far away. So what if she walked home topless in the rain. At least she was free of the leech.

Then she heard the giggles and turned to find an audience at the entrance to the pub, staring and pointing fingers. Yay. Now she would be the talk of the town for a day. Everyone could see her bra, and it happened to be white. She rushed across the parking lot. Her house only a few blocks away, she would rather walk home naked than deal with Dirk again.

A block from the pub, the rain changed from a gentle mist to big fat drops streaming from the sky, soaking her to the bone. Great, just great.

She shivered, wiping the water from her eyes. The walk would only take longer if she couldn't see. Though she'd still make it home, knew the town like the back of her hand.

An engine rumbled behind her. She kept moving, pretending she didn't hear. It could only be Dirk, or some other guy expecting to pick her up. Better to be drenched and alone than have to deal with drunken assholes.

"Need a lift?"

The voice was deep and masculine, one she didn't hear very often, but would recognize anywhere. Luke. Wonderful! He wouldn't talk to her before, but now that she was topless and sopping wet, he noticed her.

She circled slowly to stare at the leather-clad figure sitting atop his motorcycle. The visor of his helmet covered most of his face, leaving only his luscious lips and deep, jutting chin, covered in light stubble, exposed. What would they feel like against her lips? Between her legs? Her body tingled.

"Earth to Rachel. Do you need a lift, or should I leave you here in the pouring rain?"

Oh God, he knew her name. Since they'd never actually talked— she'd only heard him greeting his dates—her name on his lips came as a surprise. "Um, yes, I'd appreciate a ride." On his Harley, and if she was lucky, in his bed. Anywhere. Her romance-first rule didn't apply to him. He'd already seduced her plenty in her dreams.

Remaining on his bike, he yanked a helmet from his saddlebag and held it out to her. "What happened to your pretty blouse?"

Pretty blouse? He'd seen her earlier? "I...." Fluttering rolled through her stomach. "I don't want to talk about it."

She grabbed the helmet from him, fit it over her soaked hair, and buckled the chinstrap. Straddling the seat behind him, she fumbled with her hands, wondering where to place them, no bar behind her to hold on to. Oh, what it would be like to wrap her arms around him, lean against his wide back covered in leather. But what if he didn't want her to touch him?

Luke pushed off from the curb. "I suggest you hold onto me or you're going to fall off."

The bike lurched forward with a roar. She clasped her hands around his waist, her fingers coming together temptingly close to his manhood, cheek pressed to his cowskin jacket. His deep chuckle reverberated across her skin.

"I told you to hang on."

And she could lean on him forever. Being so close to him with pure raw power between her legs moved her better than any fantasy she had ever created. But what would happen when he took her home? Or would he invite her to his house instead?

She pressed her lips together. Sure, she wanted to know what lay under his tight pants, but she refused to be another conquest. She couldn't handle it.

He drove into her driveway too soon, leaning the bike over enough for her to slip off. She removed the helmet and handed it back to him. "Thank you. I appreciate the ride."

Tucking the helmet away, he nodded. "You want to come over for coffee?"

That and more. Though she refused to go anywhere in her state of disarray. "Um, no, I'm kind of wet."

"Another time, then?"

She nodded. Shit, why did she say no? They could strip down together and have all kinds of fun. But he drove away before she had a chance to retract her words.

A ruined opportunity. Would she ever get another?

A sudden flash of lightning sent her running up her steps. Reaching behind the outside light, she grabbed her house key and unlocked the door. In the foyer, she plucked her loose change from her pocket and placed it on the table beside her purse. She stripped down to nothing then rushed up to her bedroom. Without thinking, she opened the curtains and glanced next door, hoping for another glimpse of her rescuer.

He stood on his porch. Grinning at her, he waved.

She fell to the floor, flat on her ass. Not only had she been topless behind him on the bike, but she'd just exposed herself to him. Everything. With her tall window, he must have seen her from her head all the way down to her knees where the sill cut her off.

Had he expected her to be there? Was he waiting to see what else she'd show off? Molten heat coursed through her veins. Her heart pounded. There was no way she could sleep tonight, not without self-fulfillment while imagining being ravaged by her sexy and mysterious neighbor.

Crawling onto the bed, she ducked underneath her covers, trailing her fingers down to her heat. With so much more inspiration, this promised to be her best fantasy yet.

CHAPTER TWO

She ran her hand up and down his cock and Luke groaned. He knew she was a dream, a fantasy he had repeatedly. Yet, tonight, somehow, Rachel seemed to exist with him. Maybe having her so close to him on the bike the night before helped to make his dreams so much more real. The show from her window had fueled his desire. He didn't dare move for fear of losing her.

His fantasy woman trailed kisses down his chest, inching closer and closer to his straining cock. Was she really going to go down on him?

"I've always wondered what it'd be like to have your dick in my mouth."

Luke flicked his eyes open. The nasally voice wasn't his neighbor's. Red light flashed all around. He scrambled back on his bed, the grip on his shaft not loosening. Someone was in the room with him. He grabbed the person's wrist and squeezed.

"Ouch, Luke, you're hurting me."

"Who the fuck are you?" Sliding off the bed, he rushed to put on some pants before he switched on the light. "And what are you doing here?"

"It's me, Cindy, from Lucy's Tavern."

He stared at the huge-breasted, bleached-blonde woman. A faint memory. But he had never invited her back to his place. And the tavern was four hours away. It had been at least a month since he'd been there. Having worked several weekends in a row, he hadn't had the time to go for long rides on his Harley.

She gave him a sheepish smile. "We haven't seen you around in a while and became worried. I thought I'd drop by and pay you a visit, make sure you were okay."

"But how'd you know where I lived? How'd you get in?" Shit, he had stalkers now. What was Rachel going to think? How was he supposed to convince her to go out with him when women keep coming over? He tensed, hoping she wouldn't find out about tonight.

"I have my ways, and you left the front door open."

Great, he'd fallen into the habits of a small town. Not an ideal thing to do as an alien. He would ensure the doors and windows were locked every night from now on.

"And since there was no woman with you, I thought you could use some fun. Your cock didn't seem to mind."

They both glanced down.

Nope, it wasn't craving *her* services. He never had wanted *her*.

He pointed to the door. "Get out, and never come back. And don't expect to be seeing me at Lucy's anymore." If things didn't work out with his neighbor, he planned to move across the country. It would take a huge distance to break the hold she had on him.

Cindy drew closer. The lights pulsed faster, but she didn't notice.

He placed his hands on the woman's shoulders and guided her out of his room and down the stairs. "I'm not interested. Consider me off the market." Thank goodness she didn't see the orb going apeshit. No woman ever had. How would he explain the extraterrestrial object anyway?

At the bottom of the stairs, she stopped moving. She twisted around and grabbed his balls. "I'm sure I could convince you otherwise."

He shriveled at her touch. Prying her fingers off, he stepped to the side and opened his front door. "No. Out."

She stuck out her bottom lips and her breasts heaved.

Tempting, but no. He glared, wanting her gone. "Nice try."

She stomped down the driveway. Once in her car, she revved the engine and sped away.

Fuck. It would be a miracle if Rachel hadn't woken up with all the commotion. He ducked inside, satisfied the orb had calmed down. Would it do the same thing if he invited his neighbor over? He had to convince her to go out with him, first.

Rachel studied the night sky as she often did when her parents fought. They always waited until she'd gone to bed, but she couldn't help but hear them. And tonight was the worst yet. She pulled the blankets over her head, to try and block out the sound, but her parents' voices grew louder and louder. Leaving the bed, she sat on her toy box by the window, wishing someone would come and take her away. At least until the yelling stopped.

She continued to gaze outside, focusing on a small circle of light on the road. She'd never noticed it before. It fell nowhere near the glow from the street lamp, and there were no cars heading in the direction of her house.

Then the circle grew from the size of a basketball to a ring as big as her kiddie pool in the backyard. Trees swayed in the wind, like before a storm, but not a single cloud floated in the sky. The stars shone bright.... Except for one patch where there was only darkness. Strange.

Rachel blinked and looked again. The blank spot had been refilled by twinkling stars. The trees stopped swaying, and the beam no longer shone on the asphalt. In its place stood a boy. At least she assumed the shape was a boy.

She unhooked the lock on the window and yanked it open. The figure glanced up at her and she froze. Definitely a boy, naked except for a shiny pair of under drawers. Holding in a giggle, she became caught up in his wide eyes.

He lifted a hand and waved, a smile spreading across his face.

"Hi," she whispered, waving back.

He echoed her word, only in a deeper voice, though nothing like her father's, just like the boys in her class.

"Where did you come from?" She kept her voice low so her parents wouldn't hear her. If they caught her still awake, she would get a spanking.

The little boy pointed straight up.

"From space?"

He nodded.

Oh boy, she would rub this in Jenny Marshall's face. Aliens really did exist. One stood in front of her house.

But when she scanned the street again, he had disappeared. And she didn't even know his name.

Jumping up, she raced toward her parents' room. They would stop fighting if she told them what she'd seen.

She burst into their room. "Mom, Dad, I just saw an alien."

But they weren't fighting. They were under the covers, her dad rocking on top of her mom.

Grunting. Skin slapping. What were they doing? Her throat burned. She backed away, covering her mouth.

"There's no such thing as aliens." Her dad turned toward her and glared. "Get the fuck out of here!"

Tears rolled down her cheeks. She spun around then ran out of the room. Her father had used the F-word before, but never to her.

Out. She had to get away. Down the stairs and out into the screened-in porch. She opened the door, but came to a halt at the top of the stairs. The darkness scared her way more than her parents. She didn't want to go back inside, though.

Curling up on the cushioned wicker rocking chair, she wiped her eyes. But the tears kept falling. Her dad had yelled at her, and her mom hadn't stopped him. They didn't care where she went. If she ran away, they probably wouldn't even look for her.

But where would she go? Her friends who ran away always went to their grandma and grandpa's houses. But she didn't have any relatives nearby. She didn't even know if she had any other family besides her parents. No one ever came around.

Something soft and warm touched her shoulder. With a glance behind her, she shrieked. The boy stood there, his skin shining in the dim light.

"Don't be afraid." He smiled. "I won't hurt you."

"No, I..." She rose and turned around to see him better. "You just surprised me is all."

He had the biggest black eyes. Her parents always told not to stare, but his eyes were just so fascinating, so different than anything she'd ever seen. They contained no white, only darkness.

"You're really an alien?"

He shrugged. "I guess."

"And where are your parents?" Everyone had to have parents, even space aliens.

His bottom lip quivered. "I don't know. I was with them, and when they went to an assembly of the elders, I wandered off. I found a room with a lot of buttons. All different colors. I started pressing them and then I turned up here."

"Will they come back for you?" They couldn't leave him on a different planet by himself. They could get in trouble for that.

He shook his head. "The ship flies one direction. It won't come back for another two hundred star cycles."

Star cycles? She knew Earth rotated around the sun, a star, making a year. Was that what he meant? Two hundred years? Everyone in her life would be dead by then. "What are you going to do?"

"I don't know." He ran his hands up and down his arms. "It's so cold here."

"Hold on." She knew how to help him. Dashing into the house, she grabbed a blanket then returned to the alien. Boy clothes weren't going to be easy to find, but the quilt from the couch would work just as well. At least until the morning.

"If we cuddle together under the blanket, we'll stay warm." She would never offer to snuggle with any of the kids from school. They always tried to punch and kick her. This boy didn't seem like he wanted to do either. Maybe because he appeared a bit older than those in her class.

He sat on the chair first, and she squeezed in beside him, heaving the cover over them.

She giggled. Never had she been so close to a boy. And she didn't even know what to call him. "What's your name?"

Rachel tugged her pillow over her head, woken by another one of Luke's women letting the entire neighborhood know she was leaving. So much for him driving her home last night, asking her over for coffee. That must have meant nothing to him. She'd denied him, so he simply found someone else for the next night.

She peeked out at her bedside clock. The red numbers glared 3:00. Having gone to dinner with Christine to fill her in on her rescuer, she hadn't been around to see anyone enter his house. But the woman had left later than any of the others. Her chest ached and her eyes stung with the threat of tears. No, she wouldn't cry. Her neighbor meant nothing to her.

Images of her dream—the delusion based on her childhood memory—flittered through her mind. She winced. Why had she told them she'd seen an alien? Maybe if she hadn't, things wouldn't have changed. Two days after she walked in on her parents, her father packed up and moved out for the first time of many. And when he didn't live at home, sometimes she would see him around town with another woman. Her mother seemed to resent her, always claiming she caused her dad to leave. Mom brought other men home, prompting her to hide in her room. They weren't her father and didn't want anything to do with her, anyway. But after a few years, her dad moved back for good. Her parents didn't fight anymore, but they never paid her much attention.

Once old enough to figure out what her parents had been doing the night she'd walked in on them, she wanted to have sex, understand how it could change people. There were plenty of guys her age willing to show her. But not one of them made her comprehend why her parents suddenly shunned her. Or their actions just after her nineteenth birthday.

She cringed. Think of something else.

Her alien. Remembering him always calmed her down. There was something so innocent about him, making her feel like a child again, before everything in her life changed. And the dream of him came often. Too often. Though she would always awaken just before he told her his name. No matter how hard she tried to remember, his name remained elusive, always on the edge of her memory. The next morning, she'd woken up on the porch alone, wrapped in the blanket, and had failed to find her little alien since. Maybe his parents had returned to pick him up after all, or maybe she'd imagined the whole thing.

Rachel slammed her car door then plodded toward the grocery store. Her mind refused to settle after waking from her dream. She'd washed, dried, and folded her laundry, cleaned the bathroom, and scrubbed the kitchen floor. And minutes before the grocery store opened, she'd left her house, hoping to get in and out before she ran into her asshole of an ex-boyfriend or any of the church ladies who would insist she come with them next week to meet their *handsome, young* nephews, grandsons, and even sons who, in their forties, still lived at home. No, thank you.

Inside, she grabbed a cart and headed straight to the produce aisle. After picking up all she needed in the frozen food section, she raced for the checkout.

The high pitch cackle of Jenny Marshall froze her in her tracks. No.

She ducked down the nearest aisle only to run smack into someone else, steel grinding against steel. And who did the other cart belong to? None other than the skank and the douchebag.

"Rachel, what a surprise to see you here. We were just talking about you." Jenny pinned on her widest smile, but Dirk didn't even acknowledge her.

Thank God. Like she had anything good to say to him.

"Yeah." Her fingers dug into the handle. "Sorry about running into you." Not really. "But I've got to go."

She backed up then made a beeline for the only open checkout. Guess he must have called Jenny when she wouldn't fuck him. Just like Luke. Well, Jenny could have him. He had a pencil dick, anyway.

Driving past Luke's house on her way home, she thought of Christine's words. Could she settle for one night with him? He couldn't be any worse than her other sexual partners. But did his offer still stand?

She would fall to pieces at his rejection. No, she would rather him remain in her fantasies than become a "never going to happen."

CHAPTER THREE

Luke nailed on the last fence board, letting out a huge breath. Finally done. Working long hours all week left him antsy. Every night he arrived home too late to stop by Rachel's house. Not once did he find her staring out her window, only finding closed curtains every time he tried to catch a glimpse of her.

Today seemed especially rough. The hotter than hell weather drew on his nerves, and he swore he spotted his neighbor on the other side of the river with a young punk. Sexier than he'd ever seen her, she dressed in a short black skirt she would have to shave everything to wear, and a low-cut top. His cock strained in his pants. Then the kid groped the look-alike. He clenched his fists. He couldn't take it anymore. He had to see her, make his move.

With the extra money in his pocket, he wouldn't have to work late the next day, and after a shower, he would make the trek over to his neighbor's. Today he was too tired and his couch called to him.

Dogs yipped behind him, and he pivoted on his heels. Mrs. Yantzi waltzed toward him, her canine companions prancing along beside her. "Luke, you did a wonderful job. Are you all finished?"

"Yes, ma'am." He removed his hat and wiped the sweat from his forehead. Starting early to get the job finished before the heat of the day, hadn't made a difference. Not with the blasted humidity. "I just need to clean up my tools."

She placed a piece of paper in the palm of his hand. "Here's what I owe you plus a bit extra for working over the weekend, and in this heat."

He nodded and pocketed the check. At least the woman appreciated his sacrifice. She'd been his best client since moving back to Hanton. "Thank you. When you're ready for the deck to be done, just give me a call."

She chuckled. "That won't be until next summer, but I'll be sure to contact you." The woman and her little dogs returned to the house, leaving him to pack up.

He loaded his tools back in his truck, and took one last glance at the other side of the river.

Rachel stared in horror at her date. What on Earth was she thinking when she'd agreed to meet him? Seriously, how many adult men walked around with their pants hanging halfway down their asses with their cartoon character boxers showing? The way he strutted around, ogling her, reminded her of the punks from high school she used to avoid.

If Mrs. Norris and her group of church ladies hadn't trapped her in the cubicle Monday morning, she never would have agreed to meet the woman's nephew, Sol. She pinched the bridge of her nose, closing her eyes. Maybe she could fake food poisoning as an excuse to go home early. Flicking open her eyes, she bounced up on her toes. Time to get started.

"Mmm, all that food over there looks delicious." With reluctance, she grabbed Sol's hand. "Why don't we go eat?"

Mrs. Norris slapped their fingers apart. "It's not time yet. They're playing games out in the field. Why don't you join them?"

Sure, if she was ten.

Sol took her hand again, and dragged her in the same direction anyway. "C'mon, I know another way we can pass the time."

She groaned, but following him had to be better than hanging around with the church ladies. If they thought for one instant she wasn't enjoying herself, they would set her up with another guy by the end of the day.

Sol passed by the kids participating in the three-legged race and guided her over to the most secluded part of the park, where unkempt bushes and trees lined the riverbank.

"So, my aunt tells me you work at a bank."

"Yes, it's the only place I've ever worked." She hoped to keep the conversation going, dreading what her date would try if he stopped talking.

He twirled her around and backed her against a tree. "Well, I'd like to make a deposit."

She snorted, ducking out under his arm. "I can't believe you just said that." Lamest pick-up line ever.

His bottom lip stuck out. "What? I'm just trying to let you know how I feel about you."

God, the guy is unreal. "And how do you feel about me after knowing me for all of fifteen minutes?"

"I think you're pretty and full of spunk." He leaned in close enough his breath grazed the nape of her neck.

A cold chill ran through her.

"And I'd like to get to know you a whole lot better."

She swallowed her laughter. No way did she want what he offered. "Listen, I'm only here to get your aunt and her friends off my back."

"I am, too, so why don't we have fun while we're here?"

Why did she suddenly feel like his prey? "I'm not interested in your type of fun."

"Then why are you wearing such a short dress revealing your miles of legs?" He closed the gap between them, grabbing her hips and yanking her toward him. "You have your hair all done up. Your tits are practically falling out of your shirt, and you smell so damn good."

Bile rose from her stomach. Images of Dirk flashed through her mind. No way. Not again.

She spun away from Sol. Her feet slipped out from under her. Falling. Oh, God. Swinging her arms, she tried to regain her balance.

"Hey, Sol, long time no see. Who's the chick you're with?"

She turned her head to see who had spoken. Wrong move.

Rachel landed in the river with a splash. An eruption of laughter came from the shore, where Sol and his friend threw their heads back and held their stomachs.

"You could help me up, you know." Why did she end up wet when she went out with a guy?

"I have to stop laughing first," Sol said.

Silt tickled the backs of her thighs. She stood, her clothes dripping water and mud.

His friend clasped his shoulder. "That was fuckin' hilarious. Though it would have been better if we'd seen more of what's under the skirt."

"Hardy, har, har." After climbing up the bank, she marched over to her asshole of a date. Like she could return to the picnic in such a state. And she sure as hell didn't want to spend any more time with him. "This isn't going to work. You can tell your aunt…whatever."

"Thank God I'm off the hook." He turned his back to her. "C'mon, Troy. Let's go to the beach. I have a better chance of getting some action there."

She stood in the grass, still dripping, mouth open. What a jerk! He hadn't even bothered to help her, to make sure she was okay. Now she had to find her own way home with sopping clothes. Taking them off wouldn't work this time. The park was packed with people. Everyone would stare, and nothing bothered her more than being the center of attention.

"You like getting wet or something?"

She froze, her panties soaked, but not from the river. How did his voice have such power over her body? It wasn't as if she'd even seen him coming, heard him approach.

Oh, God, her clothes. The murky water couldn't have done anything positive for her appearance. Heat flared across her neck, ears, and cheeks. Why did he show up when she was at her worst after being ditched by a guy? Was he her secret knight-in-shining-armor? She straightened the hem of her shirt. How she wished.

With her stomach in knots, she turned around slowly, bracing for his reaction.

Wearing a ball cap, boot-cut jeans, and an oh-so-tight T-shirt, he could say anything he wanted as long as she didn't have to look away. Her fingers tingled, longing to touch him again.

He smirked. Great, she probably resembled a drowned rat. She glanced down, scuffling her sandal across the mud. "I kind of had an accident."

"Accident?" His words came out sharp, his eyes cold in their gaze. "From what I saw, you were pushed in. Was that kid your date?"

"Supposed to be." What was his problem? He'd never shown any interest in her. Why did it suddenly matter who she went out with? Though she would jump at the chance for a night with him. Never going to happen.

She nodded toward the church ladies. "His aunt thought we'd be good together."

"His aunt should mind her own business. I'm sure you can find your own dates."

"Yeah." She sighed, wishing that were true. Unfortunately, the older women were her only connection to guys outside of Hanton, unless she went hunting on her own. Like that would ever happen. Having only one friend throughout school had kept her confidence deflated.

"So, can I walk you to your car?"

Her stomach fluttered. He actually wanted to go somewhere with her, to be seen by her side? She gulped. Her car was parked at home. And she doubted he would walk her that far. "I got a ride with Mrs. Norris and Sol."

"Just my luck," he muttered.

What the hell was that supposed to mean? She hadn't asked him to come over and talk to her. "If I'm such a burden, don't worry about it. I'm a big girl."

She stormed past him. If only he'd stayed away. Then the sexy and mysterious man fantasy she took to bed with her every night would remain in her dreams, and she could forget the asshole behind her.

Fuck. He never knew what to do or say around her. Unlike every other woman he encountered, Rachel left him fumbling for words. What had he said to offend her?

He refused to let her walk away this time, rushing after her. Grabbing her arm, he swung her around to face him. "Rachel, please." The urge to draw her against him overwhelmed him, but the last thing he needed was for her to scream *alien* when she noticed his eyes, remembered how he'd changed them to look like hers. It wasn't the middle of the night, pouring rain this time. She still wore all of her clothing, even if it was soaking wet, and clinging to her luscious body. His cock stirred, and he longed to rip off the wet material.

She jerked from his grasp. "What, so you can insult me again?" With a fierce stare, she thrust a finger into his chest. "For your information, those women are the only source I have to find a date, because all of the guys who live in Hanton are assholes."

She might as well have kicked him in the junk. Anger radiated off her in waves, and since it was directed at him, he ached with the emotion ten-fold. Then her bottom lip quivered. The force of her emotions dropped, and he wanted to wrap his arms around her. He would crash to the ground if she started crying.

Raising his hands, he hoped to calm her down. "I'm sorry, I didn't mean to insult you. It's just that I have my truck with me, and I didn't want you to—"

"Get it wet? I said don't worry about me. I'll walk."

"No." Why was she so difficult? She'd seemed less spiteful when he picked her up last weekend in the pouring rain. For a moment, he considered throwing her back in the river. "The seats are really dirty."

"And I'm not?"

Her nose suddenly flared, and the glare she gave him made his cock go rigid. She frustrated him so much right now, yet his desire for her only grew. Somehow, he had to claim her, mark her as his. But, to do that, he had to stay on her good side. "The dirt on your dress can be washed off, but the oil and grime in my truck will leave stains. I think I have a garbage bag you can sit on, though."

He sensed her agitation and sadness ebb away. "*If* you're willing to accept another ride from me."

Her cheeks flushed. Maybe he still had a chance with her.

"I would appreciate a ride. Thank you."

Resting a hand on the small of her back, he guided her to where he'd parked his truck after seeing her shoved into the river. Time to take her home.

He drove, trying to think of something to say to her, to find out if she would be willing to spend more time with him. But every time he opened his mouth, he forgot what he wanted to say. Pulling into her driveway, he felt his heart pounding in his chest. No way would he let her leave without some agreement that she would see him again rather than the occasional late night wave or staring at him when she passed by on her evening jog.

She reached for the door handle, and he leaned toward her. "You're going to be at the coffee shop tomorrow morning?" Was that all he could think of?

Her eyes appeared so soft and innocent when she glanced back at him, reminding him of the night he'd first met her. "Yes. I'm there every morning."

"Well, maybe I'll see you there."

A smile lit up her entire face. "I'd like that." She slid out of his truck, and climbed the steps to her porch before he could think of anything else to say.

He didn't want to let her leave, not without asking her to dinner. But he wouldn't push his luck. He would see her in the morning, sense her emotions, and ask her then.

He backed out of her driveway, hoping she'd turn around and wave. She never did. And she didn't appear in her bedroom window either. Why did she have to be such a freakin' mystery?

Disappointment clutched her gut. Luke hadn't shown up at the coffee shop as he'd said he would. No, he'd used the word maybe. That meant no guarantee. She should never have gotten her hopes up.

Rachel took a drink of her coffee then shuffled some papers. She had no appointments until ten, but had to be at work earlier for possible walk-in clients. More time to think about how her neighbor stood her up.

After he'd dropped her off at home the day before, she'd stumbled into her house with rubber-like legs. He'd touched her. Closing the door behind her, she'd slumped to the floor.

Even now, her skin tingled with the sensation of his hand on her back.

When the chatter of women caught her attention, she rolled her chair to the farthest corner from the doorway. The church ladies came in every Monday morning, and she dreaded Mrs. Norris demanding answers as to why her date with Sol didn't work out. The woman was the last person she wanted to see when thinking about Luke. If Mrs. Norris couldn't see her in her office cubicle, maybe she would leave her alone.

"Rachel, my dear, what happened yesterday?" The woman waltzed into her cubicle.

She cringed. No such luck.

Opening a blank file on her computer, she typed away, trying to look busy. "I'm sorry, Mrs. Norris, but Sol and I just didn't have anything in common. Then he left to hang out with his friend."

"He said you dismissed him, told him it wasn't going to work."

Not until after she had fallen into the river and he'd only laughed at her. "No point in wasting his time, right?"

"I guess not." She pursed her lips. "I just wish you would have told me you were leaving. But listen, there's a dance over in Allentown on Friday night. Always a bevy of single men there. I want you to come with me, and you can pick your own fella."

God, no. Like she wanted to be eyed-up and groped by a bunch of middle-aged and old men. "I, uh… I have other plans."

"Is that right? What are they?"

She bounced her foot. How was she going to get out of this?

Christine leaned over the cubicle wall and stared at her with an evil smirk. "Yeah, what are your plans?"

Traitor.

She drummed her fingers on her desk. Why couldn't she be quicker on her feet?

"Well?" Mrs. Norris asked.

"She's having dinner with me."

Rachel gasped. Had she heard his voice, or just imagined it?

Luke stepped past the old bat, and into her office. "Good morning, Rachel. I'm sorry I missed you at the coffee shop this morning." He nodded to the other women listening. "Mrs. Norris, Miss Shaw. Would you mind if I have a few moments alone with this beautiful young woman?"

Christine ducked away immediately, and Rachel swore she heard her friend squee. Mrs. Norris, on the other hand, gave him a ferocious glare. "I've heard about you. You're no good for her."

Tension blanketed her small cubicle, but Luke grinned back at the old woman. "I believe Rachel can make her own decisions."

With one last glare, Mrs. Norris huffed off.

Alone with him in her office, she froze, unable to form a coherent thought. After a deep breath, her heart jumped back to life, pumping faster than ever. Luke Jones had more or less invited her to dinner Friday night. What was she going to wear? Oh God, she had to shave.

Luke hesitated to take a step forward. Everyone had left them alone, but Rachel remained backed into the corner, her cheeks a vibrant shade of pink. She stared at him, wide-eyed, like he was a predator going in for the kill. Was she afraid of him?

He held out his hand. Would she take it, or was it time to admit she'd never be his?

A spark of electricity shot through his body, and he groaned. Her fingers grazed across the tips of his. Grasping his hand, she stood, but still remained silent.

When she was upset, he ached for her. The emotions she gave off now were different, a little fear and something else, a tingling sensation he felt in his groin.

"So, will you have dinner with me?" He braced for her rejection.

Still holding onto him, she swallowed. "Dinner?"

"Yes, Friday night." He clenched his jaw, the wait for her answer excruciatingly long.

"I…"

Here came the rejection. "If you don't want to, that's fine. I just thought I'd save you from Mrs. Norris."

Her grip tightened before she released his fingers. "Sorry, I'd love to have dinner with you. It's just…."

She doesn't date aliens. Of course. Who would?

"I'm not into the whole one-night stand thing."

Shit. She'd seen the women leaving his house. How could she not with all the commotion they made? How could he prove to her he only wanted her? No one but her. If only she would give him a chance.

He tucked a loose strand of her hair behind her ear, and she didn't flinch. "I promise I'm after more than one night with you."

Chewing on her bottom lip, she drove him crazy with anticipation. He needed to know.

Finally, she smiled, a playful gleam in her eyes. "Okay, where would you like me to meet you?"

"I'll pick you up." He clenched his fists to contain his excitement. If they weren't in the bank, he would have wrapped his arms around her and spun her in circles.

Her eyes grew wide, terror all over her face. "But, what should I wear?"

He grinned, picturing her naked as he'd seen her at her bedroom window. "Anything you want."

A throat cleared behind him. "Rachel, Mr. and Mrs. Smith are here."

Her expression sobered. "Thank you, sir. I'll only be a moment."

Luke turned his head to ensure the other man had left before he leaned in to kiss her cheek. "I look forward to our date on Friday."

He left without waiting for her reaction. She'd said yes! Now, he had to keep himself calm until Friday arrived, and hope she didn't back out. He'd planned to take the rest of the day off, but not now. If he finished installing the cupboards for Mr. Murphy, he would have the entire weekend free. Plus, he needed something to occupy his mind so it would stop sending his dick ideas.

"Holy mother of God." Christine rushed into her office and plopped down in a chair. "Luke Jones asked you out."

"Yes," she squealed. She wanted to jump up and down, to whoop and release everything she'd held in while helping the Smiths to renew their mortgage, but the bank was jam-packed with people.

Doubt pushed her excitement aside. "What am I supposed to wear? I'm not like any of the women he's ever invited over to his house."

"Exactly." Christine leaned across her desk. "And they only lasted one night. Maybe he's ready to settle down."

Then she remembered the woman who'd left his house in the middle of the night just over a week ago. Her stomach clenched.

But this past weekend, there had been no one. And Luke had come to her rescue again. "Maybe."

"Either way, you don't want to pass on this opportunity. I have to know what he's like in bed, whether or not he's hung."

"Christine!" Her cheeks warmed. She wondered the same thing. Though she would never admit it to her friend.

"What? It's not every day you get asked out by someone so hot."

She cringed, but couldn't deny the truth. In terms of hot guys, Hanton only had her neighbor.

"I'm taking you to the spa in Allentown on Wednesday night. You're getting a full body wax and your hair done."

"But that will cost a fortune." Unlike Christine, she didn't live with her parents and paid her own bills. Every cent she spent was for essential items only.

"Is he worth it?"

God, yes. Registration for the online courses she planned to take not paid for by the bank would have to wait until next term. She yearned for a way to leave Hanton, but if her date went well with Luke, living in the small town might be a little more bearable.

CHAPTER FOUR

After a lukewarm shower, Rachel rubbed After Wax lotion over her legs and in between her thighs. She'd been stripped of every single hair below her waist, had her eyebrows plucked to almost nothing, her upper lip bleached, and her locks colored and cut to resemble the latest Hollywood style. Missing so much hair, she felt lighter, except for the heavy bundle of nerves in her stomach making her want to vomit. She'd never been so nervous in her life.

All week she'd drifted off into space, wondering what Luke had planned for their date, and whether they would have another. Tonight, she would find out.

During their trip to Allentown, Christine kept hinting to her that Luke might want a serious relationship, but she refused to get her hopes up. Two weeks since his last one-night stand could hardly mean he wanted a permanent girlfriend. He probably just needed a break after the long hours he put in that week at work. Either that, or he'd spent his evenings at another woman's house before coming home.

Her stomach twisted. No, she had to tuck those thoughts away. Tonight was about her and Luke. And he'd promised her more.

She slipped on a silk thong, very aware of her hairless skin. Every brush of material left her ready to run next door, begging for him to take her. How was she going to last through dinner? Reaching into her closet, she lifted out the short, fitted green dress Christine had helped her pick out. She slid the stretchy material over her head and down her body. After tucking her boobs into the bodice, she glanced in the mirror, twisting to observe all angles. The Lycra hugged every curve, but left her with the ability to move. Maybe she could look like the women who frequented her neighbor's house. She added some liner and mascara around her eyes and flavored gloss to her lips. As she dashed downstairs, her excitement built.

She strapped on her heels then sat on the couch and waited. *Come and get me, Luke Jones.*

Luke took a deep breath then rang the doorbell. Wiping his palms on his pants, he heard the click of her heels getting closer. He'd waited for this night for so long, too afraid of rejection to make it happen sooner.

The door opened and he stumbled back. With a sharp inhale, he gripped the porch and stared. Rachel, the woman he'd asked out on Monday, had transformed herself into a radiant beauty, and he prayed to the far reaches of the universe she would be his. Beautiful before, she left him breathless, and his blood rushed straight to his cock. Her shorter hair exposed a long neck he wanted to taste, and her dress should be illegal, even more revealing than the outfit she'd worn when she fell in the river.

"Hi." She smiled, and her cheeks flushed. "Am I dressed okay for where we're going?"

"Perfect." How could she be anything else? He lifted her chin to gaze into her stunning green eyes, a color he'd tried to emulate in his own, but never got quite right. "You look absolutely gorgeous."

Her cheeks reddened further. He longed to kiss her, press her against the solid oak behind her and taste her luscious pink lips.

"So, where are we going for dinner?" She gazed up at him, her lips parted.

He gulped. "My house." And if they didn't go now, she would likely be picking splinters out of her ass after he had his way with her in front of the entire neighborhood.

She tilted her head then peeked next door. "I thought—"

Fuck! "We can go to Chez Louis in Allentown if you'd like." He should have planned differently. Rachel wasn't like every other woman he had dated. With a dress more suited to a fancy restaurant, would she want to help him prepare a meal in his kitchen? He expected her to find it romantic to cook together. *Shit.* Overly anxious to spend the night with her, he hadn't thought his plan through.

She rubbed the back of his arm before sliding her fingers across his palm. "No, your place is fine. It's more…intimate."

Her whispered last word revived his cock. If she wanted intimate, there was no better place than his home.

Squeezing her hand, he took the first step down the walkway. "Let's go then."

Without hesitation, she strolled along beside him. He felt her rapid pulse from her palm. Nerves, or could she sense the electricity between them? Her emotions weren't strong enough for him to read, but he definitely felt an increase in her responsiveness. Making and eating dinner without exploring everything under her glove-like dress would be a challenge. He longed to rip it off standing there in the driveway, and take her over his bike. The mental image left him groaning.

He stopped at his front door. "Something wrong?"

"No, I'm just really hungry." For her.

"Me, too."

He fumbled with the handle, and rested his arm behind her waist to guide her inside. A faint blue glow blanketed the entire house. Any other woman who'd been inside had the crystal flashing red. Did it approve of Rachel? He hoped so. He wanted no one more.

Luke toured her around the main floor of his home and Rachel gawked with every turn. No way. Everything was clean lines, black leather furnishings in the living room, and stainless steel appliances, walnut cupboards, and granite countertops in the kitchen. She'd never expected the decor to be so contemporary.

Except her bed, her house contained a mish-mash of used furniture neighbors had donated to help her replace the worn-out stuff left behind by her parents. After a year of working at the bank and paying off all of their debt save for the mortgage, she'd bought herself a new bed. It was the most expensive thing she owned, worth more than the rusty tin can on wheels she drove around when needed. She always woke up free of aches and pains, except for the nights when slamming doors and squealing tires startled her awake.

Her stomach twisted. She came from nothing, couldn't compete with any of his previous dates with their expensive sports cars and fancy clothes. The funds she'd used to buy the dress would take a month to replace, and that didn't include the waxing, hair style, new shoes, or lingerie. She'd turned herself into someone else. Why had Luke even asked her out?

"Can I kiss you?"

She gazed up at him, caught off guard by his question. "What?"

He smiled and ran his hand up and down her arm. "Can I kiss you? I don't think I can make it through dinner if I don't."

His dark green eyes, a shade away from black, captivated her. They were so intense and full of passion. All for the woman she'd transformed into to spend the night with him. She turned away. She couldn't do it. God, she wanted to feel his lips on hers, to experience the thrill of the man of her fantasies making love to her, but it could never happen. Not like this. "Luke, this isn't me. The dress, hair style, and even the lack of hair south of the border is not who I am. I can't be one of those women who leave you in the middle of the night."

Would he back off, end their date before she had the chance to blink?

No, he stepped closer, backing her into the counter, his groin pressing against her belly. He cupped the sides of her face and stared into her eyes, his gaze more focused than ever. "I told you, I don't want those women. While I'm flattered you went through all that trouble for me, I'd still want to kiss you if you hadn't. I've wanted you since I moved in."

His lips grazed hers, and she closed her eyes, forgetting all of her reasons to stop him.

"I've just been too afraid."

Afraid? She didn't have time to comprehend his whispered words. He kissed down her neck and along her jaw line. Then he claimed her mouth. Gripping the edge of his shirt, she lost herself in the thrill. Finally, she was locking lips with Luke Jones.

He lined her lips with his tongue, and she opened to him, allowing his sweet invasion. He ran his hands down her arms then grabbed her hips, lifting her onto the counter. Desire flooded her every thought. She couldn't stop him even if she wanted.

Spreading her legs open, she allowed him to move between them. His hard shaft teased her core, every nerve in her body lighting up in response. She moaned. *Yes.*

His hand slid past the top of her dress, cupping a breast. Just like in her fantasies. She threw her head back as he sucked on her pebbled tip. His tongue swirled and he ground against her. Wetness pooled between her thighs. For the first time ever, she would come before dinner.

But as quick as the kiss had started, he backed away. She whimpered. *No, don't stop.*

The blue mood lighting blanketing his house when she'd arrived flashed red then rushed to purple and back to blue.

What the hell was going on?

"I'm sorry." He lifted her off the counter then rushed to the cupboards on the other side of the kitchen, plucking food out. "I didn't mean to go so far. You just tasted so…." He fixed his dark eyes on her. "It won't happen again."

Yes, it had to.

She gripped the granite behind her. What had she done to make him stop? Was she a really bad kisser? She'd never been told so before. Her past boyfriends had always said how much they liked what she did with her mouth. Maybe it was something else he doesn't like. She glanced down at her chest. Were her boobs too small?

Oh God. She never should have agreed to the date. Whether she slept with him or not, she would only have one night with him. Past observations proved the fact, no matter how much he tried to convince her otherwise. Best leave now and keep her dignity intact. "I…I think I should go. I'm suddenly not feeling well."

"Please, don't go." He returned his attention to her, his slumped posture and sad eyes revealing a vulnerability she had never seen in him. "Maybe if you freshen up in the bathroom you'll feel better."

He hurried over to her and took her hand. "I didn't mean to hurt you. I just wanted to take things slow." His thumb brushed along her cheek. "Will you at least stay for dinner?"

Despite the apprehension tightening her chest and stomach, she nodded. "I guess."

"Good." A brief smile. Then he guided her to the main floor bathroom.

She ducked inside, needing to catch her breath. No way could she deny the zing of desire that swept through her body from his touch. But part of her blamed the sensation on his charm, his way of getting into her pants before he sent her packing at the end of the night.

Staring at herself in the mirror, she blew out a deep breath. What was she going to do?

The date was going to shit all because of his stupid orb. When he had Rachel on the counter, ready to take her, the orb glowed red, as if showing disapproval. Maybe he had moved too fast. In order to make her believe he wanted more than a one-night stand, he refused to fuck her on the first date. But when he'd backed off, the emotion radiating off her no longer matched his. He'd hurt her, exactly what he wanted to avoid.

Across the table, Rachel forked the shrimp scampi and linguini on her plate, but very little made it into her mouth. She only sipped at the pinot grigio he'd been told would go well with the meal. So much for all his searching the web to find the ideal meal to make with a date. He'd prepared the entire dinner himself, wondering if she would ever come out of the bathroom.

"Are you enjoying the meal?" He yearned to break the silence. She hadn't said two words since she sat down at the dinner table.

Her eyes met his. "I'm sorry. My stomach's just a bit queasy tonight."

Guilt clutched his chest. How could he make things better? To let her go after finally working up the courage to ask her out would mean his defeat. And right now, nothing else mattered but making Rachel smile again.

She set down her fork, and placed her napkin beside her plate. "I think it's best I go home now." Pushing her chair back, she stood then headed for the front door.

He jumped to his feet and raced to catch up with her. "Let me walk you home."

He'd fucked up, been too tempted by her at the beginning of their date. He wouldn't let the evening end with her upset. "Let's do this again tomorrow night."

At the bottom of her steps, she turned to face him. "You want to see me again?"

Her hurt seemed to give way to something else, the emotion too ambiguous to read.

"Of course." He brushed his fingers along the back of her arm, enjoying the sensation he read from her. "I told you this wasn't a one-time thing."

The corners of her mouth curved up into a slight smile. "Okay. A barbeque?"

"Sounds great." Anything to get out of the house and away from the orb. Plus, he wouldn't have to look up another fancy recipe to impress her. Hanging out with the guys in his apprenticeship program, he'd learned some skills on the grill.

Her cheeks reddened. "And maybe we could come back here for dessert?"

Even better. "Sounds like a plan." He leaned forward and kissed her cheek. Best not to push his luck. "Get some rest, feel better, and I'll see you tomorrow."

He squeezed the back of her arm then walked away. If he stayed any longer, he would back her into her house and up to her bedroom. With the pain he'd caused her now gone, Rachel gave off waves of desire. He groaned, rushing back to his house. Inside, he changed into a pair of coveralls. He needed something to get his mind off her, and routine maintenance on his Harley would hopefully do the trick. He entered his garage, cranked up some old-school rock, and set to work.

Bang. Bang. Bang.

Rachel opened her eyes with a whimper. Who the hell was at her door so early in the morning? She slid out of bed then tromped down the stairs. Opening the front door, she frowned at Christine standing on her porch.

"You *are* home," her friend squealed. "So, tell me about your date. What's Luke like in bed? Is he well hung?"

"I just woke up." She spun around and traipsed toward the back of the house. "Give me a few minutes to figure out who I am and what day this is." Not only did she need a trip to the bathroom, but a strong cup of coffee wouldn't hurt. She'd spent half the night staring at her neighbor from her bedroom window and trying to understand his actions. He continued to tinker away on his bike when she'd climbed into bed. And the dream had come. She'd been on the verge of learning the little alien's name when she woke up. Had it been Luke finally going in for the night that had startled her? Too tired to care, she had rolled over onto her side and gone back to sleep. Only to be rudely awakened too damn early by her best friend.

Christine followed her inside, leaning against the bathroom doorframe while she peed. No privacy at all.

"So, did you guys do it? I need to know."

"No." She flushed the toilet and washed her hands. "We didn't have sex, so I have no idea what he's like in bed."

"Bummer." Christine plopped down at the kitchen table, resting her head in her hands. "Well, what did you guys do? Give me something."

She smiled, scooping grounds into the coffee filter. "We kissed…and a little bit more."

Her friend tapped her fingers against her mug, grinding on Rachel's nerves. "And you stopped, didn't you? You and your dreams of romance."

"I didn't. He stopped." He'd given her the fancy dinner, everything she thought she'd wanted. "Told me he wanted to take things slow."

Christine slapped her hands on the table, wearing a big grin, her eyes wide. "I told you he was ready to settle down. And you're the lucky one he picked. How I wish I was in your place."

Yet, she'd run out on him, afraid she'd done something wrong. No way would she tell her friend that.

"So, while you were with Luke last night, there was some interesting shit happening in town."

Always the gossip queen. "What happened now?" Nothing surprised her anymore in Hanton.

"Our boss came home from work yesterday to find Dirk fucking his wife in the pool."

Her stomach twisted. Even though she no longer dated the jackass, she cringed at the thought she'd let him touch her. If she'd done more with him, who knows what diseases she might have contracted?

"Bill ran back into the house to grab his shotgun and by the time he came back out, Dirk was flying over the fence, bare-assed. Bill got some of his cop buddies searching for him, but they couldn't find the weasel or his car anywhere."

Christine stood and joined her at the counter, getting her own cup of coffee. "And Jenny Marshall has disappeared, too. I say good riddance to both of them."

As much as she hated to ask, she couldn't help herself. She'd lived in the small town for too long. "What about Bill and his wife?"

"Jackie claims he works long hours and doesn't pay any attention to her, that she was just looking for affection. But we all know Bill slipped out the door every night at five to get home to her. What she was thinking, I have no idea. Bill and I both spent the night at Roy's house, but who knows what's going to happen today."

She gasped. "Roy's? You're doing the threesome thing now?" God, she needed to leave this town. Hanton would never bring her the happiness she craved. The worst part was, none of what Christine said proved to be big news. It had all happened to someone else before.

"No, Bill slept on the couch. I only *did* Roy."

"You're dating a cop now? When did this happen?"

Christine spun around without spilling a drop, and giggled. "When I left the bank yesterday, he was writing up a ticket for the silly person who parked in front of the fire hydrant."

"You." Her friend always parked there, no matter how many times she'd been warned not to. And the numerous citations never seemed to deter her either.

Christine waved her hand in the air. "Doesn't matter. Anyway, I convinced him not to write the ticket and to take me out for dinner. We'd just left the pub when Bill phoned him. Our fun was delayed a little bit."

"Wow, I'm going to have to start calling *you* Jenny Marshall." Getting it on with someone else in the house? She would never have the nerve to do something so bold. Even after two years, it had been Luke who'd asked her out, not the other way around.

"Not quite." Christine elbowed her. "For one, I would never have dated Dirk. Sorry, but I told you that all along. And second, I don't do guys who are already in committed relationships. There are plenty of single men around here willing to show me a good time. But to be honest, I think I'm going to keep Roy around for awhile."

Mug in hand, Rachel rolled her eyes and sat at the table. She gave the relationship a week. Christine got bored easily.

Her friend joined her. "But, enough about me. So what's happening next? Are you going out with your sexy neighbor again?"

She sipped her coffee then nodded. "Tonight."

"Must have been some kiss if he wants to see you again so soon."

She hoped so. But had he only asked her out again because he hadn't yet added her as a notch in his belt? No matter how hard she tried, she couldn't remove the thought from the back of her mind.

"Going anyplace special for the date?"

She blinked, returning her focus to her friend. "We're having a barbeque at his place then coming back here for dessert."

"Dessert, huh? That's original. Do you have supplies? Is your room suitable to entertain a man as hot as Luke?"

Oh God. She cringed. The thought of him actually coming into her house hadn't crossed her mind until now. "No, will you help me?"

"Sure. Hop in the shower, and we'll take a drive into Allentown." Christine poured herself another cup. "We'll have your house looking chic in no time, and your room well-stocked with everything you could possibly need."

Great, more money. But she refused to have him come into her house of odds and ends when his looked professionally designed. She, at least, had to find matching throws. And if they were going to have sex, she had to have condoms. STDs and pregnancy were not options in her life.

She gulped down one last mouthful. "Sounds good. I have no idea what I'm doing."

"Trying to land the hottest guy in Hanton. Now, get moving."

She placed her mug in the sink then rushed upstairs. If she spent time with Luke as his girlfriend, living in Hanton would definitely be more bearable.

Luke wiped his hands on the rag then tossed it onto his toolbox. He'd worked on his Harley long into the night, and again in the morning after a few hours of restless sleep. Rachel had invaded his mind with her luscious lips and soft curves. A battle raged inside him. He wanted all of Rachel, to bury himself deep inside her hot body, especially after the taste he got the day before. But he also sensed her hesitation, and refused to push her too fast. He'd heard the whispers behind his back about the women he'd invited over. And with his reputation, it would be hard to convince her he didn't want anyone else. Yet, he had to.

Leaving the garage, he trudged toward his house. He needed to grab a shower and take the food out of the freezer before she came over. Would she expect some fancy dish made on the barbeque after last night, or would she be just as happy with burgers? Damn, why had he waited so long to ask her out?

As soon as he reached his bedroom, he stripped off his grease-covered clothes. It felt so good to be out of the confines of man-made material. The one scrap of clothing he had left from his time on the ship weighed practically nothing. Not only had it stretched to fit him as he grew from a child into an adult, but there were no signs of wear and tear. He wished this planet held the same means to produce the alien fabric. But then he would have to expose what he was. That would lead him straight to a mental institution or worse, a government laboratory. He would rather be uncomfortable.

The only person he would ever reveal his ancestry to was the woman next door, and he had to hurry to be ready for their second date.

Stepping into the shower, he moaned under the warm spray. Maybe cold would be better. He grew hard already from thinking of her. Soaping himself down, he planned to be in and out, until he clutched his cock. Oh yeah.

No way could he last until dessert at her house. He needed to take care of the problem now or risk a premature release the second she touched him. With one hand on the tiled wall, he leaned forward and gripped his shaft. He started with slow, measured strokes, but increased his speed as the muscles in his thighs tightened. Rocking his hips, he imagined sinking deep into Rachel, hearing her cry out his name.

"Luke?"

"Yes. Fuck." He exploded against the wall, his body jerking from the release.

"Luke, are you home?"

Shit. He hadn't imagined her voice. She was really in his house.

Slamming off the water, he shoved open the shower curtain. Steam filled the bathroom, but not another person. Where was she, and how had she gotten into his house? He'd locked the front door. Or had he?

Without taking the time to dry off, he wrapped a towel around his waist then rushed out into the hall. The crystal sphere had stopped glowing? Damn it. He had to find her before she stumbled upon the orb. No woman had ever noticed the light, but would Rachel be able to see the sphere?

CHAPTER FIVE

Pacing her living room did nothing to relieve her nerves. Rachel had to get outside before she vomited. Christine had abandoned her hours ago—after a text from Roy looking for arm candy at the mayor's birthday party. Since then, she'd finished covering her odds and ends furniture with matching covers, fitted her bed with new linens, and dressed for the date, this time with minimal makeup. No way would she try to be someone else again. But her impatience had risen to new heights. She had to see Luke. Had he changed his mind?

She glanced at her watch and frowned. Only four. Another hour to wait. Maybe longer. Perhaps a walk around the neighborhood would help, though she dreaded who she might run into. At least she had her date as an excuse to turn down any offers from the church ladies. She slipped out the door and locked it behind her. The park down the street sat abandoned, the kids of Hanton preferring the new equipment down by the river. Starting in that direction, she paused, taking a quick peek back at her neighbor's house. He had to be home. His truck sat in the driveway. And she hadn't heard him ride off on his Harley. Perhaps she could go over there now and get the date started before she lost her nerve.

Rushing back, she stood on his porch, hand raised, ready to knock. Would he be upset she arrived early? She knocked anyway, swallowing bile.

Clasping her sweaty hands together, she waited. No answer. Maybe he was in the backyard or still working on his bike. She peered through the window of the garage and over the fence, but couldn't find him. Returning to the front porch, she banged again. With a click, the door popped open.

Through the crack, she caught a glimpse of his foyer. Empty. Had he intended to let her in then had to rush to get something?

She pushed it open farther. "Luke?" If he was busy with dinner, she would help him, make up for last night.

Gazing around, she searched for any sign of him. Nothing. The blue glow from yesterday still permeated his home, but it seemed to originate from the second floor unlike the day before. What could create such an illumination? The glow intensified then dulled over and over again as if it were alive and knew she stood there. Or was Luke playing a trick on her?

She stepped inside, curious to find the source. After closing the door behind her, she tiptoed up the stairs, and braced for him to jump out at her.

The pulsing of the light subdued, but she continued to search, drawn as if the source wanted her to find it.

She blinked. Wait. What was she doing? "Luke, are you home?"

In an instant, she heard a clunk. The rush of flowing water disappeared. Shit, he was in the shower, and she was inside his home, uninvited. She glanced around. The blue glow she'd followed disappeared. How the hell was she going to explain why she was there?

The bathroom door opened, and she froze, staring at the almost naked, and very wet, hunk down the hall. Only a small white towel covered his manly parts. From the way something hard jutted against the towel and pointed at her, she guessed very manly indeed. But would she find out for herself after he'd caught her trespassing?

"Rachel?" His towel dropped to the floor, but he paid no attention, his focus intent on her. "What are you doing in my house?"

"I...." No more words formed. She couldn't stop staring at him, gazing farther and farther down. She longed to touch every single inch. At the sight of his thick cock, she gasped. Never had she been so fascinated by a man's parts. Her mouth watered. What did he taste like?

In an instant, he stood in front of her, his erection swaying back and forth holding her attention.

"Hello, I'm up here." He lifted her chin until their gazes met. "I don't mind that you're here, Rachel, but I want to know why. And how'd you get in? I know I locked the doors."

She chewed her bottom lip, focusing on a spot on the wall beside him to avoid his stare. "I thought we could maybe start our date early. I came over here, found the door open, and followed the blue light up here. I'm sorry."

He stepped closer, backing her into a corner. "You saw the blue light?"

Her breath caught in her throat. "Y...yes. I saw it yesterday, too. But today it was different, pulsing."

"Pulsing? Are you sure?" His expression changed, as if he didn't believe her.

"Yes. I wanted to know what it was. I know I shouldn't have come in, but when the door opened, I thought you were busy with something and wanted me to come in."

"Geez." He brushed his hands over his face. "Do you see it now?"

Her lust died as she contemplated why he thought the light so important. "No. It disappeared the second you stepped out of the bathroom."

"Are you sure you even saw it?" He inched closer, sandwiching her between a wall of plaster and one of muscle. His hands resting on her hips, he claimed her mouth, drawing every thought from her mind. She wasn't even sure she knew her name.

Fingers on his waist, she grazed over row upon row of muscles. More. She wanted all of him.

Lining his tongue along her lips, he ground his pelvis to hers. God, he was so hard. She opened her mouth to his sweet invasion, running her hands along his back. Luke was everything she'd ever wanted. In no way would she ever get enough.

He broke the kiss and leaned back, gripping the edge of her shorts. "How are you feeling today?"

No, don't stop. "Better now." She no longer cared about the blue glow, only wanting him to take her with reckless abandon. Running her foot along the back of his leg, she kissed him. No more talk. Desire raced through her body, and only he could help her release it. He grasped her ass and lifted her. Wrapping her legs around his waist, she brought her mound against the tip of his cock. Oh God, she needed her clothes off now. If only she'd thought to take them off when she'd stepped inside. But she never expected to find him in the shower.

He broke the kiss, leaving her moaning. Why had he stopped? From the stiff cock separating her thighs, he obviously wanted this as much as her.

His intense gaze caught her off guard. "Rachel, what happens next is up to you. You can go downstairs while I get dressed, or we can go to my room and finish what we've started."

"Let's go to your room." Her voice came out husky, but he seemed to like it, groaning after she spoke.

"You're sure?"

"Take me." No hesitation. She wanted him now.

He swung her around and pressed his lips to hers, devouring her with passionate kisses. Following where he carried her became impossible, the power of his lips consuming her.

He laid her down on his plush bed, kneeling over her. She struggled to remove her shorts as he kissed his way down her neck. "Here, let me."

Yanking her shorts off, he tossed them across the room. But with her thong, he took his time, trailing his tongue along the inside of her leg while sliding them down.

"Oh, Luke." No guy had ever given her body so much attention. This was already the best experience ever. Even if she only had one night with him.

He moved between her thighs, playing with the hem of her top. "Let's get the rest of your clothes off."

With her top and bra on the floor, she lay back and waited for him to assess her body. Unlike his previous dates, she had extra curves. Would he still want her?

But he wasted no time examining her. On top of her again, he ran his tongue from her navel up to the space separating her breasts. "You taste so good."

She moaned at the pressure of his body over hers. He made her feel more desirable than any other man had.

Sucking on her nipple, he massaged her breasts with his large hands. She arched up until his cock pressed against her heat. God, she wanted him inside her. Moisture pooled between her folds. "Now, Luke."

He stopped his teasing and reached over to his nightstand, removing a small square package from the drawer. He tore open the plastic and slipped on the condom. His fingers trembled as he ran them along her thighs. "I've waited a long time for this moment."

Me, too. Their encounter hadn't begun as she'd imagined, but still led to the same result. Better than her fantasies.

He lined the tip of his cock with her opening. Then entered her. Slowly. Pushing in little by little, giving her time to adjust, time to fit around him.

"Yes," she hissed, gripping his arms. So thick. Finally complete.

He rocked in and out, kissing her gently, his lips lingering on hers. "Perfect," he whispered.

Tears welled in the corners of her eyes. She couldn't help herself. Suddenly, nothing seemed impossible. If she was with Luke now, if he truly wanted to change, they might have a future together.

In an instant, he pulled out of her, locked his legs around hers and flipped onto his back. She sat on his waist, a position no guy had ever wanted her in.

He lifted her by her hips then lowered her over top of him.

Her groan of pleasure mixed with his. Nothing and no one could ever compare.

"That's better. Now show me what you like." He thumbed the wetness from her eyes. "Are you okay?"

She nodded. "I've always wondered what it would be like with you."

Luke raised an eyebrow. "Well, I hope you're not disappointed." He laid claim to her mouth, his tongue dancing with hers. Grabbing her waist, he guided her back and forth. The pleasure consumed every ounce of her soul. Being with Luke, as an active participant, filled her with a longing for more. No way did she ever want to let him go after this.

Hands on his chest, she sat up, finding her own rhythm. She had to prove she was worth keeping around.

Intense pressure radiated through her from head to toe. Her walls clenched around him. He rocked her faster, bringing her closer to release. But she held on as long as possible. He hadn't come yet. He would never want to be with her again if he didn't orgasm, too. Past experience proved that.

"Let it go."

What? She gazed down at him. "I can't. You haven't yet."

"Don't worry about me. You're so close. Just let it go." He ground himself deeper into her.

Exactly the trigger she needed. Throwing her head back, she grasped his shoulders. Radiant light filled her mind. Luke kept moving as the orgasm swept through her, every nerve exploding with sensation. Crying out with pleasure, she struggled to hold onto her sanity.

When she finally opened her eyes, he grinned up at her. "How was it?"

No words could describe how she felt, but a sudden terror gripped her. "I'm sorry I didn't wait for you. I thought—"

He pressed his lips to hers for a tender kiss. "Rachel, if you hadn't released, I would have thought I did something wrong. Don't ever apologize for having an orgasm." Trailing his fingers up and down her sides, he left her body tingling.

"But how can you be satisfied?" She didn't understand. Guys like him didn't exist in Hanton. The ones she'd dated always looked out for only themselves.

He reached up and cupped her cheek. "Oh, we're not finished yet, and I plan on making you scream my name many more times tonight."

She moaned as his cock pulsed inside of her. Still hard, he took her past oblivion over and over again.

Rachel stared at the little boy with the big black eyes. "What's your name?"

He blinked, and his eyes suddenly looked human, like hers. Green, too. She gasped. How'd he do that?

"Four three seven."

"What's that?"

"My name." He smiled.

"Nuh-uh." She wrinkled her nose. "That's a number, not a name."

Some of the boys in her class who played hockey over in Allentown *signed their jersey number on their homework sheets, but always after their names.*

His bottom lip quivered. "But that's what my parents call me."

Oh no, she didn't want to see him cry. She had to make things better. "It's a very nice name, but maybe you could have one from Earth, too."

He grinned at the suggestion. "Will you give me a name?"

"Sure." But only one name came to mind, that of her dog hit by a car last summer. She ran through a list of others, but they were all boys she went to school with. Yuck!

"What about...Luke?"

He cocked his head to the side. "You'd name me after someone you love?"

"Of course." She refused to call him after someone she hated, someone who teased her all the time. The little boy was very nice and kind of cute. Her cheeks warmed. She might actually have a crush on an alien.

He pulled the blanket farther up. "I'm really cold."

"Let me help." Under the covers, she wrapped her arms around him, and leaned on his bare shoulder. He made her feel safe, and if she could stay there forever, she would.

Rachel flicked her eyes open, struggling to breathe. Luke—the alien boy. Luke—the man whose arms surrounded her in his bed. Could they be the same person? Oh God, how did she not remember him? She'd dreamed of him her entire life. Her muscled tightened. No, it couldn't be. Aliens didn't exist. She just had an active imagination as a child. And that belief destroyed her family.

But why did he haunt her sleep, repeatedly?

She slipped from his embrace and off the bed, staring at him. Was the man who'd made love to her last night really an extraterrestrial?

No! She didn't want to find out, to ruin the magical evening she would hold onto forever. She'd stayed too long anyway. As soon as he woke up, he would ask her to leave. A sigh escaped past her lips. No wonder all of his previous women had left upset if sex with him always moved mountains. After dressing back into her clothes, she took one last glance at him on the bed.

Who was he really? Had her mind simply inserted him into her recurring dream? No, the idea of him being an alien, the little boy she'd met so long ago, felt right. But what kind of relationship could they have? What if the government found out where he came from and took him away? It would never work.

Fighting the urge to touch him again, she left the room.

Luke woke to her panic like an anvil slamming down on his chest. He leaped from his bed then raced out of his room. "Rachel?"

She'd reached the bottom of the stairs before he spotted her. What on Earth had he done to make her leave? His plans to make her breakfast, and to take her out on his Harley would be ruined if she left.

She gazed up at him, her face a mass of confusion. But her radiating fear worried him the most. Why was she afraid of him?

Only wanting to stop her, he hadn't put on any clothes. He refused to let her go now that he had her in his life. "What's wrong? Where are you going?"

"Home. I…I'm sorry I stayed so late."

"Rachel, no." He raced down the stairs and tried to wrap his arms around her, to prove he never wanted her to leave, but she pulled away. "I was hoping you would stay."

"I can't. I have stuff to do at home." She blinked rapidly, continuing to step back, closer and closer to the front door.

"Later, then?" How could she walk away after last night? They had a connection, something special. What had he done wrong?

Grabbing the door handle, she stared down at it. "I don't know. I need time to think."

Shit. He'd rushed her, had sex before she was ready. "I'd really like to see you again." What else could he say?

Resting a hand on her shoulder, he hoped to understand her sudden change in attitude. Why did she hurry to get away from him? But when she winced, he backed off.

She focused on him with wide eyes. "Are you…? Oh God, this is going to sound stupid. But, are you an alien? Are you the little boy I named Luke so many years ago, the little boy I fell asleep curled up with in the wicker rocking chair on my front porch?"

If he ever wanted a future with her, he had to tell her the truth. But would he lose her? Would she leave forever? "Rachel, I—"

"Yes or no?" She screamed at him, her words laced with fear and disbelief.

Would he see her again if he told her? His chest tightened. "Yes."

Turning around, she raced away from him, stealing his hope for a lifetime with her.

With a roar, he punched the door. His throat constricted, making it hard to breathe. Her rejection stung worse than being attacked by a swarm of bees. Shit, why had he returned to Hanton?

No way could he continue to live beside her. Staring over there and being reminded of her dismissal would hurt more than anything. Starting

48

tomorrow, he would make arrangements to sell his house and move across the country. Somehow, some way, he would forget about her, make the heartache end.

CHAPTER SIX

The rain pouring from the sky, as she stared out her office window, matched her mood. Waking up in her own bed in the morning, she hadn't remembered how she got there. From the moment she'd left Luke's house, tears had streamed down her face, and they'd refused to stop.

She'd walked away from the man who showed her sex could be more than a chore. Not only that, but he showered her with compassion, with praise. The entire time she'd been with him, she thought she could fall in love with him. But now…. How could she love an alien?

Every time she tried to sleep, she saw the vulnerable little boy who had landed in front of her house. And guilt clenched her gut. She'd wanted to protect him then, stay with him forever. Had she grown too shallow over the years, doubted him because of his differences?

A sour taste filled her mouth. No, she wasn't like that. Alien or not, she wanted him, and refused to let him out of her life.

Resting her head on her arms, she struggled to keep her eyes open. They itched from crying and lack of sleep. She should have stopped at the coffee shop before coming in to work, but she'd wanted to avoid everyone, especially Luke. Did he hate her now for walking out on him? Or would he move on to the next woman? She cringed at the thought.

Tonight, as soon as she left work, she would go straight to his house, apologize for the way she'd acted, and hope he forgave her.

If she managed to make it through the rest of the day. Though she swore she hadn't fallen asleep, she fought to sit up again when someone cleared their throat inside her office.

She leaned back in her chair and focused on her boss. "Sorry, sir. I just had a bad night."

"Don't let it happen again, Rachel. I'd rather you phone in sick than sleep at your desk."

Nodding, she observed the dark circles under his eyes. He looked as tired as she felt. Was he living back at home or still at Roy's? She'd avoided Christine's phone calls yesterday and didn't know the latest gossip.

"You've been here five years now, Rachel, and performed better than any of our financial services representatives. I appreciate your dedication, and would like you to train as a management associate." He sat on one of the chairs in front of her desk. "I'm sending you to Waterton next Monday."

"Really?" All weariness fled, replaced by urgency. She had to go shopping—again—had to arrange for someone to keep an eye on her house. Christine would do it, but Luke lived next door. The request would be the perfect excuse to talk to him.

Bill slid a file across her desk. "Just fill out this paperwork and have it to me by the end of the day."

"Thank you." When her parents' died just after her nineteenth birthday, she either found a job and took over the mortgage payments or forfeited everything to the bank—too much owing to make any profit from selling the home where she grew up. She would have been left with nothing. Taking pity on her, the bank had hired her on as a teller, and she'd worked her way up to her current position. Finding a rut there, she'd remained too comfortable and scared to do anything better. But now, her time had come to move up in the world. Finally, her career had a future blossoming. And maybe someday, it would take her far away from Hanton. Would she be able to say the same about her love life after today?

Luke eyed at the *For Sale* sign on his front lawn, an ache filling him. The decision had wracked him with pain and guilt, but moving away was the only option to get over her rejection. Living next to a woman who didn't share his feelings hurt much worse. He didn't know where to go, but once his house sold, he would find another one. Far away. Things would have been much easier if he hadn't been such a curious child, if he'd remained on the ship.... But he'd gotten over that mistake years ago.

For now, he would avoid Rachel and try his best to block her emotions.

Shit. Why was she walking up his driveway? He didn't expect to see her on his doorstep, thought she would be happy with him leaving. But there she stood on the porch, her hand raised and ready to knock.

He didn't know whether to let her in or ignore her. Sensing her anxiousness, he grabbed the handle. Would she only tell him off, make it easier for him to leave her?

Waves of disappointment slammed into him when he opened the door. Did she regret coming over, sleeping with him, or knowing him altogether? He gripped the doorjamb, expecting her to crush him even more than she already had.

"You're selling your house?" She watched him with big doe-like eyes, her bottom lip trembling.

"Yes." He groaned from the slap of emotions flying off of her. Not one stood out, but happiness was not among them. A deep shadow cast over his heart. What had he done?

"When are you moving?" Her voice cracked as she asked the question.

"Depends on how long it takes to sell." Though part of him suddenly hoped it wouldn't sell, believed he still had a chance with her.

She raised her eyebrows and gulped. "Are you moving far away?"

"I was planning on it." The pain from standing in front of her proved it would be impossible to live near her if she didn't want to be with him.

"Why?"

The assault of emotion from her left him weak. She had to leave. "Why do you care? You're the one who ran out on me when you found out what I was."

"Yes, but that was yesterday."

"What's changed since then?"

She glanced away. Her dam broke, and tears streamed down her cheeks. "Everything," she whispered.

Shit. He'd read her all wrong, acted too soon. Now he had a mess of a situation to clean up, starting with the woman in tears on his doorstep. Placing a hand on her shoulder, he yearned for her to look at him again. "I thought you wanted nothing to do with me because I'm...an alien."

"No. I was just so confused. I needed time to think." Her eyelids fluttered. "I didn't expect you to do something so drastic."

Digging his fingers into the frame, he winced through the pain. "I'm sorry." He couldn't tell her that the thought of living beside her when she hated him made him want to flee. Not when he still wasn't sure how she felt. "Nothing is final yet."

"But, you're still going to move away?"

"Yes." Either way, he refused to stay in Hanton forever. His plan had been to come back, claim Rachel, and leave again with her. But fear of rejection from the beautiful woman who'd blossomed from the little girl who'd accepted him unconditionally had sidelined those plans. "I never wanted to stay this long."

"So, there's no chance for us." She spun away and rushed toward her house.

Fuck. He raced after her and managed to grab her arm just before she stepped up to her porch. She faced him, fire lighting her eyes. If she loved him with as much intensity as the anger she threw at him, their relationship might last forever. *Please give me another chance.*

"You didn't let me finish." Would she change her mind if she knew the truth? But that meant showing vulnerability. With a deep breath, he stared deep into her emerald eyes. "I came back to Hanton for you. Ever since I met you, I felt a connection to you. Growing up in orphanages and group homes where no one questioned my background, I remained determined to find you as soon as I had the chance."

"And yet, you're leaving."

"I panicked when you walked out on me. I assumed you would never be with me because of what I am." He examined the neighborhood, making sure no one had heard. "I'm sorry."

Releasing her arm, he blew out a heavy breath. So much for being the alpha male every woman desired.

At the touch of her hand, he looked up.

"Maybe you can come in, and we can talk about it?"

Sensing her hope, he thought he might still have a chance with her. "Sure."

His phone vibrated in his pocket. "Excuse me for a moment." He fished the device from his pocket and heard his real estate agent on the other end.

All his hope deflated as the woman announced someone would be viewing his place in an hour. Tucking the cell away, he turned to Rachel. "I'm going to have to take a rain check. There's someone coming to look at the house soon, and I have to make sure it's presentable before they arrive."

"Maybe I could help?"

He shook his head. "No. I couldn't ask you to do that." The reminder of his ill-timed decision would be hard enough without her with him.

"Well, do you have a place to go while they're there?" She rocked up to the balls of her feet. "You could come over here. I can make something for dinner."

"I'd love to." No way would he refuse her offer. Leaning over, he kissed her on the cheek. "I'll see you in about thirty minutes."

She smiled. "Okay."

His heart pounded all the way home. The cleaning had already been done earlier in the day. Now, he just needed to find a place to store the orb while some stranger traipsed through his house. Should he take it with him to Rachel's? She'd already seen its glow. If he was going to have any type of relationship with her, he had to tell her everything, about the orb and his ability to read her emotions. Her reaction tonight would determine if they had a chance at a future together. He rolled his shoulders and stepped into his house. Might as well get it over with.

Rachel blinked as she opened the door to find Luke on her doorstep. She hadn't expected him to return, still unsure if he was playing her or really did want her in his life. One week wasn't enough time to figure out his intentions. But if he moved away while she trained for her new position she would be devastated.

He reached for her hand, rubbing his thumb over the back. "Does the offer still stand for dinner?"

"Of course. Come on in." With an almost bare refrigerator and cupboards, she'd thrown a meatloaf together with mashed potatoes—a staple growing up. Sundays were always reserved as her grocery shopping day, but she hadn't felt up to going anywhere yesterday, only finding a pound of ground chicken. Though with Luke's intense gaze, she didn't think it mattered what they ate. She'd seen the same look right before he carried her to his bedroom and showered her with passion only two days earlier.

He followed her, but stopped on the porch, staring at her wicker rocking chair. "You still have it?"

She nodded. "I would never get rid of it. It reminded me of…you."

With a wry grin, he stepped closer. "I captivated you back then, didn't I?"

So much for the vulnerable alien she'd seen earlier. He'd returned to the confident man women everywhere admired. How would she ever keep his attention?

Setting down his duffle bag, he gripped her hand tighter. "Why don't we take a seat, for old times' sake?"

She led him over, and he sat down first, guiding her onto his knee. "We don't quite fit now, do we?"

"No, but I like it just the same." Several people had suggested she get rid of the chair, including Christine, but she could never bear to part with it, or the memory of the little alien boy. And now he'd come back to her, a grown and sexy man.

Still unsure of his feelings for her, she leaned on his shoulder, seeking the same comfort she had gained when trying to escape her parents. He ran his hand down her arm, her own nerves lighting up with need. "You feel so good in my arms."

Yes, if only he had never left. They could have grown up together. Her childhood would have been so much different. Maybe she would have had more than one friend. For a moment, she held onto the hope of finally having everything she'd dreamed of. A good career. A man who cared for her, loved her. And a chance to leave behind the town she grew up in. She never wanted the feeling to end. He had to know about next week, and with any luck, he wouldn't find someone else.

"Um, Luke, starting next Monday, I'll be out of town for training. I was wondering…."

He gently squeezed her thigh. "Yes?"

Lifting her head from his shoulder, she gazed into his mesmerizing eyes. "Would you check on my house while I'm gone?"

"That's it? That's all you want?" With one eyebrow raised, he cupped her cheek. "What happens if I move away before you get back?"

She drew in a deep breath. He had to be joking. "I'll only be gone for a week."

"Good, because I don't think I could stand not seeing you spy on me from your bedroom window for more than that." He caressed the side of her face. "And I couldn't stand not kissing your for that long, either."

His lips brushed along hers before he devoured her. Gripping his shirt, she gave into her desire. With every touch, he made all of her worries disappear. The passion of his kisses filled her soul. He made her feel like no other man had, wanted. Though it didn't matter. She only wanted him.

A car door slammed behind them at the same time the buzzer on her oven went off.

Gasping for breath, she pulled away.

"I take that as our cue to go inside," he said. "Sounds like dinner's ready, and I don't want to see who's trolling through my own home."

She nodded, sliding off his lap. "Yes, might be a good idea before the food burns."

On their way inside, he grabbed his bag. "While we eat, I need to show you something."

Show her something? Apprehension twisted her gut. Sure, she trusted him, but why wait to tell her? She lifted dinner from the oven and served it onto plates, trying to calm her shaking hands. When she'd waltzed into his house, uninvited, she'd done so with more confidence.

With a deep breath, she circled around, plates in hand, and set them on the table. On the corner, Luke had placed a cantaloupe-sized object resembling hundreds of tiny crystals formed together. A pale blue light emanated from inside, growing in intensity until it filled the entire kitchen. The same glow from his home.

"It seems to like you," he said, a wide grin plastered on his face.

Like her? "But what is it?" Some kind of high-tech device she'd yet to hear about? Wouldn't surprise her since she didn't even own a cell phone. Never had any need. No one called her but Christine. And most of the time, her friend came over rather than call.

Luke pushed back from the table and guided her onto his lap. "It's my orb from home. That's why I left you. My parents had kept it by my bed for as long as I can remember. I carried it with me the day I came to this planet. I thought I'd dropped it before being transported from the ship."

He glanced down at the floor, loosening his grip on her. "I thought maybe they would come back for me."

Her chest tightened at the hitch in his voice. If anyone knew what it was like to lose parents, she did. Even though she never had the best relationship with them, her life had shattered when they died. They'd abandoned her just like Luke's mother and father.

"I'm sorry." She trailed her hand down his arm, needing his comfort as much as she wanted to give the same to him.

His eyes became glassy. "You don't need to be sorry. You're the one who, as a child, accepted me without pause. I can't say the same about everyone else I've met. And they never knew of my origins."

God, how she could relate. Yet, everyone had known about her parents. Christine had been the only one who didn't shun her because of their actions.

The orb began to pulse. She leaned closer. "What did you mean when you said it likes me? What does it do?"

He squeezed her against his body. "It's like a guardian, glowing red when it disapproves of my actions and blue when it approves. You're the only woman who can see the light from the orb, and also the only one who has ever made it turn blue."

How had no one ever noticed? She immediately observed the light when she entered his house, though never thought much of it until it had turned red.

Wait! "The first time I went to your house, it glowed red when we were in the middle of...."

Squeezing her thigh, he chuckled. "Yes, it disapproved of me moving so fast. Yet, the next day my *guardian* wanted you upstairs."

She stared at the giant crystal again. At least it approved of her. Now, she just had to be sure of Luke's true intentions. Was he ready to commit?

He ran his hand down her back. "Why don't we eat? You made this wonderful dinner for us. Let's not waste it."

Conversation flowed freely for the next half hour. She shared parts of her childhood, while he revealed what he'd experienced growing up. Like her, he'd been an outcast, not due to his parents, but because he didn't have any.

If only he'd remained in Hanton.

Yes, if only.... She focused on him. "Why did you leave? Why didn't you stay here? With me?" Maybe her life would have gone differently if he'd stuck around.

Setting down his fork, he gripped the edge of the table. "I didn't have a choice. When I went outside to grab my guardian, a police car drove by. Because the cop didn't recognize me from town, and I couldn't tell him where I came from, he turned me over to Children's Services."

She gasped. "You must have been so scared." Many times she wished she would be taken away until her father told her what happened to children in foster homes. Remaining with her parents seemed to be the lesser evil.

"What I went through does not compare to the day you lost your mother and father."

A chill ran through her body. How would he know how she felt? And how did he even know about her past? She'd kept that part of her life out of the conversation. Even after so many years, her stomach still churned when she remembered the night of their deaths. "You don't know anything about that."

He reached out for her hand, but she shrank back. Why did he have to mention her parents?

"I do, Rachel. I experienced the same terror when you found them, the shock, then anger, and even the regret. I felt it all along with you."

A tear trailed down her cheek. "How? You have no idea what I went through." Nobody knew.

He left his chair to stand behind her, squeezing his fingers into her shoulder muscles. "Ever since the first day I met you, I've had an emotional connection to you. I experience all of your joy and sorrow, as you do."

A new pain clutched her heart. She glanced back at him. "Then why didn't you come back, then?" On the night she discovered her parents' bodies—dead after her father had shot her mother then turned the gun on himself—she'd really needed someone for support. Anyone.

Stepping away from her, he stared at the floor. "Because I wasn't ready to face your rejection."

With a deep inhale, she stood. She'd faced enough rejection in her life to understand. Craving the comfort he provided, she leaned against his chest and wrapped her arms around him.

"I'm sorry," he whispered, holding her tight.

Pressing her palm to his heart, she let go of the painful memories. "It doesn't matter anymore. We're together now."

Luke stroked the soft skin of Rachel's cheek, enjoying her naked body tucked into his. The morning would come soon enough, taking her away from him for five long days. Until that time, he planned to study every inch of her body in the moonlight shining through her bedroom window.

He'd spent every night with her since he'd revealed his secrets, and it would be hell to let her go in a few hours. Aside from the initial alien bit, nothing he'd told her seemed to scare her away. She accepted him just as she had as a child.

With a soft moan, she turned onto her back and opened her eyes. "Hey. Is it morning already?"

He smiled as she fought to keep her eyes open. "Not yet. Go back to sleep. I'm just not tired."

Turning onto her side, she reached over and grabbed his aching cock. "Maybe I can keep you company, or make you sleepy again."

Want coursed through his body, eliciting a deep groan. But as much as he craved her—never stopped—he didn't want to deprive her of sleep. "You have to drive to Waterton later today. You need to be well rested."

Her supple lips met his, and she crawled on top of him. "Once in Waterton, I'll have plenty of time to catch up on my sleep. Until I leave, I plan to make the most of our time together."

Condom in hand, she rolled the thin barrier over his cock then slid easily onto him. Gripping her hips, he released a growl. How was she ready for him after just waking up? He'd been the one with his cock lingering between the cheeks of her ass, fighting off the temptation to take her from behind. Had she sensed him the whole time?

With each sway of her hips, she moaned, voicing her pleasure. He palmed her breasts and tweaked her pert nipples. Her cries rose in pitch. Her body moved with its own ancient rhythm. For someone whose previous lovers had always taken control, she certainly took the reins well. Grabbing her waist, he rocked her faster. The satiny walls of her pussy clenched around him, tighter and tighter, until she burst.

But she didn't stop. Her unwavering motions continued, ramping up the intensity of his own impending orgasm. Wrapping his foot around her ankle, he flipped her onto her back, stealing the power. As much as he enjoyed her having the control, he loved taking charge. He lifted her legs onto his shoulders, thrusting as deep as possible. If he had the stamina to do this all day, he would. She fit him like a glove.

Panting, she dug her fingers into his arms, her wide eyes focused on him. "Holy fuck! You're going to make me come again."

His goal every time they had sex. She deserved more than just one. And his release drew closer. Faster and faster, he plunged into her, until he exploded in a frenzy of sensation. The orgasm rocketed through his body. Her release came at the same time, heightening his waves of pleasure, milking his pulsating cock until he'd lost every last drop.

Sliding off, she lay down on the bed beside him. "You tired yet?"

Damn, he would miss her. "No." The rush of euphoria zinging through his veins kept him from being able to settle.

Yet, the next thing he remembered, he woke up to the sun shining in the window and a showered and dressed Rachel rushing around, throwing things into her suitcase.

Sitting up, he rubbed his eyes and groaned. "What time is it?"

"Almost six," she huffed, plopping onto the lid. "I've got to go before I'm late."

He tossed the covers off. "Why didn't you wake me?" His plans to make her breakfast and help her pack no longer mattered. Not enough time. Now, he only needed to convince her to take some food with her. No way would he let her drive three hours on an empty stomach.

Pulling on his pants, he cursed the ancient alarm clock he'd thought Rachel had set.

She shrugged. "You needed more sleep." Grabbing a carry-on, she shoved more stuff inside.

He rolled his eyes. Why did she need so much?

Lifting her mountainous suitcase, he headed down the stairs. With the struggle he had, she would likely lose her balance if she tried to carry the luggage down herself. In the kitchen, he flicked on the coffee maker then mixed together granola, yogurt, and some blueberries he'd found in her fridge. Better than nothing.

Meeting her at the bottom of the stairs, he shoved the bowl in her hands. "Eat this before you go. Coffee is ready, and I'll take your baggage out to the car." He waited for an excuse.

Instead, she smiled, losing the harried expression he'd woken to. "Thank you."

Satisfied, he removed the other bag from her shoulder, and carried the gear out to the rental car. Not trusting her rust bucket, he'd offered to drive her himself, but she refused. She wanted a car to get to work from the hotel and didn't want to take him away from his work. So, he'd done the next best thing, rented a car for her to drive there and back.

By the time she met him outside, he'd already dressed and grabbed a cup of coffee for himself. "All set?"

She gave him a half smile. "I guess. I'm a little nervous, and I'm going to miss you."

As he would her. Reaching for her hand, he gave it a squeeze. "You'll do fine. And I'll call you every night. Mornings, too, if you want."

Her eyes lit up and she handed him her house key. "Okay, and I'll be home late Friday night."

"I'll be waiting." He kissed her goodbye then tucked her into the driver's seat. "Be safe."

Starting the engine, she nodded.

After tapping the hood of the car, he stood back. Five days. Not long at all. Watching her drive down the road, he waved.

Now, if only he could get rid of the bundle of nerves she'd passed on to him on top of his own. For, on Friday, he planned to ask her to marry him.

CHAPTER SEVEN

Rachel pulled into her driveway, sighing with relief. Her training had gone well, and she'd talked to Luke every night—sometimes more often—but she couldn't wait to be back in his arms again, beside him in bed. Sleep hadn't come as easily as she'd hoped in the hotel. She'd missed her own bed and her boyfriend's warm body. Hard to believe she'd grown accustomed to him so fast.

With a quick glance over at his house, she grinned. No truck. She'd beat him home. Finishing her training earlier than scheduled, she'd wanted to arrive before him and make him something nice for dinner. Perhaps chicken pasta parmesan. Not fine dining by any means, but her parents had never taught her how to make anything. She'd learned how to cook from the free recipe magazines she received in the mail.

Dragging her luggage, she struggled to reach the front porch. Maybe she should have waited for Luke. Finally, she made it up the steps. Key in hand, she tried to unlock her door, but found it already open a crack.

Strange. Had Luke forgotten to lock it behind him when he'd last come over?

She bumped the door, peeking inside. "Hello?"

"By Jesus, you scared me."

Jumping back, she shrieked. "What… are you doing… in my house?" Had something happened to Luke?

Mrs. Yantzi, the old lady whose house backed onto the river, stared at her, palm pressed to her chest. "I was cleaning, but now I think I'm going to have a heart attack."

She rushed over to her. "Oh gosh, why don't you sit down? I'll call for an ambulance." Like she needed someone else to die in her home.

The lady swatted at her. "I'm fine. Really. You just gave me quite a fright." With the cock of her head, she furrowed her pencil-thin brows. "What are you doing home so early? Luke said I'd have time to clean up before you arrived."

"I finished my training early." Not that it was any of her business. "Where is he, anyway?"

"Oh, it's been a busy week for him. First he sold his house…."

What? She missed the *Sold* sign on her way in?

"…and then he was asked to be a guest carpenter on that renovation show on the home improvement channel." She glanced at her watch. "His first episode should be on any minute now."

Rachel stood rooted to the floor, her mouth hanging open. What the hell had happened while she was gone, and why hadn't he told her about the show?

"Well, don't just stand there." Mrs. Yantzi sat on the couch and flicked on *her* television. "Come join me, and we can see how well he does."

Every step felt like she had a brick tied to each foot. Her boyfriend still kept secrets from her. Why? She knew he was an alien. How much bigger could things get than that? She choked down a sob and eyed the woman. "I still don't get why you're here."

Mrs. Yantzi shrugged. "Luke just wanted me to check on your houses while you were both gone. I thought since I was here, I'd clean it up a little."

She didn't know whether to be offended or thankful. But the vise gripping her chest overpowered all thought. Talking to her every night, he never once mentioned being on some television show, or even being away from home. He had a good reason, right? But the rock in the pit of her stomach disagreed. And her mind flashed back to all the women who'd come knocking on his door before her. Perhaps this time, he went to one of them.

Mrs. Yantzi tapped her arm. "Oh, look, it's starting. That host, Pepper, she sure is a pretty thing."

As much as she wanted to, she couldn't disagree. Jealousy ate at her every time the pretty host laid a hand on Luke, batting her eyelashes, and rubbing her double D breasts against him, over and over. His only reaction? A maddening grin. No wonder he hadn't told her. He didn't want her to know about his other woman.

"Look at those two flirting," Mrs. Yantzi said.

At least Rachel wasn't the only one to notice. She blew out a heavy breath, trying to maintain her composure in front of the other woman.

"They're both so attractive. Wouldn't they make a gorgeous couple? Imagine how adorable their babies would be."

The woman's comments slammed into her like a knife to the heart. A sob escaped from deep inside. And then the tears came. She'd been rejected and cheated on by guys before, but with him, the pain hurt much worse. For once, she had actually believed she had a future with a guy.

She saw Mrs. Yantzi staring at her through her tear-blurred eyes. "Oh, honey, did you have a thing with Luke? I'm sorry. I thought, living next door to him, you knew how he was with women."

Yeah, seemed no one but her believed he could change. *I'm such a fool.* She swallowed hard. No more.

She struggled away from the woman. She didn't need her comfort, only to banish all the love she had felt for Luke, the alien boy. But he wasn't a boy anymore, but a man who'd grown up on Earth and now acted like he belonged. A cheating bastard, just like every other man who lived in Hanton.

"Are you going to be okay?" Mrs. Yantzi asked.

"Yes." She didn't want to be around anyone, let alone the woman who he had asked to come into her house. The one he'd told where he'd be, but refused to tell his own girlfriend. Ex-girlfriend. The bullshit had to end.

"But...."

"Leave." Grabbing the bat she kept by the door—just in case—she swung it over her head.

She almost giggled at how fast the Mrs. Yantzi stumbled out of her house. Then she turned her attention to the wicker chair. It certainly didn't bring her a sense of peace and comfort anymore. Over and over again, she slammed the bat down on the chair. Bits and pieces flew all over the porch. And she kept smashing it until nothing but small twigs were left.

Setting down the bat, the stabbing pain in her heart only grew more intense. She'd come to love him, and in such a short time. Only to find out aliens could be assholes, too.

A sharp-edged knife plunged into the back of Luke's skull. Or so it felt. He swerved onto the side of the road. Once stopped, he massaged his head.

He had to get home. Something had happened to Rachel. Her emotions spiked worse than he'd ever experienced. But driving with the blinding pain in his head proved impossible. He palmed the back of his neck. If only someone could calm her down until he arrived. Where was Mrs. Yantzi?

Reaching into his pocket, he grabbed his cell. He thumbed through his few contacts, and dialed Rachel's number. *Please pick up and tell me you're okay.*

The phone rang and rang. She didn't answer, and the pounding in his head ramped in intensity. Shit. She must be mad at him. But why? Had she found out about the show? How would that make her mad at him? He had his reasons for keeping it a secret from her. And working on the show had helped him to secure a new place to live.

Oh no! She would have found out he'd sold his house. And he hadn't revealed that, either. No wonder her anger left him fighting to see through the pain. He'd planned to tell her, right before he asked her to marry him. With all of the events over the past week, the hope she would be his wife had kept him grounded. No one else accepted him the way she did. But would she forgive him? Would she spend the rest of her life with him?

Tucking his phone away, he gripped the steering wheel. He had to push past the pain and hurry home. She needed him. And he needed her.

Rachel tried to ignore the incessant banging on the door, but the noise served to increase the throbbing in her skull. She'd cried enough to fill a tub during the past couple of hours. No tears remained, only a splitting headache.

"Please let me in, Rachel. I can explain," he called.

Explain what? He'd fooled her into believing he loved her? Yeah, she'd already figured that one out. "Go away!"

"No, I won't." His voice faltered.

"Rachel, if you don't let me in, I'll...."

"What?" What could he possibly do from the other side of a locked door? She never wanted to see him again. Hopefully the closing date on his house would come quickly. He'd be gone, and she could forget about him. But would she ever be able to truly purge him from her mind? Her heart? Even as a young boy, he'd haunted her dreams. She'd yearned to find him again. Back then, she wasn't even sure he existed outside of her mind. Now, she knew the truth. Everything about the sexy alien broke her heart.

A fresh set of tears trailed down her cheeks.

A roar echoed from her porch. He really did feel her emotions. Good. He deserved to feel the pain he'd caused her.

A click came from the front, like a lock coming undone. She held her breath and turned toward the door. Luke dropped to his knees in front of her, grasping her hands.

She reeled back. "Get out! You broke into my house."

He stood slowly, propping his palms on his knees. Taking a step away from her, he still remained in her kitchen. "I didn't. The orb opened your door, just as it did to mine. It's been flashing red, unhappy with this situation. It doesn't want us to fight."

Balling her fists in her lap, she glared at him. "Yeah? Well, how did it feel when you cheated on me with Pepper?" She spewed out the woman's name like a bad taste in her mouth.

"Pepper? What does she have to do with anything?"

Her blood boiled. How could he act all innocent? She rolled her eyes at his feigned surprise. "I thought you loved me, Luke. Then I find out, while I was gone, you sold your house, got a gig on a TV show, and cheated on me. Why did you lie?"

His brows furrowed. "Cheated on you? With who?"

"Pepper," she spat out. "Even Mrs. Yantzi noticed how cozy you two were during the first episode. I'm sure everyone who watched the show figured out the host and the guest carpenter were fucking." Saying the words deepened the wound. She gasped, struggling to breathe. She just wanted him gone.

He drew a hand over his face. "I deserved that, I know. With my past reputation and the secrets I've kept from you this week, I can't blame you for not trusting me. But, I promise you, nothing happened between me and Pepper. Nothing happened with the women who came to my house, either. I always asked them to leave before we…. I only want you. I love you."

"Bullshit. How do you expect me to believe that? I saw how cozy the two of you were on television. Don't lie. Just leave."

"No." He pulled out his cell and dialed. "Hey, Pepper…."

As if! Calling his new fuck-buddy right in front of her?

"…my girlfriend wants to ask you something." Holding out the phone, he raised his eyebrows. "Ask her."

A wave of terror washed through her. Had she made a huge mistake in her assumptions? Or maybe he was covering his ass. Maybe they had an agreement.

Her fingers shook as she put the cell to her ear. "Hi, Pepper?"

"Yep, it's me. Let me tell you, you are one lucky lady."

What, did Luke fuck her then reveal he had a girlfriend? Wouldn't surprise her, since he hadn't even told Mrs. Yantzi they were dating. No point in holding back. "Did you fuck my boyfriend?"

Laughter burst through the phone before she heard, "I wish."

"Listen, Rachel. I admit that Luke is extremely hot, and I wasn't shy in my advances on him."

Her stomach turned. Actually hearing that he really had cheated on her would hurt worse than anything.

"But, he made it very clear from the first day that he had a girlfriend and was very happy with her. In fact, he ditched the production party tonight to get home to you. Seems he had something big planned."

With a sharp inhale, she glanced up at him. Had she just made the biggest mistake of her life?

He stared at her with hard eyes, his lips pursed.

"Is that all you wanted?"

She turned her attention back to the phone. "Yes, that's all."

"Okay, well, good luck." Pepper hung up, leaving her with a whole lot of groveling to do.

She gave the cell back to him. "I… I'm sorry." How could she ever make up for what she'd accused him of?

He grabbed his phone. "I hope you believe me now." Spinning on his heel, he left, slamming her front door behind him.

What the hell? How could he walk out on her like that? She'd said sorry. And he'd still kept stuff from her. Why hadn't he told her all along?

She gripped the seat of her chair. Was this the end? Had he left for good? She squeezed her eyes shut. If he truly felt her emotions, he should know how much guilt consumed her. He should know.

Springing from her seat, she headed for the door. He couldn't walk out on her. She wasn't finished with him yet.

She raced outside and over to his house. He still had to explain why he hadn't told her about the show or his house. And what *did* he have planned for tonight?

Reaching up to knock, she found the door open. Again. If he could walk into her house, she had no qualms about walking into his.

Peering inside, she gasped. He lay in the foyer, sprawled on his stomach.

Dropping to her knees beside him, she grasped his wrist to check for a pulse. Still strong.

"Luke? Are you okay?" She brushed hair away from his eyes. They were closed. Had he fallen asleep? Did aliens just drop like that? He'd never done so around her, but how well had she really known him?

Her heart thudded. What was she supposed to do? If she dialed 9-1-1, they'd take him to the hospital, and someone would be sure to discover he was an alien. And if he'd only passed out, calling for help was overkill.

The orb! Could it help? He'd brought it over, but where was it now? She examined the foyer for his bags. Nothing.

He must have left it at her place. She ran a hand across his back. "Luke, I'll be right back."

Sure her feet never touched the ground, she rushed back home and found the orb on her porch, in the same duffle bag he'd brought it over in the first time. Bright red light flashed, making it impossible to stare at the orb directly. Glancing away, she grasped the handles then zipped up the bag. She didn't need any nosy neighbors questioning her about his giant alien crystal. Racing back to his house, she fretted, finding him still on the floor. If the orb didn't work, she had no idea what to do next.

She slipped her hands into the bag and removed the flashing crystal. Now purple, it still flared with a blinding intensity. Laying the orb on his back, she hoped to revive him.

When its color changed to blue, she leaned back against the wall. Blue was a good thing, right? The flashing stopped, but still, the crystal pulsed, a warmth radiating from inside.

He moaned and turned on his side. She lunged to grab the orb before he rolled on top of it, returning it to the bag. Then she stared down at the man she loved. Never would she doubt him again. But was he okay? She stroked the side of his face. The secrets didn't matter anymore, so long as he woke to hold her in his arms again. If he forgave her.

Rolling onto his side, Luke whimpered. Every part of his body ached. Yet, something soft brushed over his cheek. Rachel. He opened his eyes and gazed up at her. Was she really there, or just an image created by his unconscious mind?

He'd tried to make it to the couch, but Rachel's emotions had weakened him so much. Managing to shut the door, he'd turned around before everything went black. And from the pain radiating through his body, he must have fallen flat on the floor.

"Luke, are you okay?"

He tried to answer her, but no words left his mouth. Still too weak.

"Oh, Luke, please be okay." She placed her other hand on his chest. "I love you. I have since we were children. God, I just wish I knew how to help you."

A new sensation radiated from her palm, flowing through him. Hot and cold at the same time, flushing out all of the pain. He gasped, struggling to sit up. She backed away, but he grabbed her hand, placing it back on his chest, above his heart. "You healed me."

Chewing her bottom lip, she nodded. "Yes, I put the orb on your back—"

"No." He drew in a quick breath. If only it were that simple. "The orb can't do that. When you rested your palm on me, I felt your concern, your love, your forgiveness. It all flooded into me, pushing away everything from before."

"I'm sorry I didn't trust you."

He shook his head. "Doesn't matter anymore." Ushering her onto his knees, he kissed her soft lips. Less than an hour ago, he had been sure he'd never have the chance to touch her again.

"Can we put it all behind us? Can we move on?" He swallowed down the nervous lump in his throat. "Because I have something very important I want to talk to you about."

Her eyes grew wide, and he sensed her trepidation. She rose from his lap, brushing off her ass. If all went well, his hands would be there later tonight. So long as he didn't screw everything up.

Pushing off the ground, he stood, his head spinning. But he took a deep breath and planted a palm against the wall to steady himself. He had to ask her. The only reason he'd come back to Hanton was for her. And now he planned to leave. Would she agree to leave with him?

Grasping her hand, he guided her over to the couch. She sat while he remained standing, too anxious to sit next to her.

With her arms crossed, she gazed up at him, her bottom lip caught between her teeth. "So, what important thing did you want to talk to me about?"

"Well, you know now that my house is sold."

She nodded, throwing off a hint of anger.

He cringed. This was already heading in the wrong direction. He had to save himself, and quick. "I'm sorry for not telling you. But you should know that I already have a new place lined up. It's a year-round cottage on the shores of Lake Barnaby."

"Sounds wonderful." She tried to sound excited, but her emotions betrayed her. Instead, he felt her bracing for bad news.

No. No. It wasn't supposed to go like this. "The problem is, the cottage isn't built yet. I'm going to need a place to stay until then."

Her hands dropped to her sides. "I have an extra room. If you want to stay in my rundown home."

Her extra room? But that's not what he meant. Her disappointment stung. Shit, this wasn't going well at all. He had to stop talking about the house. *Just ask her!*

Fishing in his pocket, he fumbled for the diamond ring he'd bought a week ago. Back then, he'd been much more sure of himself, confident Rachel would say yes when he asked her to marry him. Now, he didn't even know if she wanted him as her neighbor.

Only one way to find out. He yanked the ring out and lowered to one knee.

She covered her mouth.

"I know we haven't dated for very long, but I've never wanted anyone but you. Never." He reached for her hand, and she didn't pull away. "When I move into my new place, I want you to move in with me, as my wife. Rachel, will you marry me?"

A single tear trickled down her cheek. Her bottom lip quivered.

Shit, she was going to say no.

Silence lingered, eating away at the single shred of confidence he had left. He tried to read her emotions, get a sense of what to expect. But he got nothing.

Finally, she stroked his face. "I've waited a long time for my alien to come and rescue me from this life, this place. And now you're here. Finally." She kissed the corner of his mouth. "Yes, Luke, I will marry you."

Relief mixed with intense joy washed over him. Hers blended with his. He slipped the ring on her finger and grinned. Nothing could make him happier than this moment.

She wrapped her arms around his neck, and joined him on the floor. Grazing her lips across his, she tortured him with her adventurous tongue. He had to have her. Now.

Lifting her in his arms, he carried her up to his room. Since the night he'd arrived on Earth, he had waited for this moment. And now he had everything he wanted. Rachel. Always Rachel.

She waved goodbye. A hint of sadness washed through her as she watched Christine and Roy drive away. She hadn't expected their relationship to last, but they'd remained together for almost two years. And even her old boss, Bill, had found love again. With Pepper, of all people. Maybe Hanton would one day lose its reputation as the cheating capital of the province.

But she was happy to be gone, leaving behind her old house and the memories of what had happened there many years ago. Her new life had begun.

She turned around to face the lake, where oranges and reds danced across the water and sky as the sun dipped below the horizon. Absolutely beautiful. The same view would greet her every night from inside the house her husband had built in between his numerous contracts. LJ Construction became a much sought-after company after Luke's appearances as a guest carpenter. And she'd finally finished her accounting courses in order to run the financial side of the business.

"We're finally here." Her husband, an alien, wrapped his arms around her, laying his hands on her ever-growing belly. "Is he still active, or has he calmed down a bit?"

Covering his hands with hers, she guided them across her stomach to the spot where their baby's foot pressed against her insides. "He's sleeping now, but I think he's a bit squished in there. Only two more weeks. I hope I don't burst beforehand."

Luke chuckled then kissed the top of her head. "We were cutting it close with the construction, but we finished. Now, let me carry you over the threshold and into our new house."

Even with her big belly, he scooped her into his arms, carrying her up the steps and inside their cottage. "Welcome home, my love."

God, she adored her husband. Her alien. She rested her head against his chest. Not long ago, her life now had been an impossible dream. But her spaceman had returned for her, and now her dreams had become their reality.

JUST ANOTHER WEDDING
A BONUS STORY

Another wedding. Another event where people recognized and interacted with her based on the image she portrayed on television. Though paid to be a flirt, in real life Pepper Dobson preferred to blend into the wall, go unnoticed by those she didn't know. Because if everyone ignored her, they wouldn't judge her, make false assumptions.

Kicking off her shoes, she leaned back in her chair. The rest of the cast and crew invited to the wedding had abandoned her ages ago, off with their spouses or one-night stands. And yet, she continued to watch the happy couple dance.

A pang of jealousy rose in her stomach. Of all the guys she'd met since starting on *House Switching*, Luke had been the only one who hadn't tried to get in her pants. Sure, they'd had plenty of on-camera chemistry, but as soon as the show finished filming for the day, he placed a barrier between them, treating her like a lady rather than someone he wanted to score with. Once she learned he had a girlfriend back home, she understood why he kept his distance. He remained faithful and loyal, something she didn't see much in any man in the last couple of years. No, she attracted players who easily left her for the next pretty face when she turned them down.

Luke's new wife radiated with happiness, waltzing across the dance floor in her chiffon wedding dress. What Pepper wouldn't give for one ounce of her joy.

The lights rose. Very few guests remained; only the wedding party and her. But she resisted the walk up to her empty hotel room.

Slipping her heels back on, she stood, ready to help clean up the banquet hall. It was the least she could do after a fabulous meal and free alcohol. Or simply an excuse to avoid the loneliness.

"Pepper, I'm so glad you came, and I hope you enjoyed yourself." Rachel wrapped her arms around her with a squeeze, a far different exchange than their first conversation.

"Thank you," she said. "And congratulations! I wish you both the very best." Pepper had come to like her, so opposite of the superficial women she often met in the television industry. She really was the typical girl next door, didn't care much for the latest styles, but always presented herself well.

Luke came over to give her a hug and a kiss on the cheek. "Thank you for coming. Do you need a ride home at all?"

"No, I'm spending the night here at the hotel." Unable to predict how much she would end up drinking, she'd booked the room long ago. Though she'd always envisioned spending the night with someone else. Even if with just one of the crew too wasted to go anywhere.

"Well, have a good night, then." He scooped his bride up in his arms, carrying her out of the hall.

Talk about an awkward moment. They were going up to consummate their marriage, and she had to rely on her own devices for company and pleasure.

"Need a lift back to town?"

A deep voice resonated behind her, one of concern rather than the cocky tone of someone trying to pick her up.

She spun around, expecting an older gentleman. Not so. Taking a step back, she gazed into the rich blue eyes of a handsome man. With a strong jaw, wavy blond hair, and a styling three-piece suit, he made her heart race more than any hunky contractor she'd met in her past. "Um, I...."

The man's face paled. "Oh, I'm sorry, Miss. I thought you were someone else."

At least he didn't call me Ma'am. Though, she'd never been mistaken for another person. Not since the show started, anyway.

Pepper shrugged. "It's all right. Who did you think I was?" Best to make sure he wasn't trying a pick-up line she hadn't yet heard.

"I thought you were from Hanton. But when you turned around, I realized my mistake." He stuck out his hand. "I'm Bill, Rachel's former boss."

She offered her hand in return, surprised by his firm yet gentle grip. He didn't crush her knuckles together like other guys had tried to that night.

"Pepper. I'm...." If he didn't already know who she was, she didn't plan on telling him. No point in giving him false hope. "A friend of Luke."

"He sure is a popular guy. Considering neither of them have any surviving family, it's nice that so many of their friends came, especially those from the show he was on for a bit."

"Yeah, that home improvement show." Time to test whether he was playing her. "What was it called again?"

He shrugged, his mouth twisting to the side. "I don't know. I hate to admit it, but I've never seen it."

"Really?" She smiled, her eyes sparkling.

No woman had ever looked at him or glanced his way lately without an expression of pity or disdain. And during his recent divorce settlement, his ex-wife wouldn't even turn his way, as if their five years together meant nothing.

He sucked in a deep breath. "Yes. I just haven't had the time. Though, I guess I should have watched it with so many people here tonight from the show."

"Phew." She stepped forward, adjusting the boutonnière on his lapel. "I'm glad I'm not the only one."

Blood rushed straight to his cock. He hadn't come to the wedding to pick up, only to support Rachel and Luke as one of the ushers. But that didn't stop his libido from craving more. His hand wasn't cutting it anymore. Besides, the worst possible answer was no. And that would never hurt as much as finding his wife in the pool, fucking the town's male slut.

He balled his fists, trying to conjure up the courage. "Would you like to get a drink? I think the hotel bar is still open. And we can talk about what other shows we don't watch."

God, that sounded so lame. Though he'd never had the need to pick up women in his earlier years. Every girlfriend in his life had asked him out. And that added up to two.

Pepper's smile widened.

He held his breath, bracing for her rejection.

"Sure, I'd like that. And maybe you can tell me what it's like to be the bank manager in the small town of Hanton."

Hallelujah! He dug his fingers into his palms, resisting the urge to fist pump the air. *Maybe tonight won't be a total bust after all.*

Pepper sipped her martini, gazing into the alluring eyes of Hanton's bank manager. She knew tonight would lead to a one-night stand, to never see Bill again once he slipped out of her hotel room. But she no longer cared. She couldn't face spending the night, alone. And for once, a guy hadn't asked her out based on the character she portrayed.

"So, what kind of hours does a bank manager work?" A lame question, but she wanted to know if he'd be leaving first thing in the morning or if they would have extra time to cuddle. Noticing the lack of a wedding ring, and the hard-on pressing against his zipper, she had no doubt he would join her in her room. But even with a one-night stand, she enjoyed the pillow talk after. If he was into that.

"I used to work nine to five, Monday to Friday. Though lately, I've been putting in more hours, plus taking care of Rachel's clients while her replacement is being trained."

Something he wasn't telling her. Another reason for him working later. But that didn't matter. Tonight would be about their pleasure. Rubbing her hand up his thigh, she squeezed, satisfied when she heard him groan. "Do you get any time off?"

"I...I get Sundays off."

The hope and desperation in his eyes reflected her own feelings. She refused to let him walk away without having her needs satisfied, and fulfilling his as well.

"We're closing." The bartender rubbed his hands in a cloth. "Sorry, but you two are going to have to find someplace else to chat. Breakfast isn't for another four hours."

Perfect! Gripping Bill's tie, she leaned closer. "Why don't we continue this up in my room? And I'll buy you breakfast."

Bill gulped, his Adam's apple riding the length of his throat. When he first realized he'd mistaken her identity, he never expected to spend the night with Pepper, especially after the way she'd backed away from him. But now that she was offering, he would not refuse.

She moved her hand closer to his aching cock. Gripping her fingers, he slid off the stool. "Sure."

But as they ventured through the hallway toward the elevator, she became quiet.

Has she changed her mind? Would she abandon him in the elevator once they reached her floor? Sweat beaded across his forehead. He wasn't ready to start dating again, couldn't handle the pressure, the rejection.

Did she have any expectations beyond tonight? Inviting a stranger up to one's hotel room usually meant uncommitted sex. At least, he assumed. So much time had passed, he didn't know the rules of dating anymore.

The door dinged open. He reached for her hand, waiting for a sign she still wanted him.

Yet, she ignored his gesture, rushing into the elevator. Without an outright refusal, he followed, confused by the woman, and intrigued at the same time.

"Are you sure you want this?"

He'd barely said the words when she jumped him, wrapping her long legs around his waist. Her lips crashed down on his, sending a rush of lust straight to his cock. *Holy shit! This woman goes from cold to hot in an instant.*

Grasping her ass, he spun her around, to press her against the wall. Sure, he'd waited for her to make the first move, but now he wanted the control.

A startled gasp. Pepper pulled away from Bill's hungry lips and looked out the open doors in horror. A mother and her young son—she assumed—stared at her with wide eyes. Her cheeks warmed. *Should've pressed the emergency stop.*

Without any awkwardness, Bill held her tight, carrying her out of the elevator. He nodded to the woman. "It's all yours."

She hid her face in his neck, not wanting to be recognized, and out of sheer embarrassment. *Why on Earth are people up at this ungodly hour?*

Breathing in his musky cologne, she let all of her tension melt away. The sweet and insecure man she'd first met in the banquet hall had transformed into a confident hunk. And she wanted him. Now.

Sliding down his body, and back onto her feet, she reached under her strapless bra for her room key.

Bill placed his hand on hers. "Here, let me." Within seconds, he unzipped the back of her dress and snapped open her bra.

Breasts free, she heaved a sigh. *And I thought I'd be all alone tonight.*

Leaning down, he sucked one of her nipples into his mouth.

Electric fire rushed through her veins. She pressed her palms against the wall behind her. Holy hell, the guy knew what he was doing. In between using his teeth and tongue to ignite her pleasure, he slid her dress farther and farther down her legs.

Soon, she would be naked in the hall, but she refused to stop him. Any guy who put her own needs before his was worth whatever awkward and embarrassing situation she might find herself in. Heck, she didn't even know what had happened to her room card.

Bill ran his fingers along her bare thighs, reaching higher until he pressed his palm to her pulsing mound. The thin cotton of her thong remained the lone barrier between her and ecstasy. He brushed the material aside and drew the tip along her swollen nub. Her breath caught at the sudden overload of sensation.

Bill stood, still fingering her clit, feeding her desire. "You need to tell me your room number, or I'm going to take you right here in the hall."

Her pussy clenched at the thought. *Talk about exhibitionism.* Though she didn't need that kind of publicity for herself or the show, her reputation being tainted enough. "Four sixteen. Hurry."

He scooped her into his arms, rushing down the hall. Never had she understood the term *swept off your feet* until then. A total loss of control. Nothing existed beyond him, her need, and her want to satisfy him.

Holding her against the door, he swiped her key card. The door clicked and he carried her inside.

Her heart slammed in her chest. She kicked off her dress which had settled around her ankles, craving him with reckless abandon.

With a chuckle, Bill set her down, before quickly picking her back up again. He pressed her against the wall, like in the elevator. This time, the door would stay closed, no one to interrupt. He fumbled with his fly. Legs around his waist, she rocked into him until the tip of his cock rubbed along her clit. The she froze.

"Shit." Bill lowered her to the ground, shaking his head. "I never expected this tonight. I didn't come prepared."

Prepared? She gripped his shoulders, hoping he wasn't going to walk out on her. Not yet, anyway. "You mean condoms?"

With a nod, he released a heavy breath. "Yes. When I was married, I never needed to carry them around."

A recent divorcee. The slight hope she held onto that Bill would be more than a one-night stand flew away. She would be his rebound fuck, a nudge for him to get back into the dating world. *So be it.* Her own itch needed to be scratched. "I packed some in my bag. Let me grab them."

Them? She brought multiple condoms for an overnight stay at the hotel? How many guys did she expect to have in one night? "Um, I only need one."

Pepper yanked out a strip of foil packages, brushing them across her nipples. "I'm willing to bet otherwise."

He groaned. Head spinning, he gripped the door frame of the bathroom. He'd hit the jackpot with this woman. Or so he hoped.

Legs spread open, she trailed her fingers along her wet pussy. "Get over here, Mr. Bank Manager. Let's get started."

Not caring if he ripped something, he stripped off his clothes before joining her on the bed. He expected to crawl on top of her, plunge right in. But she met him on her knees, her more-than-a-handful breasts pressed against his chest. His muscles tightened when she grabbed his balls. Yet, as she massaged him, he relaxed, save for his engorged cock.

Wrapping his arms around her, he reclaimed her soft, full lips, imagining them wrapped around his dick. With a strangled groan, he thrust toward her. Need consumed every last thought.

He grabbed her ass, pulling her tighter. His entire body shook with restrained control. She made him feel desirable for the first time in months.

Slipping from his grasp, she leaned down in front of him, her fingers surrounding his cock. She licked the tip, the movement sending him straight to heaven.

"Don't tease me. I like that way too much."

She took him in her mouth, sucking his swollen head, circling his shaft with her tongue. Though he tried to stop, he couldn't fight the urge to drive into her. And she didn't stop, simply taking him deeper with every thrust.

A heavy weight filled his body. *God, no. It's too soon.*

He pulled out, the orgasm barreling through him, his seed spilling into his open hand.

"I'm sorry." He couldn't look at her, shame quickly taking the place of the satisfaction of release.

Something soft touched his skin. A towel. Pepper wiped his hand and his softening shaft. She stared up at him, a light smile across her lips. "No need to be sorry. Now, lie back. We're far from finished."

His stomach twisted. He hadn't gone for a second or third round in years.

Settling on the bed, he stroked his shaft, praying he had at least one more in him. The rip of a foil package did the trick, making him instantly hard and ready to go again. This time, he would make sure Pepper came first.

Pinching the tip of the condom, she rolled the thin barrier over him. With the taste of his salty syrup still on her tongue, she met his lips for a chaste kiss. The foreplay in the hallway had not been enough. He left her hungry for more. An entire night of ecstasy. Even with his quick release, she yearned for her own satisfaction.

She straddled his waist, lining the tip of his cock to her folds. Taking in a little at a time, she adjusted to his thickness. Then she let go, sinking all the way on. A whimper escaped from her lips. Exactly what she'd been craving. She placed her palms on his chest, arching back. The perfect angle. He'd touched her G-spot the instant she settled on top of him. "Fuck, you feel so good."

His cock pulsed. With a groan in response, he clutched her hips. She rocked along with him, her nerve endings lighting up with every movement. Pressure built inside her, a bomb about to detonate. She dug her fingers into his chest, losing control. With a strangled cry, she burst, shattering into a million pieces.

Bill grunted below her, not yet letting go. His motions became more frenzied, extending her orgasm. Her breaths came in short gasps. She couldn't handle much more, her head ready to explode.

A roar echoed through the room. He bucked under her, his cock convulsing inside her sensitive walls. Her own release leapt to new heights, setting off fireworks in her mind. She collapsed onto his chest, her entire time with him filled with new experiences.

A one-night stand, the best of her life. Though she hoped for more, more stress-reducing releases, and more of Bill. A future? If he was willing.

Four orgasms. Three used condoms. And one long nap. Though now that he'd opened his eyes, Bill couldn't get back to sleep. At this time back in Hanton, he would be out jogging the streets with his cop buddies. Now, even with the sexy, naked woman beside him, his mind focused on the need to feed his rumbling stomach.

Slipping from the arms of his most adventurous lover, he left the bed and collected his clothes off the floor. He ducked into the bathroom to relieve himself then dressed in his suit from the night before, tucking the tie into his pocket.

With one last glance at the beautiful woman who'd invited him into her bed, he left the room, hoping the hotel had a continental breakfast.

Pepper rolled over, stretching her muscles, tired from a night of the most amazing sex ever. *Bill. Oh shit!* She turned to the other side of the bed, but found it empty. He'd already left. A glance around the room confirmed it, his clothes gone, too.

Disappointment clutched her gut. She'd known all along their time together would end like this. Though she couldn't deny the hope for something more. One-night stands and casual dating were no longer enough. With no husband, or even a serious boyfriend, each passing day filled her heart with more loneliness. Her parents, after thirty years of marriage, were still unbelievably blissful, as were her recently married friends. Would she ever find the same happiness?

She slid off the bed, swallowing her pride. *It's my own fault. I need to start looking for the right guy. Not the right now guy.*

With a heavy sigh, she plodded to the bathroom. *Why can't I have both in the same person?* Because keepers don't sleep with someone they'd just met. She knew that, and yet she'd still invited Bill up. Maybe at another time and place, the night may have gone differently. If he hadn't been fresh out of a divorce.

A knock sounded at her door. *Shit. Housekeeping already?* She hadn't meant to sleep so late. But after an all night session with Bill, she'd forgotten to set her alarm. The shower would have to wait until she arrived home.

She grabbed a robe and wrapped it around herself. Hopefully, she'd at least be able to change before they kicked her out.

Opening the door, she held her breath, prepared to argue for that one concession.

"Good morning, sleepy head." Bill waltzed into the room, his arms filled with food. "I didn't know what you wanted for breakfast, so I brought a variety of things."

Tears pooled in the corners of her eyes. Her heart swelled. "You...you came back?"

He furrowed his brows. "Of course I did. I just needed something to eat, especially if we go another round or two. I know you said you were buying, but I thought it might be more intimate up here."

She chuckled, wiping her tears. "I don't think we'll have time. I have to check out soon."

"Oh." He frowned. "Well, maybe you'd like to come back to my place? Hanton is only a half hour away. That is, if you don't already have plans."

She shook her head. "No. No plans. I just didn't think this would go beyond the hotel. I thought once you'd left, I'd never see you again."

After setting the food on the wooden desk, he turned and faced her, looking as vulnerable as he had last night when he realized his mistake. "I'm sorry. I thought... never mind." He headed for the door. "Goodbye, Pepper. Thanks for last night."

"No!" She rushed to him, grabbing his arm. "I do want more. It's just that when I woke and you weren't here...."

Pulling her against him, he held her tight, pressing his lips to hers. She moaned at the sweet invasion, and the taste of a chocolate chip muffin. Gripping his ass, she felt the swell of his cock against her stomach. Ready to go all over again.

But he pulled away, leaving her breathless.

"You'd better get dressed and eat before it's too late. I'll pay for the extra night if you don't check out in time. Though I'm really anxious to get you into *my* bed."

Sweet and sexy, and God, she wanted him. She expected last night to be just another wedding. Yet, with Bill, it turned out to be so much more. Perhaps she'd finally found her keeper? *Only time would tell.*

ALIEN ADMIRER

CHAPTER ONE

Staring out the window at his next door neighbor, Adam cringed. His buddies had already left for Morty's Pub, needing a break from a week of twelve hour days to finish building another house. He was the only licensed carpenter among them, though they all put in the same effort. Instead of spending his Friday night with them, he'd chosen to lounge in nothing but boxer briefs, and pine over the woman of his desires, but not his reality. Not because one of his parents came from a planet many light years away—a part of his life that he kept secret from everyone. Neither did their eight-year difference in age weigh into his decision to stay away from her.

No, Sera's husband had died about a year ago and she'd refused to start dating again, saying her kids didn't want a replacement for their father.

Adam longed for a way to convince her to take a chance on him. Her children, Melody and Zach, clung to him every time he offered to take them swimming in the lake, or treated them to ice cream from the convenience store up the road, or any other time they spotted him outside.

He adored them.

Sure, Sera needed time to grieve. He understood that, but his mental comprehension didn't stop his dick from stiffening every time he had her in his sight. No woman had left his body humming with one simple glance in her direction. Except Sera.

He yearned to read her thoughts, sense more than her emotions. Her sadness and grief he empathized with, but nothing explained the confusion he sensed around her. In the few moments alone he'd had with her, she always changed the subject when asked if she'd considered dating again. Sure, she trusted him with her kids, but that trust didn't extend enough to open up to him. She remained a mystery, one he desperately wanted to solve.

Adam groaned, grabbing a shirt. *I'm going out.* He'd been through all of this before. No point waiting forever for her to change her mind. So what if his dad said his ability to read her emotions pointed to Sera as his soul mate. She'd probably never view him as anything more than a handy sitter.

Pulling on a pair of jeans, he considered a trip to the local pub. The same women always frequented the place, but at least he'd be guaranteed some action. His fist, and fantasies of the woman next door, no longer brought him much satisfaction. He craved the real thing.

Not going to happen.

After a quick spray of cologne, he peeked out his window one last time. And froze. His neighbor stood naked on the dock, her luscious body glowing in the moonlight. That image ingrained in his mind, his cock stiffened. Screw going to the bar. He either finished the job based on the recent sighting, or acted fast to get even closer to her.

No harm in trying. He rushed down the stairs.

A settlement. That's all the company had to offer. *More fucking money.* Though none of it would bring Rob back.

They were supposed to be happy together, enjoying their lottery winnings in their dream home. But all of their dreams crumbled into one horrible nightmare. An electrician by trade, her husband had his own company and bid on tenders for work at factories and other businesses in the area. After they'd won ten million dollars, he'd agreed to take a few years off and spend more time with her and their children. On the day they were set to move into their newly-built fantasy home, Sera received a phone call that changed her life. Her husband had been killed on the job.

Sera wiped away the tears. She'd shed enough of them already. Anger consumed her, aimed at the factory that contracted her husband for allowing a faulty forklift on the floor, at Rob for taking that one last job, working one more day, and at herself, for allowing his memory to slowly slip away. She didn't want to lose him, let him disappear from her life, but her kids and the small collection of pictures of him remained her sole connection to him. Although he'd done all of the electrical work in her current home, she'd never lived there with Rob. All of her memories with him happened at their previous house.

He'd been so busy those last few months, driving between his local jobs and their future quarters. *We'll have all the time in the world together once we move*, he'd promised. But he didn't make it, killed on his last day of work, changing fuses in an electrical panel. An easy task, something he'd done many times. The forklift driver hadn't noticed him until the last second.

Not enough time to stop with brakes that don't work.

Over the past year, she'd struggled not to break down each and every day, hiding her heartbreak from Melody and Zach. But, at night she lost control, sobbing and yearning to have Rob beside her again, making love to her, holding her.

She used to be able to imagine all of that. Not anymore. Instead, the man next door invaded her fantasies. A man too young for her to be thinking about in such a way. Stomach rolling in shame, she closed her eyes. Sure, Adam treated her children as his kin and had incredible patience with them for someone without any of his own. But everything else about him was so wrong.

Sera stood, extending her taut muscles. She'd waited all day to hear from her lawyer, only to wind up disappointed. The company had offered their money, and expected her to go away. They didn't care they'd ruined her life.

Across the lake, the sun dipped below the horizon, spreading long, red tentacles over the surface of the water. They reached for her, called her into the dark depths.

A quick dip wouldn't hurt. Anything to help clear her mind, let her find the sense of peace she'd yearned for since Rob's death.

She gazed over her shoulder at the cottage. The kids had already fallen asleep before she'd come out. And no lights remained on in the house next door, or the loft above the garage. Everyone had gone to bed, or at least settled for the night. No one to see her.

Fingering the hem of her shirt, she pulled it over her head and tossed it on the beach. She stepped out of her shorts, then removed her bra and panties, enjoying the quiet moment of freedom. Fate may have stolen her husband from her, but it would not take away times like that when she could be herself. She wasn't Rob's widow, or mother to Zach and Melody. Right then, she was just Sera.

Stretching out her fingers and toes, she stood at the end of the dock. A warm, gentle breeze nudged her forward and she jumped.

Plummeting into the frigid water, Sera tensed, her skin breaking out in goose bumps. Instead of gliding, she pushed off the silt-covered bottom and broke the surface, gasping for air.

"Holy shit, that's cold." She wiped droplets from her face. *Why the hell did I think that was a good idea? Next time I'll dip my foot in before taking the plunge.* Sure, she'd temporarily forgotten her grief, but at the expense of her body temperature and pride. *Total epic fail.*

Rushing over to the dock, she placed her hands on the first plank and hopped up. She rubbed her arms, hoping the warm air would dry her off fast. Her teeth chattered so hard, her jaw ached. After gathering her clothes, she raced for her house, craving a cozy blanket.

A hot body would be better.

"Need a towel?"

Sera shrieked and jerked to a halt. *Oh, hell.* Everyone was supposed to be sleeping. She squeezed her eyes shut, hoping she'd imagined the voice. Opening them again, she took a quick look to her left.

Adam. Great! The last person she wanted to be anywhere near before bed. While naked. She held her clothes across her breasts and groin to cover them from his view. How much had he already seen? Obviously enough. *God, why can't this be a dream?* Yet, a fantasy about the man next door wouldn't leave her shivering. Just sweaty.

"Adam, what are you doing out here? I thought I was alone." *Don't ever assume again.*

He stared at her, his blue eyes sparkling in the diminishing light, filling her with sudden warmth.

"I came to offer you a towel. To dry off. I noticed you didn't have one when you jumped in."

He'd spied on her the entire time? He'd definitely seen her naked, then. Watched her splashing around in the lake. She stepped away, needing distance.

"Watch out!"

Her feet slipped out from under her, and flying backward, she fell in the water, landing on her ass in a pile of seaweed and sand. The clothes she clutched sank to the murky bottom.

Adam strode over and scooped her up before she had the chance to object. After setting her on the shore, he wrapped a towel around her, holding her close. Too close. His musky cologne tingled in her nose. Bundled in the towel, she sneezed, unable to cover her mouth in time, spitting all over his shirt.

"Oh, God, I'm so sorry." Though the sudden space between them gave her the breathing room she wanted.

He wiped the front of his shirt. "I guess you're allergic to me."

"No, it's just your cologne." Just like meat, cologne shouldn't come in a can.

His face paled. "It's gone. I'll never wear this stuff again."

How sweet. What he wore didn't matter. She wanted to get inside and wash away the grit and sand crusting on her body. "Thank you for the towel. I'll return it tomorrow."

"No need. You can keep it."

The teenage girl inside of her wanted to hold onto the towel forever, while the grouchy old widow told her to throw it back at him and skedaddle.

"Thank you." She crept to her house, needing to escape the awkwardness, dreading him following her. Like she needed any more fodder for her already wicked fantasies.

Racing the last few feet, she dashed onto the covered porch, letting the screen door bang behind her. He made her want to be with a man again. He made her want *him*.

Before entering the house, she shed the towel, giving it a quick shake to get rid of any dirt. In the bathroom, she twisted on the shower taps until steam billowed from the glass stall, although Adam had already taken away her chill the moment he held her. So close to him, pressed to his hard body. Those thick arms. His full, tempting lips. *Oh, to have kissed him... No! He's off limits.*

Not trusting what her erotic thoughts of her neighbor might lead to, she cut the shower short, slamming down the faucet and drying off. She crawled into bed, pulling a picture of Rob from the nightstand drawer. With a body pillow tucked under the sheet, she tried to imagine cuddling with her late husband. But every time she closed her eyes, Adam intruded instead.

Why can't I picture Rob? She wasn't ready to date again, still hoping to wake one morning with him beside her, find out the accident had been a bad dream.

Yet after what occurred with Adam, she had a hard time banishing the man next door from her thoughts. *What if I had invited him inside?*

No! Stop it. She scooted out of bed, needing to flush away all thoughts of her neighbor. Other than being courteous by offering a towel, he hadn't made any type of pass. She'd read too much into his actions. *Wishful thinking.*

Maybe it'd been a sign to consider dating again. Rob would never return to her. Time to find comfort, and possibly love, for a second time. But she had to quit looking for the attention she craved next door. She needed a man her own age, one who already had his life established, settled down.

Slipping out to the porch, she grabbed the towel Adam had lent her.

Gotta wash this tomorrow and give it back to him. I don't need a reminder of him lying around. She caught a whiff of his cologne on the material. Where the scent had bothered her earlier, this time it left her craving another warm body in bed all the more.

Time to stop turning men down when they asked her out. She was on the market again, done with giving the cold shoulder.

Tonight, in her fantasies, she belonged to her neighbor. Raising the towel to her face, she breathed in, letting the same warmth from his arms fill her again. With an aching need between her legs, she returned to her room. She lay on the bed, placing the towel beside her. Spreading her legs, she began the seductive sweep of her fingers, picturing Adam between them, teasing, licking, sucking…. Arousal skyrocketed at the mental image of him gazing at her from below. The tormented pleasure she'd denied herself over the past year left her head spinning.

With a shriek, she detonated, the orgasm shooting through her. "Adam," she cried, thrusting her hips in the air. The rolling waves continued and she shuddered, gasping for air. God, it had been so long since she'd had that kind of release.

Way to betray Rob's memory. You cannot do that again. Why had she imagined her neighbor while doing it? Of all the men to fantasize about…. Every time she encountered Adam again, she'd remember that fantasy, yearn for her fantasies to become real. And he came around often.

But as eye candy, he is so worth the awkwardness. She turned on her side and curled up to the body pillow, more content than she'd been in a long time.

CHAPTER TWO

Adam thumbed the button on his key fob, waited for the garage door to open, then started up the Harley his father had passed down to him. Revving the engine, he wished he didn't live in the loft above his parents' garage.

It wasn't the first time. Then he wouldn't have had to witness Sera leaving with another man. To make matters worse, she hadn't asked him to watch her kids while she went out, having his sister, Angela, come over instead. A double kick to the nuts. Sure, he wanted Sera to be happy, but with *him*, not some other guy looking to prey on a lonely widow and didn't care about Melody and Zach. Or so he told himself. Though the thought didn't make her rejection sting any less.

Riding into the night, he headed toward Asterdale. By the time he'd reached the bar, none of his hurt ebbed, instead festering into a pool of anger. He needed an outlet, a release. After parking his bike, he strolled across the gravel parking lot. Once inside, he checked out the selection of females through the thick stench of stale smoke, alcohol and cheap perfume. Nothing about the women, not the halter tops, miniskirts and spandex, caked-on makeup, or the cloud of hairspray above their heads held any appeal for him. Because they weren't Sera.

He slid onto a stool at the end of the bar, hoping to drink thoughts of her away. A thin film of stickiness coated the log-milled, cherry tree bar top. Such a beautiful piece, neglected for far too long.

"What can I get for ya?" the bartender asked.

"Whatever you have on tap." The safest bet. He placed his cash on the bar, careful not to touch the surface.

Within a minute, he had a frosted mug full of beer in front of him and a woman to his left, her tits brushing against his arm.

"Hello, Adam. Long time, no see."

Her alcohol-laced breath left his stomach rolling. He recognized her from high school, but her name eluded him. He didn't want to remember, anyway. "Hey."

She cupped his balls through his pants, and he groaned. He'd rather cut his testicles off than fuck her, but his cock had other ideas.

"Wanna buy me a drink? I promise I'll make it worth your while."

He surveyed her. Not Sera. Not even close.

Maybe it wasn't a good idea to come here. The chick had already drunk too much, her face slightly green through a layer of blush. Getting puked on held no appeal.

"I'm not interested." He removed her hand. "And you can tell all of your friends the same thing. I want to be left alone."

Grumbling the entire way, the woman returned to the table of intoxicated females. He took a mouthful of beer. Horrible. Never had he tasted such a bitter brew. He shoved the mug aside, and slipped off the stool. *This was a mistake.*

He needed to suck up the heartache and get over his neighbor, look for someone closer to his age. *But not at this place.*

Without a backward glance, he left the bar and headed home.

Far too soon. Sera never should have started dating again. Her stomach had twisted and churned all day, but she shrugged it off as nerves. Until her date arrived, that is. He kissed her cheek in greeting, and a cold chill traveled down her spine. She wanted to hurl every time he touched her after that.

A wave of relief swept over her when he dropped her off. *Date over. Never to happen again. Or at least not anytime soon.* With Melody and Zach still up when she arrived home, she'd paid Angela, then tucked them into bed. All alone once more, she sat on the porch, again wishing for company. The disastrous evening proved she wasn't ready to date.

What's wrong with me?

She gazed next door at the loft above the garage. *Adam.* Why did her pulse race whenever she thought of him?

She didn't feel uncomfortable around him, not until she decided to go to dinner with Peter, a man she'd met at the grocery store. Then guilt ate at her. She feared asking Adam to watch her kids while she went out on a date. *But why would he want to?* What young man wanted to be strapped down, babysitting on a Friday night, when most went out drinking and picking up girls? Their own age.

Her chance to live that life had come and gone. She had little ones, and they always came first. Her libido had to wait until they'd grown up and left the house. By then she'd be an old maid—and long out of the dating world—too dried up and bitter to want to hunt for a boyfriend. She slumped deeper into the wicker chair. *Life sucks.*

The deep, throaty rumble of a motorcycle caught her attention. *Adam coming home. Probably with some young floozy on the back of his Harley.* The back of her throat ached at the thought, and she stood. *I don't need to see that.* Her fantasy, the one thing left that brought a smile to her face at the end of the day, would end if she watched him escort another woman into his home.

She didn't escape fast enough. Adam pulled into their shared driveway before she grabbed the door handle. At the sight of the empty spot behind him, she breathed a sigh of relief. In her dreams he wouldn't leave her for another woman.

He waved, and she waved back, filled with a sudden giddiness. *Geez, what is it about him that makes me feel like a teen again?*

Without another glance, he disappeared into the garage. She remained on the porch, staring like a fool. *These fantasies have to stop.* He had no reason to give her a second thought, at least not in the way she hoped.

Time to go inside and purge him from her mind. Plenty of celebrities her own age to take Adam's place and ravage her in bed.

She pulled open the screen door.

"Sera?"

Every muscle tensed. She circled slowly, expecting him to disappear if she turned too fast.

Standing at the bottom of her porch, he clutched the railing, one foot on the first step. "How was your date?" His eyes were hard, far different from the gaze he'd given her when holding her in his arms the day she'd gone skinny-dipping. But her love life wasn't any of his business.

She threw up her arms. *Who am I kidding?* "It was horrible."

He climbed the steps, his proximity sending a tingle through her. Would she ever get over the sensations she experienced around him?

"Do you want to talk about it?"

No! She flinched, crossing her arms. Not a topic she ever wanted to discuss with him. "I'd rather just forget about it. Why don't you tell me about yours?"

He chuckled, sliding past her to sit on her steel glider, his hands behind his head. A bold move for a stranger. Yet, he wasn't. They lived next door to each other, and she trusted him with her family.

"I wasn't on a date." He turned away from her. "I went to the bar to try and drink away the sight of you with another man."

She gripped the outside ledge of the window, trying to wrap her head around his mumbled words. "You didn't drive under the influence, did you?"

He raised his eyebrows. "Of all the things I said, that's what you picked up on?"

"No, I just want to make sure it's not the alcohol talking. Because if you are intoxicated, I'm going inside and pretend you didn't say that the sight of me with another man bothered you." Though, his words were already embedded in her memory.

"I can assure you I'm not drunk. Didn't even finish my first beer. It wouldn't have helped anyway. I can't get you out of my mind."

She shook, running her hands down her arms. *This has to be a joke.* She wasn't a cougar, didn't go after younger men.

"You don't want me. I'm an old widow with two kids." What young man looked for a girlfriend with wrinkles around her eyes, flabby arms, and stretch marks? "I'll tie you down."

He rose, stretching out his perfect, muscled body, and drew closer. "I adore Melody and Zach, just as I adore you. I may only be twenty-seven, but I know what I want. You're the most beautiful woman I've ever met."

He traced his fingers along the side of her face, leaving her lightheaded. How did he have this effect on her when her date had given her the creeps?

"I'm looking for a long-term relationship with the right woman. That is, if she wants me."

God, yes. She wanted him more than anything. But she needed more than a fling. Her children already told her almost every day she should marry Adam.

She spun away, needing some space to think. *What would Rob think about being replaced by a younger man?*

What is it going to take to convince her I want her? On the ride home, he'd persuaded himself to give up on Sera. Until he'd seen her on the porch. He had to seize what might be his lone opportunity.

"Why do you have such a problem accepting that I'm attracted to you?"

She faced him again, her cheeks glowing with color. "I don't have a problem with that. In fact, I'm flattered. I have a problem with how much I'm attracted to you, how even on my date, I couldn't get you out of my head."

It was all the invitation he needed. Closing the space between them, he held her, pressing his lips to hers. Sera moaned, her body tight against his. She didn't push him away, instead wrapping her arms around him, running her foot up and down the back of his calf.

He clutched her thighs, pulling her up to straddle his waist. Every moan encouraged him to keep going. He wanted more.

"Inside," she said in a breathless whisper. "Take me into the house."

All right! Grasping and fumbling with the handle, he managed to open the door without letting her go. Focused on her in his arms, he shuffled around blindly until his knees met her couch. He laid Sera on the cushion, but she clung to him.

"No, my bedroom. And be sure to close the door."

Her room? *Holy shit!* Before that moment, he'd expected several days of trying to win her over before she invited him to her room, if she ever even acknowledged his feelings.

He carried her up the butcher block wood steps, to the bedroom he'd helped construct. While he'd helped build every part of the house, the master bedroom remained the one room he hadn't entered since Sera moved in.

Sacred, just like her body.

Setting her on the bed, he took in her pleasant, feminine scent, vanilla with a hint of peach.

Absolutely delicious. He shed his boots and jacket, unsure how much more to take off. He didn't want to get ahead of himself, nor give her the chance to stop him from going any further.

He slid onto the bed, between her legs. Counting backward from ten, he tried to calm his raging hormones and the urge to fuck her right away. He growled, hiking up her sundress to stroke the soft skin of her thighs. "I've waited a long time to do this."

"Well, hurry up already." She lifted her hips, slipping her black silk bikinis off.

He shivered in anticipation. How had a night that started out so terribly turn into this? Finally, everything he'd ever dreamed of.

Following the trail of her panties, he licked her leg from knee to toe, and repeated the process on the other side. She tasted as exquisite as she smelled. "Fuck, Sera, you have no idea what you do to me."

She sat up and kneeled in front of him, hand on his groin. "If the bulge in your pants is any indication, I think I do."

As she unbuckled his belt and jeans, he grunted. If she wanted to take control, all the better. *Sit back and enjoy the ride.* So long as she didn't change her mind…that would kill him.

Sera pulled his jeans and boxer briefs down to his knees then palmed his balls with a touch so gentle, so warm. He ached in anticipation.

"Raise your arms." She grabbed the hem of his T-shirt, lifting it over his head, then grazed her fingers down his chest to pause at his abs. Tracing each muscle, she stared at his stomach as if confirming it was real. "You know, I've viewed six-packs in pictures, but not in real life. I thought they were just Photoshopped onto the models."

He chuckled, stroking her arm. "I assure you, it's all real." Though the muscles hadn't gotten that way on their own. He used the gym equipment in his loft at least once a day. No short cuts. None with Sera, either.

With trembling hands, he fumbled to remove her short, flowery dress, and tossed it on the floor, then finished stripping out of his own clothing.

He froze, able to admire Sera's naked form. *Sweet Jesus, she's gorgeous.* Long brown wavy hair, which she usually wore up, flowed across her shoulders. Her full, creamy breasts swelled with each breath she took. But she frowned at him, the smile he adored gone.

"What's wrong?"

She grabbed a pillow from the bed, holding it in front of her. "I'm too old for you. I have two kids, and the pregnancies weren't kind to my body."

Drawing closer, he kissed her quivering lips. "You're not old," he whispered, nuzzling her shoulder. "And I don't care how many times you gave birth. You're the most beautiful woman I know."

He kissed her neck, down to her collarbone, wanting to taste every inch.

Wrapping her arms around him, she halted his journey. "You could have any woman you want."

"And I want you." No time to waste. He laid her on the bed, devouring his way down to her breasts, grazing his teeth over each erect nipple. Her gentle cries encouraged him on. He reached down to her pussy, drawing a finger across her swollen clitoris.

She bucked under him. "Oh, my God!" Spreading her legs farther open, she rocked back and forth.

Grabbing a condom and plunging right in would be so easy, but the best things came if he remained patient. Dipping two fingers into her wet heat, he circled her clitoris with his thumb.

She writhed on the bed, her whimpers growing louder, then she orgasmed, her pussy clenching around him. Riding his digits, she panted and twitched for several moments.

"Holy fuck!" *One down and so many more to go.* If he proved himself, he hoped she'd invite him another time.

Lying flat on the bed again, she smiled. "Thank you. I really needed that."

Wait! What? "I'm not done with you yet." He eyed the door, praying she wouldn't kick him out so soon.

She drew her thumb along his lips. "I know. It just seems like forever since someone else brought me to orgasm." A pretty blush spread across her cheeks. "Sorry, I shouldn't have said that."

Resting beside her, he circled her breasts with his fingers. So supple. "Do you know how adorable you are?" After all she'd been through, she still had an innocence that left him yearning to protect her from the world, from any more pain.

"Adorable is a word one uses to describe a child. Considering I'm older than you—"

He leaned over to kiss her forehead. "Age doesn't matter. What matters is that I make you come again."

"Wait," she said, rolling him onto his back. "It's my turn."

Shifting between his legs, she gripped his cock. He tensed, anxious for her next move.

She sucked him into her mouth. Liquid fire rushed to his extremities. Nothing better than living out his fantasy. He moaned with every thrust. *How did I get so lucky?*

As quickly as she started, Sera stopped and lay over his body. Kissing him, she pressed her perfect breasts again his chest. *All mine.*

He rolled her over until he lie on top, wanting all of her. Would she give herself completely? Without reservation?

Scrambling off the bed, he found the condom in his jeans pocket, and rolled the latex across his shaft. Not enough time for her to have doubts. He hoped.

He settled over her, his head spinning with the heat between her legs. *Need. Just like mine. No more waiting.* He licked her neck, savoring the delicious taste that was Sera. She thrust her hips up, her hands gripping his waist. He met her actions, plunging deep inside.

Sweet heavens! Being inside her felt like coming home for the first time, the most perfect place in the universe. He didn't want to move, wanted to stay there until the end of time. But her gentle sways amplified his longing. He rocked in and out, slow and deep.

From Sera, he sensed nothing but happiness, complete satisfaction. Exactly what he wanted to give her. *Now and always.*

CHAPTER THREE

Sera inhaled, catching the musky scent of sex still heavy in the air. That and the desire-inducing smell of masculinity coming from the man whose chest she lay on. She couldn't help the smile tugging at her lips. Instead of her fantasies to keep her company, she'd spent the night with her dream come true. *Adam.* Perfect in every way. She hadn't expected to find a man who both satisfied her, and treated Melody and Zach so well.

Shit! The kids. What time is it?

Seven a.m. glared at her in bright red letters.

She gasped and shot upright. *What have I done?* Tossing the covers off, she scrambled out of bed. Melody and Zach would be up soon. They couldn't find her naked, in bed with a man. With Adam, of all people.

Yanking open her pajama drawer, she pulled out a cotton shirt and shorts set and slipped them on. She gazed at the man who'd rocked her world. Her kids didn't need to know about him spending the night. They already adored Adam and wanted him around more. If they discovered him there, they'd have him and Sera down the aisle after one night of sex—earthmoving, mind-blowing sex. She couldn't let them get hurt because of her own desires. Heck, she didn't even know if the previous night was a one-time thing.

She hurried over to the bed and shook Adam. "Wake up. You've got to leave."

Not how she wanted to thank him, but she didn't have time for anything else.

He yawned and stretched, showing off his delicious muscles. She yearned to taste him again and her mouth watered. *No!* The clock tick-tocked away. Most days, her son woke up earlier than her. The fact that Zach had stayed up late would extend his time in bed, but she couldn't count on how long.

Adam gave her a lazy smile. "You sure are sexy in the morning. Why don't you climb back in here with me?"

"Can't." Having a hard time squashing the urge to join him, she picked up his clothes and tossed them on the bed. "You have to get out of here before Melody and Zach get up. Move it."

"Shit." He shimmied into his boxer briefs. "I should have known you'd regret this."

"No!" God, no, she didn't regret the night one bit. "I just need you out of the house before they wake up. And that's going to be soon."

"I thought I would make us all breakfast."

Crap, why isn't he getting out of bed? What didn't he understand? "Adam, as much as I loved last night, and as much as my kids think you're amazing, they can never know you stayed here. They will get hurt when you don't show up again."

"This isn't a one-time thing."

Her heart skipped. How she wanted to believe him. But common sense rolled its eyes in her face. "Fine, when you realize I'm too old for you and leave me for a younger, prettier girl, they will be crushed. I can't do that to them just for a great fuck."

His nostrils flared. "It's nice to know that's all you think of me."

He rushed to get his clothes on, leaving her with the guilt of her bluntness. But she refused to deny the truth. She'd wind up hurt too, if she hoped for too much.

Adam opened the door then paused. "I'm leaving today for a job in Hanton. I'll be gone all week. But when I return, I'm taking the kids swimming again. I hope we can talk about what's going on with us as well. I'm looking for more than a fling."

She nodded, swallowing her shame. "Okay." Maybe she'd assumed wrong, but she had to be careful.

In the blink of an eye, he stood in front of her, pulling her against him. She melted into him, surprised by how much he'd already affected her. He kissed her hard, stealing her breath away. And then he left.

She suppressed the urge to follow him. The bedroom door clicked open again—one of her children had awoken.

Back to being Mommy.

"Same clothes as yesterday, and a big grin?" His sister gave him a once-over. "Someone got laid last night."

"Angela!" his mother snapped.

Adam plopped down at the kitchen table, glaring at his sibling and wished he were an only child. "My sex life is none of your business." If he didn't have a job to go to that day, he'd be in his bed, catching up on his sleep, rather than being questioned by his sister.

"Or mine." Their father peeked over his newspaper, scowling in disgust.

"It may not be my business," Angela said. "But I don't want any of them to get hurt."

"I don't know what you're talking about." Adam didn't want to discuss what happened, especially not at the breakfast table with his parents and younger sister. He simply wanted to eat and get on with the day.

"I saw you come home alone. Then you went over to Sera's house. I assume you left only minutes ago."

"Adam Lucas Jones!" His mother set a plate of bacon, home fries, and an omelet in front of him with a huff. "I can't believe you took advantage of that poor widow."

He closed his eyes. Nothing he said would make him look any better in his mother's eyes. *Doesn't matter that I'm an adult.* Why couldn't his sister keep her mouth shut?

"Calm down, Rachel." His father folded the paper and laid it on the table, along with his reading glasses. "She's his soul mate."

"That's impossible," his mother said.

Adam wished he had her support. He'd doubted the feeling for a long time, but after the previous night, the title felt more than right. But, he had a long road ahead of him to convince Sera of their connection.

His mother flung a dish towel over her shoulder and sat at the table. "The woman is several years older than Adam. Plus, she has two young ones and, until just over a year ago, had a husband."

"It's not like Adam can pick and choose," his father said.

No, but if he had the choice, he'd still want Sera.

"I'd hoped he'd be paired with a woman without baggage."

He held up a hand. "Stop, please." She had no right to say that about Sera.

"I'm more concerned about Sera and the kids. We all know his dating history." Angela snorted loudly. "How long do you think this relationship is going to last?"

Great! "If you want to talk about me like I'm not here, you could wait until I leave." He pushed away from the table and stood. "Dad, I'll meet you out by the truck in an hour."

Listening to his sister and mother squabble held no appeal. Their opinions didn't matter. Only Sera's. With a sigh, he left the house and headed for the loft. He had to have a shower and pack his bags, anyway.

"Adam, wait."

Ignoring his sister, he trudged up the stairs to the entrance of his loft. The conversation was over. His business, nobody else's. He let the door slam behind him. Maybe the time had come for him to move away. The convenience of being so close to work and family wasn't worth sacrificing his privacy and sanity. But that meant living farther away from Sera. His soul mate.

"You're so stubborn sometimes." Angela waltzed into his apartment, flopping onto the couch. "I want to talk about Sera and the kids."

"I'm the stubborn one?" He grabbed his duffle bag from the closet and tossed it onto the bed. "You're the one who can't let the issue go."

"I mean it. I don't want to see them get hurt."

He turned and scowled. "Neither do I."

"But it's only been a year since her husband was killed. She's likely still healing."

"You think I don't know that? I want what's best for Sera, Melody, and Zachary as much as you do, if not more. And she has the final say, not me." He packed some work shirts into the bag. "But I can't stop how I feel about her, no matter what she decides."

He threw more clothes inside the duffle, along with his toiletries. Angela's sudden silence increased his frustration level. *Why is she still here?*

"So, she's really your soul mate?"

He nodded. "Yup."

"How does it feel?"

What the hell did she mean by that? "How does *what* feel?"

"To have a soul mate. How do you know she's the one?"

He sat on the bed with a huff. How *did* he know? "It's weird, really. I can't stop thinking about her. Not in an obsessive way, like a stalker. But she's the first thing on my mind when I wake up, and the last person I think about before going to sleep. Whenever I see her, I get this warmth inside. I want to make her happy, make her smile."

"That's the most romantic thing I've ever heard you say."

He threw a bundle of socks at her. "Conversation over."

"Wait! Do you think I'll have a soul mate?"

"Probably not. You're too much like Mom." Though, he did hope his sister found happiness one day. "Now, please go. I've got to have a shower before I leave."

"One more question. What are you going to do when she learns you're half-alien?"

He raised his brows and shook his head. "She's not going to find out."

Adam ushered his sister out the door, locking it behind her. No, Sera didn't need to know the truth about his family. He was born and raised on Earth, and that's all that mattered.

CHAPTER FOUR

Butterflies swarmed in Sera's stomach. After a week of deliberation, she'd decided to take a chance on a relationship with Adam. And now, she waited anxiously for him to return.

Melody sat on her knee, gazing up at her. "Adam really is coming back, right?"

"Yes." Sera tickled her daughter, hoping she hadn't picked up on her own fears of the same thing.

Zachary bolted into the room, naked. "I'm ready to go swimming."

"Ewww." Melody covered her eyes. "Adam's not here yet."

Sera sighed. At least they had kept her occupied over the past seven days. "And I think you need a bathing suit."

"Oh yeah." He flew back upstairs. Hopefully, to get dressed.

A huge diesel work truck roared up the driveway. Her heart raced. Finally, Adam had returned. She gripped the cushion, restraining herself from rushing out to meet him. She couldn't show the kids anything had changed until sure Adam still wanted her.

An hour passed, then several more. Melody and Zach demanded supper, holding their bellies and grumbling. *Too late for swimming anyway. And no chance of Adam coming over tonight.* If he ever wanted to visit again.

Enough! As tough as it was to raise them on her own, she managed. She could very well cope without the boy next door.

Boy. Who was she kidding? Adam was all man. Hard muscles, big cock, and the feeling of him inside of her.... She pulled out the frying pan and slammed it on the stove top. Thoughts like that lead to disappointment.

Opening a package of ground beef, she dropped it in the pan for the tacos Melody and Zach had requested, but she'd eat something else, her stomach too unsettled to digest anything spicy. If she ate at all.

She jumped at the loud knocking on the door. With her palm on her chest, she tried to catch her breath. Her children stampeded like a herd of elephants for the door.

"Adam!" Their excited cries revved up her own enthusiasm.

He'd actually come over. But for what? To tell her he'd changed his mind? He'd found someone else? Someone younger?

Sera clenched her fists and headed toward the front of the house, bracing for his rejection.

"And there's the most beautiful woman in the whole world," Adam said as she entered the living room.

With a wickedly handsome grin directed at her, he held both of her children in his arms. She smiled. Why he wanted, at his age, to be saddled down with young ones, she had no idea, but she refused to turn him away, though his tardiness nagged at her.

"My very own Prince Charming has returned. You've been home for a few hours already. What kept you?" An elastic band tightened around her chest.

His smile faltered. "I'm sorry. I really wanted to come over right away, but I had a mountain of paperwork, and wanted a shower to wash off all the grime."

God, why did I worry?

He hadn't spent the last week partying. The tension drained away and she longed to be in his arms and beside him in bed again.

He raised his eyebrows. "You okay? You sure you want me here?"

She nodded. *Time to take a chance.*

Setting the kids down, Adam walked toward her. "You're certain?"

She nodded again, more sure than she'd been of anything over the past year.

He opened his arms and she leaned into him, yearning to have the support of another once again. Before she could turn away, he kissed her, drawing her under his spell. Excited squeals echoed all around her, but she rejected the idea of pulling away from his sweet lips. *Just a moment longer.*

"Adam and Mommy, sitting in a tree, k-i-s-s-i-n-g."

Adam backed away with a laugh. "I guess they're okay with us."

"Yes, more than okay." Considering they'd asked her all week when Adam would come home, she hadn't expected them to have a problem with her dating him. "Will you stay for dinner tonight? We have tacos on the menu."

"Sounds delicious. And maybe we can have an after-dinner swim?"

Melody and Zach's heads bounced like bobble-heads.

"Okay." She headed back to the kitchen. "I've got to return to the stove before everything burns."

"I'll take the Melody and Zach outside to play then."

As much as she wanted him in the kitchen with her, they wouldn't get a moment of peace until her children had gone to bed. She hoped he'd stick around until then. Maybe spend the night.

Standing on the dock in her white string bikini top and matching boy shorts, Sera resembled a swimsuit model. If Adam were a cat, he would've purred. Good thing he stood in water past his waist so no one saw what she did to him.

Every time Sera had swum with him in the past, she'd worn a one-piece suit. Except for the time he'd caught her skinny-dipping. But the bikini was new.

She crossed her arms and legs in front of her, one step away from running to hide. If she only knew how hot she looked, like a sexy angel fallen from the skies. Whether she was fully dressed or naked, he wanted to claim all of her. And when Melody and Zach went to bed, he would do so, leaving the white two-piece on the floor.

He shivered with anticipation. Gliding toward the dock, he forced his thoughts on something else…anything to calm his raging hormones and get rid of the tent in his pants. Like his sister dating one of his buddies. That always hit a nerve.

"Do you like her swim suit?" Melody asked. "She bought it just for you."

Sera flushed, and he couldn't help but smile. She'd thought of him while he'd been gone. Just as he'd thought of her. His thumb still hurt from when he'd whacked it with a hammer while daydreaming on the job.

"I like it very much. Your mom is so pretty."

Melody giggled, while Zach rolled his eyes. "It took her hours to pick this one out. I don't know what was wrong with the other one."

With a chuckle, Adam grabbed Sera's leg, pulling her into his arms and dropped her in the water. "It's time to test the bathing suit."

Sera fluttered and splashed water before finally standing again. "You're going to pay for that."

Something he very much looked forward to, since any form of punishment was worth the sight of water droplets falling down her most delicious body. He longed to lick every last drop.

Shit. Way to keep your mind out of the gutter.

A human cannonball landed in front of him, spraying water in his face. *Well, that works.* He wiped his eyes to find three smiling faces staring at him.

A family. One he desired to be a part of. Groaning, he turned from them. As much as he wanted Sera, and treated her offspring as if they belonged to him, could he ever truly call them family until they knew the truth? About everything, including his alien DNA?

Family meant no secrets. At least, not from Sera. Maybe one day he would tell her, though not anytime soon. On the day he proposed marriage, perhaps? Or on their one-year anniversary? Then it would be much harder for her to walk away.

"What's wrong?" Sera touched his shoulder. "Did Zach hurt you?"

"No, no. Just a cramp. Guess I didn't wait long enough after I ate." Like he didn't think through the relationship before plunging in.

Shit, what if his parents or sister let something slip when they came over for dinner? His family remained careful and cautious, but occasionally the word, *alien,* tumbled into the conversation, and tracks had to be covered. Most of their friends brushed it off as a joke, but Adam always worried about the day that didn't happen, when someone contacted the tabloids claiming to know extraterrestrials.

"Why don't we go inside then?"

Sera helped Melody and Zach out of the water, and she kept pulling at her bikini as if uncomfortable. He wrapped an arm around her waist and nuzzled her neck, kissing her soft, wet skin. "And once the little ones are in bed, we can find out how quickly this new bathing suit of yours comes off," he whispered.

She sighed. Before desire took over, he scooped her up and set her on the dock. Hands on the edge, he hoisted himself out of the water then followed them back to the house.

One day, she'd have to find out about his ancestry. He hoped she accepted him as an alien, because no matter how she reacted, she would always be a part of him.

CHAPTER FIVE

Sera's head spun and her stomach churned. Why had she agreed to go on a ride called *Death Mountain*?

"Why don't you sit the next one out?" Adam rubbed her back while an eager Melody and Zach yanked on his other hand.

"C'mon. We want to go on *Tower of Doom*," Melody and Zach pleaded.

She glanced up at Adam, not sure how many of him really stood in front of her. "That would be great. I'll sit here, and once my vision returns to normal, I'll go get us some drinks."

"You sure you're okay? I don't want to leave you alone if you're not." He touched her forehead like a parent checking a child's temperature.

She shooed him away. "Go. I'll be fine."

"Okay, if you're sure." Holding Melody and Zach's hands, he strolled off to the next ride.

God, how had she been lucky enough to find a guy who cared so much? He'd taken them to the aquarium the week before. *And today, an amusement park.*

He included her children in just about everything, never complaining they were a hindrance to getting her in bed. And once they fell asleep, he made her feel all woman, leaving her oh-so-satisfied and always wanting more. Except for Thursday nights, when he played poker with his friends, and the occasional night out of town for work, he spent every evening at her house. Where he belonged.

When she'd decided to start dating again, she hadn't expected their relationship to progress so fast. Once it had though, she didn't want to go back to her life without Adam.

Sera headed toward the closest concession stall while eyeballing the line for *Tower of Doom*. Adam had Zach in his arms and played a counting game with Melody. A familiar tingle swept through her. After only a few weeks, she loved Adam Jones.

He peered over at her from his place in line smiled as if reading her mind. More than once, she'd wondered if he had telepathic abilities, since he always seemed to know when she needed comforting, a moment to herself, and even an extra boost of confidence. Was she that transparent?

While they stood in line, she bought drinks, hoping to meet them once they'd finished on the ride. Propping the cups on the bench beside her, she waited near the exit.

"Sera? Is that you?"

She turned toward the familiar voice, shocked to be face-to-face with a friend of Rob's. "Derek, is that really you?"

He'd lost weight and toned up since the last time she'd seen him. "Wow, you look really good." Not that she held any attraction to him, but she considered Derek a friend.

His cheeks reddened at the compliment. "Thank you. When I moved out of my mother's house, I also joined a gym. Best two decisions I ever made."

She chuckled, happy for his success. "Did you buy a house then?"

"No, I rent an apartment. But it has three bedrooms, two bathrooms, and a huge galley kitchen. If you ever return to the city, you should stop by some time."

"I will." Her trips back home occurred less and less frequently, though she did miss visiting with their old friends.

"So, who are you here with? Where are Melody and Zach?"

"They're in line with my...boyfriend." Sera swallowed the sudden lump in her throat. *What are Rob's friends going to think?* She hadn't thought about that.

"You're dating already? I thought you'd wait longer, at least until I had a chance to ask you out."

Sera crossed her arms. She didn't expect her friend to make her so uncomfortable. Fingers clenched onto her shoulders and someone cleared their throat behind her.

"Hi, Zach. Hi, Melody," Derek said.

They waved and grabbed their drinks before sitting beside her.

"And this must be your boyfriend. A little young, isn't he?"

Adam's grip tightened.

"Derek, this is Adam Jones, my boyfriend, and a wonderful role model for my children." Age didn't matter so long as he treated them well.

Neither guy reached out to shake the other's hand.

"They're Rob's children, too," Derek said.

He had no right to judge her or tell her who she could and couldn't date. "That's enough, Derek."

"Fine, but they need a real man in their lives, not a guy who's just a kid himself."

And he definitely had no right to tell her what Melody and Zach needed when he hadn't had a girlfriend for as long as she'd known him. And only *just* left his childhood home. "Goodbye, Derek."

"You know how to get hold of me when you're ready for someone better." He pivoted and left.

Gah! How could he say such things when he didn't know Adam? She refused to date Derek, but he was supposed to be a friend. Losing weight did not give the guy the right to be a prick.

Sera rose and kissed Adam, rubbing his arm. "You have nothing to worry about."

"I know, but I didn't like the way he talked to you. You deserve more respect than that." He balled his fists then relaxed them again. "It was all I could do to refrain from knocking him out. But I knew you wouldn't approve. And I would never do such a thing in front of your children."

She passed him the remaining drink. "I know. And that's one of the many reasons why I love you."

Adam dropped his cup, spraying colored ice across the pavement. He gave her a blank stare. "You love me?"

"Yes, I do." Though maybe she should have waited longer to say the words, or at least when they were alone. Because instead of the deer-in-headlights reaction he'd given her, she'd hoped to hear the same words in return.

She loves me. Adam clutched the steering wheel to keep his joy from bubbling over. He wanted to show Sera how much he loved her, too. But he had to wait until they arrived back at her house and had the little ones tucked into bed.

The DNA condemning him to be happy with only one woman had lost. His soul mate loved him. He wanted to shout it out to the world, the universe. He'd won, found his soul mate, and received her love in return.

With Sera's reluctance for any bond at the beginning of the summer, he hadn't expected their relationship to progress as fast as it did. And now he was one step closer to securing a future with the woman he was meant to spend a lifetime beside.

As he pulled into the driveway, the sound of faint snores drifted toward him from the back seat. "They're asleep already."

"Yes." Sera crossed her arms and sighed. "It's been a long day for all of us."

Pain burrowed into the front of his head and he pressed the brakes, careful not to wake the little ones. "You're mad. Sera, why are you mad?"

"I'm not mad. I'm just tired. And I want to go to bed."

"To have some fun?"

She glared at him. "No, to sleep for a change."

What the hell? When had she turned from the woman who loved him, to sitting beside him, throwing off waves of anger? "Tell me what's wrong."

"Nothing. I just want to get the kids to bed."

A total one-eighty. For no reason. Completely out of the blue. She was mad, and directing all of her animosity at him. He parked and turned off the engine. "What did I do wrong?"

Her nostrils flared. The pain in his head intensified.

"Nothing."

Yeah, right. Sliding out of the truck, he opened the rear door, unhooked Zach from his booster seat, and carried him to the house. Sera met him there, but her emotions hadn't ebbed at all. Shit, he wished he had the ability to read her mind rather than just her emotions. He laid Zach in his bed then returned to the truck for Melody.

Sera waited in Melody's room when he arrived. He set the child on her bed. "I'll wait for you downstairs."

"If that's what you want."

He cringed at the cold response. Trudging down the steps, he remembered the encounter with Derek. Had she thought about what the man had said? Did she consider Adam too young to help her raise her children?

He sat on the couch and buried his head in his hands. What the hell had happened?

Several minutes passed before Sera entered the living room, her face red and puffy.

Adam rushed to her, holding her tight. Rubbing her shoulders, he yearned for the ability to fix the problem. "What's wrong? Please tell me."

"Do you still want to be with me?"

"Of course. I wouldn't be here if I didn't." What on Earth had prompted her to think he didn't? "I love you, Sera."

She glanced up at him with tear-filled eyes. "You do?"

"Yes. I have for some time, but didn't want to scare you by saying it too soon."

"Then when I told you I loved you earlier, why you didn't say it back?"

Hence why she's mad at me. He guided her over to the couch and sat beside her. "I'm really sorry I didn't tell you I loved you at the amusement park. I wanted to wait until we were alone, because it's not about simply saying the words, it's about showing you at the same time. I love you, Sera."

Leaning away, she gave him a pained look. "Do you think we're moving too fast? Do you need your space?"

He reached for her hand, clasping it in his. "No, not at all. If I have a problem, I'll be sure to talk to you about it. Now, do you need your space? Am I over here too often?"

"No." She squeezed his fingers. "I really enjoy having you here. It feels so right. But, I do have one question for you."

"Go for it."

"Why is it that when I'm down or mad, or even really happy, you always seem to know? Today, I was thinking how much I love you, and you looked over from the line and smiled. And just now, you knew I was mad, wouldn't leave me alone about it."

"Because you wear your emotions on your face." He didn't want to reveal the truth too early.

"You couldn't have been able to tell from that far away. You're more perceptive than my friends, more than Rob ever was."

Adam gulped. She needed to drop the subject. He never wanted to be compared to her late husband, and it wasn't the time for confessions of the extraterrestrial kind. "You're exaggerating."

"And you're deflecting. C'mon, Adam. What's your secret?"

His secret. A huge one. Had the time come to confess? Tell the truth?

Sera lifted off her shirt and snapped open her bra, exposing her full, creamy breasts. "I'll let you play if you tell me your secret."

Torture. Adam groaned, his cock hardening.

Shit. Eventually, he'd tell her, right? Why not now?

Capturing her breast in his hand, he licked a pert nipple. "I'm an alien and you're my soul mate."

With a laugh, she shoved his chest. "Liar."

"Sorry, you're right...I'm only half-alien. My mother is from this planet. It's my father who's from Space." He pulled her onto his lap, not wanting to give her any time to think about what he'd just said. Sucking the other rosy nipple into his mouth, he rolled his tongue around the hard peak, longing to do the same to her clit.

"Prove it."

Fuck!

Apprehension bubbled inside her. Being able to read her emotions didn't help him at the moment. He shouldn't have said anything, or made something up, instead.

"Forget about it. I was just joking."

"No, I don't think you were. When you're joking, your eyebrow twitches. This time, it didn't. But I've seen you naked, and you look totally human to me."

"Forget it, Sera. You don't want to do this."

"Then why would you say such a thing?" She slid from his lap and stood. "Is this your way of breaking things off, making me think you're crazy? One last fuck and you'll never talk to me again?"

What the hell have I done? "No."

"Then prove it. Prove to me why you think you're an alien. Otherwise, leave."

"Sera." He grabbed her wrist to pull her closer, but she shook free.

"Are you an alien?"

"Yes." He glanced down and let go of the disguise he'd kept since he was two. Returning his gaze to Sera, he held his breath, waiting for her reaction.

She recoiled, radiating fear. "Your eyes...they're totally black. Even the whites of your eyes. Y-you really are an alien?"

He nodded.

"Get out!" She pointed at the door. "Get out of my house, and out of my life. Don't talk to me or my kids again. Don't even look at us."

His chest constricted. How could she go from loving him to fearing him? He hadn't done anything to bring her or her children any harm. Yet, there was no mistaking the anger and betrayal rolling off her now.

Without trying to explain, he left, since she wasn't willing to listen. The door slammed behind him, followed by the unmistakable click of the deadbolt. She wanted him gone forever.

Fate had won after all. Stepped in and stolen his soul mate from him, snatched away his chance at happiness.

After climbing the steps to his loft, he'd barely made it in the door before collapsing.

His head pounded, so much pressure he expected it to explode. His ears rang. His vision blurred. Bile burned its way up to his throat. Every ounce of hate Sera felt toward him blazed through his body. All because of his father's DNA.

His stomach revolted and unable to prevent it, he vomited on the floor. Then his world went silent and everything disappeared.

CHAPTER SIX

Aliens. I live beside aliens. They'd befriended her, deceived her, and one had made her lust for him, made her believe she loved him. Beings from another planet. How could she have been so blind?

Maybe he'd fabricated the entire story, performed some kind of trick with his eyes to turn them black. Eyes that had haunted her for the past week. She didn't sleep without waking to dreams of the guy she once considered spending her life with, turning into a green-skinned extraterrestrial, with multiple tentacles and abducting her, leaving her children behind.

"Mommy, can we please go outside?" Zach tried to reach the chain lock she'd added to the rear door to prevent him and his sister from trying to sneak down to the lake. Now, it protected them from the neighbors.

Melody stared at her, hand on hips. "Adam is waiting to give us more swimming lessons. You always said it was important we learn how to swim. But you're keeping us locked inside so we can't see him."

God, how she wished for a way to help them understand. Though, she'd never tell them about the aliens next door. They didn't need extra ingredients for their own nightmares. No, it was time to find a place to live in the city, get away from the sparsely populated wilderness. She'd thought she wanted a place in the middle of nowhere, but after Adam's confession, she worried for the safety of her children, as well as her own.

"I'll sign you up for swimming lessons at a real pool."

"No, I want Adam to teach me." Melody kicked the door and her brother on the way past.

Zach screamed, shoving his sister to the floor.

Sera grabbed them by their shirts. "Go to your room. I've had enough."

Tears fell down her cheeks. Being confined to the house grated on her nerves, too. Her kids never fought, at least not to such an extreme. And she tried not to yell at them. The past week had been hell on all of them, but she hoped the start of school in two days would improve everyone's mood.

Glancing out the kitchen window, she caught sight of a wet, bare-chested alien. She sighed, remembering lying on his hard chest, how he elicited the most extreme orgasms she'd ever had, and how he treated Melody and Zach like they were his own. Why had she kicked him out?

Because he's an alien! Or he thought he was, anyway. What kind of a person went around telling people that? And why wait until she'd told him she loved him? She had to purge him from her mind and her heart, forget about the eight weeks of bliss she'd spent with him.

Maybe she should talk to him again, find out if there was a misunderstanding, if she'd heard him wrong. He had treated her so well, and she'd been on an emotional rollercoaster that day, running into Derek again, then realizing she loved Adam and telling him.

Sera walked to the door and grabbed the knob. Time to apologize, swallow her pride and admit her mistake for the sake of her own happiness. Then she'd forget the mention of aliens.

The phone on the counter rang and she picked it up, forgetting to check the caller ID. "Hello?"

"Hey, Sera, it's Derek. I wanted to apologize for the way I acted last weekend."

"That's okay." Rolling her eyes, she tapped her fingers on the granite counter. *Hurry up, I'm busy.* She returned to the window, anxious to get outside and be near Adam again. "It was kind of a surprise for all of us."

"Yes, well, I've got another surprise for you. I'm in the area, and I thought I'd drop by to check out your new house—visit Rob's dream home. You up for it? I'll bring dinner."

What happened to the shy Derek I remember? "Um, I guess." If he wasn't her late husband's friend, she'd slam the phone down in an instant. No way was she interested in him.

"Great, I'll be there in an hour. Just you, me, and the kids, right?"

"Sure." *Unfortunately.*

She peeked out the window again. Adam had already left the lake. She would straighten things out with him in the morning. With the holiday, he shouldn't have to work.

"Perfect. I'll be there soon."

Sera hung up and rushed outside. Did she have time to catch Adam on his way to his loft, ask him if he'd be around the next day?

Nope, gone. Disappointment clutched her gut. She refused to chase after him, not with Derek on the way. The last thing she needed was another confrontation between the two of them. But she hoped she wasn't too late, that he still believed in their soul mate connection. Because she wanted to believe, and she could only know for sure by spending more time with the man she loved. Alien or not, she could not deny her feelings for Adam Jones.

With the headache finally subsiding after several bedridden days,

Adam slipped into the water. All week, he'd stayed home from work, unable to function due to the symptoms of Sera's emotional state. His mother, concerned about his inability to keep anything down, threatened to take him to the hospital, but he refused. He didn't need anyone else to learn of his otherworldly heritage. He simply waited for the ailments to go away, or, at least, become less severe.

But what had finally eased his pain? Had Sera accepted him as an alien, or moved on? Would she ever talk to him again?

He spotted her gawking at him through her kitchen window. Did she know he saw her? Fuck, he yearned for her to come out, to talk to him again, to race around with the kids once more, and teach them to swim like fish. Even if things with Sera returned to the platonic relationship they'd had before sleeping together, he didn't care. Anything to have her in his life again.

In an instant, she disappeared from his view, his brief connection with her gone. Was she on her way outside? He waited several minutes, but nothing. She remained in her home, and out of his life.

He slammed a fist on the water's surface. How long would she take to come around? Hopping up on the dock, he left his hope for a reunion behind. His swim hadn't been as relaxing as he'd expected. Not with Sera still avoiding him.

Up in his loft, he grabbed a beer and flopped on the couch, peering out the window. How was he supposed to get over her? Dating another woman wouldn't help him forget about Sera. And none of his friends would understand, most of them still working on their scorecards. Although, he couldn't condemn them. He'd had his share of casual relationships until meeting Sera. After her, no one else mattered.

Gravel crunched on the driveway below. Adam leaned forward, catching sight of a shiny black SUV pulling up to her house. He squeezed the cushion beside him, waiting for her visitor to get out. Better not be a guy. Had to be just a friend.

The asshole from the amusement park exited the vehicle. *Derek.* Adam's stomach twisted. *How could she?*

Sera appeared instantly to meet him. Her voice carried up to Adam. "You're early."

"I couldn't wait to see you again."

Derek bent forward for a kiss, but she turned her head, letting his lips brush her cheek. Still too much touching for Adam's liking.

She caught Adam staring and quickly glanced away. "Let's go inside."

Fate plunged a knife deep into his heart before reaching into his chest and ripping it out. Adam may not be able to move on, but she could, and had, with a man totally not right for her. She deserved more respect than that guy gave her. If not from Adam, then someone else. Just not Derek.

Adam paced, seething with frustration, then sat on the weight bench, but wanted to punch something rather than lift weights. A ride on his bike wouldn't take him anywhere to make things better, only let him temporarily stop thinking about his soul mate with another man. Yet, nothing else came to mind.

He opened the door to leave and slammed into two little people.

Attaching themselves to his legs, Melody and Zach clung to him. "Adam, we've missed you."

"And I've missed you, too." *Just as much as I miss your mother.* They were a part of her. He rubbed their heads, smiling for the first time in days.

Melody peered up at him, her bottom lip sticking out. "Then why haven't you come over?"

"I've been very sick. Didn't want any of you to catch anything." And he didn't know what Sera had told them.

"You're feeling better now?" Zach asked.

"Much." At least they still wanted him around, even if their mother didn't. "Does your mom know you're over here?"

Shaking her head, Melody peeked into his loft. "No. Derek told us to go out and play so he could be alone with Mommy. We decided we wanted to visit you."

Adam's stomach twisted. A week had passed since Sera kicked him out of her house, and she was already dating another guy, letting Melody and Zach out to play while she got it on? That didn't sound like the Sera he knew. And why would she allow them out alone, near a lake?

Sudden, intense waves of apprehension rolled through him. Something wasn't right.

"Stay here." He rushed down the stairs then stopped at the bottom. Was his queasiness due to Sera's need for help, or pure jealousy? He didn't want to knock on the door and look like an asshole. Then again, Derek hadn't had a problem looking like one at the amusement park. But, she was with that guy and Adam had nothing to lose.

He stalked up to the porch and knocked, ready to ream someone out for not watching the kids. No answer. She couldn't possibly be fucking him already, could she? Pain sliced through his brain, trying to rip out his eyes from the inside.

A high-pitched scream echoed from the house. "Let go of me!"

Adam kicked open the door and scanned the living room. Empty. He refused to let anything happen to Sera, and raced for the kitchen.

"I'm going to have you, bitch. If you can screw the boy next door, you can have just as good a time with me. I've always wondered what it would be like to fuck you. But you never gave me a second glance."

Adam spotted Sera, face down on the kitchen table, her dress pulled up and legs spread. Derek held her arms behind her back, pinning her with his weight.

Fire rushed through his veins. Gripping the man by the throat, Adam tore him off her, tossing him across the room like a ragdoll. *How dare he touch her*. The man lie slumped on the floor, no longer a threat.

He helped her up and held her. "Are you okay?"

Before she responded, Derek ripped her from his arms and shoved him down on the table. A sharp object pressed against his throat.

"You shouldn't have interrupted, boy."

Sera shrieked. "No! Derek, let him go. You don't want to do this."

"What I want is you, Sera. I've always wanted you. And since this boy's here, I'll make him watch."

Derek's weight shifted above him. Grasping the hand behind his head, Adam bucked, his head slamming into Derek's face. The crunch of bone echoed in the kitchen.

"Fuck!"

He must have hit his target. Adam spun, smashing his fist into Derek's nose. Blood spurted and the knife he clutched clattered across the floor. *The fucker was going to kill me!*

"You asshole! You broke my nose."

Adam held him by the throat again, knocking him against the wall. "That's not all I'm going to break."

"Please don't." Sera tugged at his arm and nodded toward the entryway.

Melody stared at them, her wide eyes filled with tears, then ran to her mother.

Shit. How much had she observed?

"Mommy, why are Adam and Derek bleeding? Were they fighting?"

I'm bleeding, too? Didn't matter. *Get Derek out of the house, make sure the others are okay, and take care of everything else later.* He gripped the man's shirt, pushing him out of the kitchen. "Let's go." Adam shook with the urge to beat the shit out of the guy. But he wouldn't. Not in front of the people he loved.

Once they'd reached the porch, Derek grunted. "You're going to pay for this, boy. You never should have interrupted. I have a lot of friends."

Shoving him down the stairs, Adam laughed. "So do I. And they will beat any man who tries to rape a woman within an inch of his life. Want to meet them?"

Derek stumbled on the walkway, searching for balance. "She'll never be yours."

"I think that's up to her. But if you ever set foot anywhere near here again, you'll be leaving in a body bag."

"Are you threatening me, boy?"

Adam stepped forward. "Yes."

Rushing to his SUV, Derek gunned the engine and threw it into reverse.

Adam caught a glimpse of brown hair a few feet behind the vehicle. *No!*

He bounded down the driveway. "Zach, move!" Scooping him up, Adam raced to get out of the way.

The steel bumper slammed his knee and he fell forward, letting Zach roll out of his arms to the grass. Heavy rubber rolled over his knees, grinding his legs into the gravel. Bones snapped. His vision wavered and dust coated the inside of his mouth. So much pain. *Help me.*

He coughed and his lungs burned as if shards of glass ripped through the tissue. His legs were on fire and he wanted to tear them off, get rid of the agony.

Figures surrounded him. Faint voices buzzed, but their words remained foreign. Unable to focus, he tried to reach out, get someone to help him, but his body refused to respond.

Save me, please.

CHAPTER SEVEN

A restraining order. All she got for now. The rest took time. After Derek tried to rape her, nearly ran over her son, and left Adam in the hospital with broken legs, Sera pressed charges. More counseling, lawyers, and an upcoming date in the courtroom, though this time, she had to testify. Today, she craved a break from it all. Rob's case had tormented her enough. She yearned for a different life, one far away from all the pain.

She peered around her home. Could she really leave the house Rob built behind? *As long as Derek stays away, I'll be okay.* And she always had Adam, the man who believed himself an alien, to look out for her. He'd promised. If she left, she'd have to leave his security behind.

Blinking hard, she rubbed her temples. Regardless of his crazy talk, she loved him. And he'd nearly sacrificed his life to save her and her son. *I need to stop hiding. Thank him, at least.* When, though? Sure, she had more time with Melody and Zach in school, but she couldn't waltz into the hospital and pretend nothing happened. All the blame for his injuries lay on her. She swallowed her guilt. He'd come back after she kicked him out and locked herself away. So, how was she going to face him again?

Knock, knock.

Please don't let it be another detective. She wanted to be done with the police and the incident altogether.

Rising from the couch, she sucked in a deep breath. A cold sweat washed over her. *Why can't things go my way for once? For every good thing that happens in my life, something worse follows.* She hadn't lost Adam, she'd pushed him away.

With a shaky hand, she opened the front door. But, instead of a detective, she found Adam's mom.

"Hello, Sera." The woman gave her a weak smile, holding onto a rolled-up brown paper bag. "I was wondering if we could talk."

Talk to the woman who'd married an alien and given birth to extraterrestrial offspring. According to Adam, that is. Yet, those were her son's crazy beliefs, not Rachel's.

Sera held open the door. "Come on in." Maybe her neighbor could clear up the issue.

"Have a seat. Would you like some tea? Coffee?"

Rachel sat on the edge of the center couch cushion, still clutching the bag. "No, thank you. I only have a few minutes before I have to leave for

114

the hospital."

Panic, like a wave of fire, rushed through her. "Is Adam okay?"

"Besides being anxious to leave the hospital, yes," his mother said. "His bones are mending well, but after one week in bed, he's going stir crazy."

Sera grinned and sighed with relief. She'd experienced the same need to leave after giving birth to her children. One night had proved long enough for her.

Yet, she hadn't bothered to visit him, too disturbed by what he'd told her. "What about...? Did they find out what he is? What he thinks he is?" Waiting for her neighbor to tell her Adam had made up the story, Sera gripped the chair.

Rachel's eyebrows rose. Her soft smile disappeared. "Did they find out that he's part alien? No, but that's why I'm here. I had a hard time believing his father was, too."

Sera gasped, covering her mouth to hide her shock. *No way. The tale can't be true. They're all delusional.*

"I was a young child when Luke arrived on this planet." The woman set the paper bag down and folded her hands in her lap. "For years, I believed I'd imagined the entire thing. And my parents made me think the same thing, that the little alien boy I saw magically appear on the street in front of my house was simply a story I'd made up to get attention."

If Melody or Zach told her they'd met an alien, Sera would assume the same thing. Drumming her fingers on the chair, she waited for the woman to continue.

"Then I met Luke again. When I realized he was the same little boy, that I hadn't made it all up, I freaked, running out on him and refusing to let him explain."

Similar to how she'd reacted to Adam. "And yet, you married him?"

"Yes, because regardless of where he came from, I loved him, and I knew he loved me."

Sera circled around to the front of the chair and sat. "You really believe he's an alien?"

"I know it's such an awkward concept to accept, but yes, I do. Though, I completely understand your skepticism. If I hadn't seen Luke arrive with my own eyes, I would not have believed his claims, either."

"Then why are you here?" Sera sprang to her feet again, too jittery to stay in one spot. "If you understand why I won't talk to him, why are you trying to convince me otherwise?"

"Because he's my son, and I know how much he loves you and your children. He would never have risked his life, risked being found out, if he didn't."

Her chest tightened. "Do the doctors know?" She didn't want to be responsible for turning him into a lab rat, too.

"No. Except for his dark eyes, and his emotional connection to his soul mate, he's no different than any other male on Earth. He's learned to transform his eyes like his father. As for the link with his soul mate, you're the only person who can fulfill that destiny. You're the woman he's meant to be with. No one else. And he knows that."

Sera swallowed the lump in her throat. Regardless of the alien blood flowing through his veins, he'd saved her. God, why had she been so stubborn?

"Um, maybe I could get a ride with you?"

"Tell you what…why don't you go up to the hospital on your own? I'll stay home."

"But…."

"You two have a lot to talk about. I'd just be in the way."

Sera's stomach rolled. *By myself?* "I…I don't think I can."

"Tell me something." Rachel's stare hardened, her brow creasing. "Before my son confessed his ancestry to you, did you love him?"

Yes, I loved him. I still do. "I…."

"Did you ever worry about him hurting you or your children?"

Not until he told me he was alien. She suppressed her pride. "Okay, I'll go. But will he forgive me?"

"I'm sure he will, but you have to talk to him first."

Sera grabbed her purse. If she didn't go right away, she'd lose her nerve. "What room is he in?"

"Three-seventeen. It's a private room."

Easier for them to talk, yet did she really want to be alone with him?

Rachel held out the paper bag. "Oh, and would you take this to him?"

"Food?"

"No. It's an object from his father's planet, so please be very careful with it."

Reaching for the bag, she almost dropped it, surprised by the heavy weight, and supported it from the bottom. "Will it hurt me?"

Rachel chuckled and rose. "No, it's meant to heal. And you both could use some of that right now."

Before Sera responded, her neighbor left. As if the woman had left her in charge of healing Adam. She had no idea how to use the object, let alone anything about alien internal anatomy. She didn't even know what the object looked like.

Curiosity won out, and like a child at Christmas, she peeked inside. Red light flooded her vision and she snapped her lids shut, closed the bag and hoped the flash hadn't caused permanent damage.

Opening her eyes again, she blinked to regain focus. *Good, I can still see. But how's this supposed to heal Adam?* If it did have healing powers, wouldn't it draw the attention of the entire hospital? *And how is he going to explain the miraculous mending of his bones? Witchcraft?*

Grabbing a sweater off the stair banister, she shrugged into it. He and his family had survived for this long without their secret being discovered, but trusted very few with the knowledge. They likely wouldn't blow it now. And he'd trusted *her* enough, too. She owed him an apology, her thanks, and a chance to explain.

Adam cursed the straps holding his legs immobile. *Stupid-ass contraption won't let me move.* He longed to get out of the bed and use the bathroom instead of pissing into a catheter all the time. He had broken legs, not a fractured spine. Surely, he could get on his feet by now.

And with the stench of body odor, he dreaded anyone coming to visit. Sponge baths only cleaned off so much. Not even after a weekend of camping and drinking did he and his buddies smell so disgusting.

Adam peeked at the wall clock. *Already eleven.* His mother, the one person who saved his sanity in the hospital, didn't arrive any later than ten-thirty. Had something happened to her?

Reaching for his cell phone, he dialed his parents, when someone knocked on the door.

"Hello? Adam?"

Desire stirred low in his groin at the familiar voice, and he set the phone down. Too much time had passed since he'd last regarded the woman he loved. Had he really heard Sera, or simply imagined her in desperation?

He lifted his head from the pillow, trying to peek past the curtain to the doorway. "Sera, is that you?"

She peered into the room, a wary smile on her face, her shifting eyes giving away her apprehension. Yet, he sensed a glimmer of something else. Hope? He held onto his own optimism, wishing one day she looked beyond his alien ancestry and let him be a part of her life.

"Hi, Adam." She walked into the room, keeping her distance, as if a wide dome surrounded his bed. "How are you feeling?"

A loaded question. He refused to tell her of his anxiousness to leave, and all the pain he'd suffered after saving her from Derek. He already felt enough of her guilt. "I'm doing better now that you're here. I've

117

missed you."

Tears rimmed her eyes.

Shit. He'd purposely tried not to make her cry, yet failed.

"I'm so sorry, Adam. Sorry for treating you the way I did, and sorry that because of me, you ended up in here."

"Hey, none of this is your fault. I knew the risks before I acted. Aware of the outcome, I'd do it all again. In a heartbeat. If that asshole hadn't—"

"No. I was the one who kicked you out, avoided you for a whole week, all over something silly."

"It's hardly silly." Hence, why he'd waited for so long to tell her, and had doubts even then.

Sera shook her head. "That's not what I mean. What I meant to say is that it doesn't matter. I can learn to deal with it, if you can ever forgive me."

Fuck! He wanted to get out of the bed and hold her in his arms. "I already have. I could never stay mad at you, my soul mate, the woman I am madly in love with."

Her bottom lip trembled and a tear escaped. "How can you be so sure? You're still young, and yet you're ready to give it all up for an old widow with two kids?"

"Geez, Sera. We've already been through this. I know what I'm doing. And you're only eight years older than me, nowhere near being old." He reached out, longing for some contact. "Now, get over here before I break loose of this contraption to come to you."

Inching closer, she stopped a foot away and held up a paper bag, as if suddenly remembering it. "This is from your mom."

Her hands trembled as she placed it on his overbed table.

"What's wrong?"

"Nothing." She glanced to the left. "It's just, I kind of looked at it before I came here, and the thing was glowing red. In the parking lot, it changed to purple."

With a chuckle, Adam opened the bag. "And now, it's likely to be blue. I should have known Mom would do this."

Sure enough, the crystal orb, passed down to him from his father, glowed radiant cerulean, the same shade as the sky on a clear day. *Perfect.*

"What is it?" Sera leaned closer, her eyes wide.

"Close the door and I'll tell you. This isn't something I want anyone else to know about."

After shutting the door, she returned to the side of his bed. "Is it really from another world?"

"Yes." Adam pulled out the orb, careful not to drop it. "My dad brought it with him when he came to Earth."

"And what does it do besides flash different colors?"

"I'm not exactly sure. My father always said it told him right from wrong, flashing red when it disagreed with his actions, and blue when it approved. And that only we can observe the colors, along with our soul mates."

"So this...us...it's right?" Her gaze held so much hope.

"I've always thought so." From the moment he'd felt their connection, the first time he set eyes on her after her husband had died, he'd thought so.

Sera swatted his shoulder, smiling, something he hadn't seen her do since their day at the amusement park. "Does it have special powers?"

"Well, my mother believes it has the power to heal, to bring two people together and heal their hearts."

Taking the blue crystal from him, Sera returned it the bag and set it on the table, shoving the overbed aside. She pulled the sheet back "I like your mother's explanation."

"Ugh, as much as I want you in my arms again, I don't think you want to get that close. I stink."

She grinned. "You're right. But it's not any worse than that canned deodorant spray you used to use."

With an unexpected release of tension, he inhaled Sera's soft vanilla scent, content to have her by his side again. "I love you, Sera. I will always love you."

Tilting her head, she kissed his cheek. "And I love you, too, Adam. My alien."

"Half-alien."

"Doesn't matter."

Her eyes filled with lust and she trailed her fingers under the sheets, across his chest, sparking his hunger.

"Now, does my alien have any special powers I should know about?"

He groaned. "Only the never ending desire to please the woman I love."

"Knock, knock," came a sing-song voice from the doorway.

Sera scrambled off the bed.

Shit. Adam stared at the nurse sweeping the curtain aside, dread pooling in the pit of his stomach. *How much had she heard?* He shifted to hide his hard-on, but the restraints didn't give him any room to move.

"Mr. Jones," the nurse said. "I know you're frustrated at being confined to your bed, but you are not healed enough to engage in hanky-panky. And this is definitely not the place."

"Sorry." He willed his erection gone. "Won't happen again." *Not without locking the door first.*

The nurse laughed. "I'm just glad you didn't try to take the catheter out. I've had that happen before. Not a pretty sight." She clapped her hands together. "Now, let's get you up to X-ray before lunch."

Horrible timing. He hated to leave Sara after she'd finally come to visit, but the sooner his bones healed, the sooner he could leave and start his future with her.

CHAPTER EIGHT

"Careful, watch the top of the ramp." Sera rushed to open the door, aiming to get Adam inside without causing him any extra pain. After eight weeks in the hospital, he'd been released and was coming home. To live with her.

With Adam in a wheelchair, the steps up to his loft were too much of an obstacle, and he needed to recover in a place with no stairs. Sera immediately offered her home, having a ramp installed in the back, and converting the unused office on the main floor into a spare room. She wanted him under the same roof, now and forever. And once he was given crutches to use instead of a wheelchair, she'd invite him into her bed. Their bed.

"Geez, I feel like an old man." Adam rolled over to the couch. Grabbing the arms of the couch, he heaved himself out of the wheelchair and onto the closest cushion. "I hate being so limited in what I can do."

After dropping off his duffle bag in the transformed office, Sera settled in beside him. "Yes, but I'm here to take care of you. Enjoy it while you can."

"You have kids. I don't want to be an extra burden on you."

"We've already discussed this—you are not a burden." She rubbed his thigh. "I invited you, remember? To live, not just to stay until your bones are healed."

"But, I didn't want it to happen like this. Right now, you feel obligated to take care of me, but I need to be here because you want me."

"Gah!" She pinched his arm. "I want you, all right, and I want you living with me more than anything. What is it going to take to convince you of that?"

The roar of an engine clamored through the open window behind her. She checked her watch.

Crap! The school bus. Sera jumped off the couch and rushed to the door. *The kids. I lost track of time.* Melody yanked Zach up the driveway, her son dragging his feet all the way.

And Adam wants to be a part of this? She squeezed the bridge of her nose. "Okay, that's enough. Hurry inside, because I have a surprise for you both."

"A surprise?" Zach ran the rest of the way to the house and flew past her, dropping his backpack and coat on the floor.

Melody followed behind with an ear-piercing squeal. "Adam, you're out of the hospital!"

They launched toward Adam and Sera gasped. "No!"

Panicking, she reached out to pull them away, but didn't make it in time. She cringed as Melody and Zach crashed down on Adam's knees.

"Get off of him! Oh my gosh, you're going to hurt his legs even more." She gasped, squeezing her eyes shut. *Maybe this wasn't such a good idea.* She didn't want to send him back to the hospital right after he'd been released.

"Sera, I'm okay."

Slowly, she opened her eyes again. Instead of the wince of pain she expected, Adam grinned, receiving hugs from both of her children.

She placed a hand on her chest to catch her breath. "I'm so sorry. I didn't think they would jump on you."

"They're kids." He chuckled. "Besides, I'm sure they won't get as excited after I've been here for awhile.

Melody stood, rising up on her toes. "He's staying? For good?"

With a smile, Sera nodded. "Yes, he's going to live with us now."

Her daughter giggled and danced around the room, cementing Sera's confidence in the decision.

But Zach stared at her, a deep crease between his brows. "He's going to sleep in your room, right?"

She gulped. Did her son have a problem with Adam's permanence? "Yes, eventually. Although, until he's allowed to walk up a flight of stairs, he'll be sleeping in the office."

Zach bounced on the couch, the concern gone. "Okay, as long as I don't have to share a room with anyone. Tommy, a boy in my class, has to share a room with his older brother who snores when he's sleeping, and he punches Tommy all the time, for no reason."

The concerns of children. Sera shook her head, abandoning her worries.

Melody stopped beside her, tugging on her shirt. "So, does that mean you're going to get married?"

"I think that's something we'll discuss in the future." She didn't want to scare Adam away already. After a month, he might change his mind about living with her. Or maybe after a week.

Patting the cushion next to him, Adam raised his eyebrows. "No, let's talk about it now."

What's he up to?

She shuffled over, her muscles tensing with every step. Her head spun as she sat beside him. *Is this the end, or just the beginning?*

Melody and Zach kneeled on the floor in front of them, beaming, as if they already knew what Adam had planned.

"Sera, you know this isn't how I wanted things to happen between us…."

Her stomach flipped. *Oh, God.*

"But, I'm not going to be deterred, either. Remember, you asked me what it was going to take to convince me you want me to stay?"

Her mouth suddenly dry, she picked at the non-existent lint on her flower-print dress.

"Well, I've already talked to your kids about this at the hospital, and…." He reached into his pocket then placed his hands over hers. "Sera, will you marry me?"

The Hallelujah Chorus played in her head. An overwhelming rush of joy burst from within and tears slipped down. "You mean it?"

He chuckled. "Of course I do. I wouldn't have asked if I didn't."

Wiping her cheeks, Sera asked her children, "And you guys are okay with this?"

"Yes, Mom." Melody rolled her eyes. "We wanted you two to get married at the beginning of the summer."

Sera focused on Adam's rugged, handsome face. "Yes, Adam, I will marry you."

After sliding a gorgeous diamond ring on her finger, he brushed his thumb along her lips, then kissed her. His restrained passion filled her heart with bliss. She'd found love again, from the most unexpected place, a man younger than her, with otherworldly ancestors. And she wouldn't trade him for the universe.

ALIEN ATTRACTION

CHAPTER ONE

Soul mate. The one person Angela would marry, spend the rest of her life with. Did she have one somewhere on this planet, or was she destined to spend the rest of her life alone?

Holding the crystal orb passed down to her by her father over a year earlier, she willed it to give her a sign, flash red or blue. Or any other color for all she cared. The extraterrestrial sphere hadn't provided any guidance in her life decisions as it had her father and brother, hadn't shared its thoughts on the two guys she'd dated since moving to the city, not even whether she should stay there. Had the battery died? Or was she too human to make it work? Her brother Adam, had told her to be thankful she shared little of the extraterrestrial DNA, that her life would be easier. Instead, she didn't fit in. Anywhere.

The last few years had been brutal as she waited to locate her one true love, especially after Adam had married Sera. Angela had given up on all the guys she'd gone to high school with, none of them interested in anything other than drinking and one-night stands. Moving far from home had been the best decision she'd made in her life, but hadn't brought her any closer to finding love.

Tempted to slam the orb on the floor and smash it to pieces, she instead tucked it into a nest of tissue paper inside a cardboard box. Next time she drove the four-hour trip to visit her family, she would return it to her father and give up on the idea of celestial intervention. After fitting the lid on top, she shoved the box into the rear of her bedroom closet. No point in leaving it out for another year to collect dust.

With a sigh, she plodded over to the bay view window in the main room of her tiny apartment, the only saving grace to being on the fifteenth floor. She picked up her plum-colored pillow and plopped onto the matching foam seat. Glancing across the city, she gazed at the setting sun, the end of another day on her own. Growing up, she'd never imagined living so far from her parents, in a city full of concrete, steel, glass, and people. So many people. Yet, she failed to make a connection with very many of them, save for the sweet old lady next door who had passed away from a heart attack a month earlier. Angela didn't regret her decision to move though, not when the friends she'd grown up with were alcoholics, or in prison for dealing drugs.

Knock, knock.

She jumped. Except for her former neighbor, no one visited her. Plus, the building had a controlled entrance, so anyone who did decide to pop over had to call up first.

The sound came again. She rushed to the entrance, curious as to who stood on the other side. No one at work had mentioned stopping by. Heck, she was lucky if her co-workers remembered her name for an entire day.

Peeking through the peephole, she gasped. A guy. And a damn hot one from what she could tell through the tiny hole. Shoulder-length brown hair, a prominent nose, and radiant green eyes. Though his scowl left her wanting to sneak away from the entrance and pretend she wasn't at home.

When he raised his fist to knock again, a burst of courage swept through her. She yanked the door open before he made contact. "Can I help you?"

He jumped, his scowl momentarily gone. "You're Angela Jones?"

"Yes...." How did he know her name when she'd never met him before? Usually it was the other way around. People knew her face, but couldn't get her name right if their lives depended on it.

The stranger held out a couple of envelopes. "I believe this is your mail. Seems the postal carrier put them in my box instead of yours."

She took them from him. "Thank you." Maybe it was a good thing the mail lady kept mixing up Angela's box in the lobby with the one next to hers. That was how she'd ended up meeting sweet Mrs. Kersley, her neighbor before the handsome man in front of her had moved in. She could get to know him better. "You.... You're new here, right? Would you like to come in for coffee?"

"No." He furrowed his brows, looking even more disgusted than he had through the peephole. "See that this mix up doesn't happen again. I don't want this to be a daily trip. I have better things to do."

What an asshole! Like she had any control over which slot her mail ended up in. As he turned away, she slammed the door behind him. The mail snafu had happened for as long as she'd lived there. Mrs. Kersley hadn't minded bringing the misdirected letters and packages to her. She would often make extra food and invite her for dinner when the older woman did stop by. Angela doubted the same would ever happen with Mr. Too Busy. Time to get the computer out and switch everything to e-billing with the hopes of never running into him again.

With a huff, she headed back to the window. Lights flickered to her left. She spun toward her bedroom, where blue and red beams danced across her walls and ceiling. *What the hell?*

A few cautious steps and she reached the entrance. Peeking inside, she searched for the source of the luminescence. Inside her closet, the box she'd tucked in the back corner less than an hour earlier, lay on its side, with the orb in the middle of the floor, lighting up her bedroom like a disco ball. What had caused it to fall over? And why was it flashing two colors? According to her father and Adam, it pulsed with lights of red *or* blue, not both. Knowing Angela's luck, the orb had little life remaining, giving one last show before it finally died.

Shaking her head, she picked up the extraterrestrial object, not at all surprised it stopped flashing with her touch. Why would it start working for her after so many years anyway? *Stupid ball.* She tossed it in the box and used her foot to shove it to the far corner of her closet. Time to face the fact she lived alone in the big city, with no help from anyone or anything. And when her work contract expired in a few weeks, she would consider moving elsewhere rather than sign a new offer of employment. Because she had no chance of stumbling upon her soul mate here, not when people chose to ignore her rather than invite her to group events. Didn't seem to matter she carried more human DNA than Adam.

Cosmos! His second day in this city and Chal had already come face-to-face with five locals. Not exactly low-key as he'd promised his brother, second-in-command of the Memonon. Slade agreed their kind could not survive many more cycles on their aging ship, and unless they booked it to another solar system, the third planet from this system's sun remained their only refuge.

Chal had always yearned to live amongst the people of Earth—beings so close in physiology to his own—and show his kind they could stop hiding beyond the system's asteroid belt and live with so much more freedom. So, Slade had snuck him off the ship, transported him millions of miles to the blue-and-green sphere. Unfortunately, Chal's stay in what was called Russia hadn't turned out as he'd planned. A group of thugs had hunted him down, their boss hoping to dissect him and sell him in pieces on some kind of black market. But North America had a reputation as the home of the free, a place where people could live together in peace, regardless of their differences. Hopefully the same would hold true for his own kind.

Closing the apartment door behind him, he leaned against it, guilt enveloping him after the confrontation he'd had with his neighbor. She'd seemed...bubbly upon first seeing him. When he'd told her to avoid the mail mix-up happening again, her emotions had changed, happiness evaporating into anger and contempt. His fault. But he couldn't avoid his rudeness. If he wanted to stay undetected, he couldn't make nice by having relationships with humans. Not yet. Maybe never. A lonely life, but necessary until he could convince the rest of his kind to join him on the planet.

Yet, there was something familiar about the fair-haired young woman named Angela. He hadn't yet met her in Alerto, but had she followed him from Moscow, changed her identity to track him down? He couldn't be too sure. And he'd have to keep an eye on her, at least from a distance. Best to be prepared than caught off guard. But, if she simply turned out to be his attractive next door neighbor, he'd use the information he gathered to win her affection once his kind arrived on Earth. Because the best way to blend in was to become one of them. And from what he'd observed, that meant claiming a mate.

CHAPTER TWO

With a heavy sigh, Angela slipped on her running shoes. Five o'clock in the morning remained far too early for any sane person to head to the gym, but if she didn't go down to the apartment facilities at that time, she wouldn't have the chance to claim a piece of equipment. Finally getting her shoes tied, she stood and grabbed her water bottle. She planned to plop her butt on the exercise bike and cycle for forty-five minutes, because she doubted she could concentrate long enough to remain standing on the treadmills or elliptical trainers.

The damn orb had decided to work again, sending pulses of light around her room in the middle of the night. Not as bad as a fire drill, but at least the fire alarm stopped, and she had the chance to go back to sleep. Not so with the stupid extraterrestrial sphere. After a sleepless Friday night, she'd shoved the orb in the oven to try and dim the pulsing light. Instead of being awoken by bright flashes, she'd heard the thing banging around, as if alive and trying to escape. Last night, she'd simply buried her head under the cover and pretended she didn't see it.

Come morning, she yearned to leave her apartment and escape from the malfunctioning alien technology. With little energy, she rode the elevator to the first floor. The trek to the end of the hall took forever. For some reason, the corridor sensed her tiredness and expanded, making her walk even farther in her sleepy state. Thankful to finally reach the entrance to the gym, she grasped the handle and pulled.

A man kept a good pace on the treadmill. Her gut clenched. *No way. Not this morning.* She considered turning around and heading back to her apartment. She didn't need another confrontation with the asshole from next door. But she'd lived there longer, claimed this time at the gym long ago, and she'd be damned if she let him restrict her movement. Thank goodness he didn't occupy her desired machine.

Avoiding eye contact, she ambled over to the stationary bike. It was all she could do not to take a quick peek, catch a glimpse of his breathtaking eyes. No, even that view couldn't redeem his horrible attitude.

Placing her water bottle in the holder, Angela stuck one foot into the pedal strap before she hopped onto the bike and buckled her other foot. She reached for her phone to turn on some tunes. *Shit!* It wasn't clipped to her arm. She'd forgotten it in her apartment with her towel and keys. Great, not only did she have nothing to distract her from Mr. Attitude, she'd left her apartment unlocked, open to strangers. Anyone could walk in and steal her phone, furniture, or even the orb. Although, she hoped someone did steal it, take away the blasted piece of alien junk forever.

Beginning to spin, Angela programmed the tension for a nice, steady ride. No rolling hills or uphill climbs that morning. She closed her eyes, imagining a trip along the roads back home, wood lots on either side and birds chirping all around. If she couldn't get lost in her music, she would in her daydreams.

When she opened her eyes again, she checked her watch. Twenty minutes had passed. And someone occupied the elliptical trainer immediately beside her—her pain-in-the-ass neighbor who had, at some point, taken off his shirt and moved closer to her. Bronzed skin covered ripple upon ripple of toned muscle. He had his dark, wavy hair up in a man bun, accentuating the tribal-looking tattoos across his chest, back, and shoulders. Swallowing the saliva forming, she glanced away from the man who resembled an Ancient Roman Gladiator. But no matter how attractive he appeared, she couldn't forget his piss-poor attitude.

"Good to know you're awake and not pedaling in your sleep."

She turned her head to him, unsure if she had heard him talk to her in a pleasant tone, or imagined the whole thing.

Slowing his pace, he met her gaze, a smirk playing across his lips. Part of her yearned to swoon at him for talking to her, but a much larger portion wanted to reach over and kick him in the shins. Taking his shirt off to reveal his godly physique and a half-hearted smile did not make up for his rudeness.

Staring straight ahead, she stood and cycled, giving her ass a break from the seat. She didn't want to make conversation with an arrogant prick. If her orb did begin to function properly, it would definitely tell her to stay away from him.

Change of plans. Staying away from the woman next door wouldn't work. They were bound to run into each other every once and again. And from the look of disdain on her face when she'd seen him in the exercise room, there was no way she had purposely followed him. Not unless she faked her anger well, because it rolled off her in waves. Even more so after he'd spoken to her.

"I'm sorry." Oh gods, he'd said it. No turning back. "I'm sorry for being rude the other night. I'd just had a really bad day and shouldn't have taken it out on you."

"Whatever." She sat back on the bike, not even glancing in his direction.

Her anger never faded, not a single inch, her emotions boring into his temples like an electric drill. She was no actress with the way she projected her feelings. What else had he done to offend her?

"And I'm sorry I took your time in the gym. I'm still learning how things work around here."

"Don't worry about it." She stopped spinning and stepped off the equipment before taking a drink from her bottle. Her emotions retreated, though mistrust still lingered. "I should get cleaned up for work anyway."

She was leaving already? Chal jumped in front of her. For some reason, he couldn't stand the thought of her having any negative feelings toward him. "Wait. Do you come here every day at this time?"

"I try to." She met his gaze then quickly turned away. But Chal didn't miss the hint of a smile before she did.

"Would you have a problem if I joined you occasionally? Of course, you'd have first pick of equipment. I wouldn't interrupt your routine."

A faint blush spread across her cheeks. "No. It's open to everyone who lives here."

Stars, she made conversation difficult. But then again, he hadn't made the best first impression. He stuck out his hand. *Time to start over.* "Hi, I'm Chal, your new neighbor. Come here often?"

She choked out a laugh then took his hand. For the first time that day, he sensed a bit of the bubbliness he'd noticed when he'd first met her. "Angela. And, yes." A gentle grip, but not delicate. She didn't hold on long, letting go before sidestepping toward the exit. "See you tomorrow morning."

Chal nodded. Yet, he couldn't shake the sense of familiarity around her, no matter how sure he was she hadn't followed him from Moscow. Watching her exit, he searched his mind for some epiphany, a revelation to confirm the feeling he had. Nothing. Only a deep desire to spend more time with her, and in doing so, solve the mystery of how he knew her.

CHAPTER THREE

"Well, that's a nice view first thing in the morning." A guy's voice, but not the one she'd hoped to hear.

Angela paused in the middle of her sun salutation, holding her downward-dog position. Glancing between her legs, she spied two sets of muscular calves. *Great!* Two strange males stared at her ass in the air. Abandoning her pose, she slumped onto her yoga mat.

"I've heard women who practice yoga are very flexible in the bedroom."

The comment wasn't directed at her, but she turned to face the men anyway. Her gut clenched when she recognized one of them. With his thick, dark-blond hair and crystal blue eyes, he'd caught her attention the day she moved in. After her family had headed home, he'd offered to help her unpack and sweet-talked his way into her bed, professing his love as he fucked her. Then he'd stomped on her heart a week later when she'd caught him making out with another woman in the foyer. A few minutes later and she would likely have seen much more. If only the orb had worked for her then.

"It's true. I've experienced her flexibility and not just in the bedroom, if you know what I mean." Grant slapped his friend on the shoulder before winking at her. "It's Amber, right?"

She rolled her eyes. Even sleeping with the guy hadn't helped him remember her name. "Angela, but it doesn't matter. I'm leaving." In no way did she plan to stick around and listen to sexual comments from these jackasses.

She rolled her mat then rushed out the door. Down the hall, in front of the elevator, stood the man she'd hoped to see in the exercise room all week. Chal hadn't returned since Monday, and she wondered if he'd been avoiding her. He hadn't seen her yet. Should she turn around, avoid a possible uncomfortable elevator ride?

"Angela, wait!"

She spun around to Grant's friend heading out after her, crooking a finger in her direction. Refusing to get any closer, she cocked her head to the side. "What?"

"Whoa! No need to be so harsh." He stepped toward her, letting the door close behind him. "I wondered if you wanted to go out tonight. You know, dinner, dancing, and then back to my place. Or, your place if you prefer."

The cocky grin on his face revealed exactly what he expected from her, and she wanted no part of it. "Sorry, I already have plans."

The elevator dinged and she rushed toward it.

"Another night then?"

"Sorry, I'll be busy then, too," she called over her shoulder.

When she reached the elevator, Chal held it open for her, a rolling suitcase at his side.

"Thank you." Angela ducked inside and moved to the far corner.

He laughed. "Well, that was a definite brush-off."

After a heavy sigh, she smiled. "Yeah, but his ego is too big to comprehend."

As the elevator closed, Chal pressed the button for their floor. "Sounds like you really don't like the guy."

A definite understatement. "I dated his friend last year. I know exactly what he's looking for, and I'm not interested in that kind of relationship."

"Last year, huh? How long have you lived here?"

The casual question caught her off guard. Was he actually trying to make conversation? Better than being seen as nothing more than a sex object. "About a year."

The elevator reached the fifteenth floor and opened. Chal gestured for her to exit first. Instead of rushing down the hall to her apartment, she lingered. "So, you were away for a couple of days?" Maybe he had a good reason for not showing up in the gym in the mornings as she'd hoped he would. He'd been the one person she'd secretly looked forward to seeing after the stupid orb had wakened her in the middle of the night and before she'd headed off to another day of work as a nameless face. Yet, every morning had led to disappointment when he didn't show.

"Yes, got called away for a family emergency." Chal walked beside her, not seeming to be in any hurry to get away.

Pausing, she touched his forearm. "Oh, I'm sorry. Nothing too serious, I hope."

He placed his hand over hers, sending an electric spark shooting through her veins.

"Thank you, but it was nothing like that. Only...." The rest of his words never came as he stared into her eyes.

Time stopped. The walls evaporated around them. Nothing existed but her and Chal, the energy radiating from him into her, filling her with a sense of peace, yet igniting desires she'd never experienced.

And just as quickly, the sensation disappeared. Angela let go and sighed. She'd likely imagined the connection, thinking too much about a soul mate in recent days. But that didn't mean she couldn't have a purely human relationship with him. Digging her toes into the insoles of her sneakers, she delved deep for some courage. "Would you, um, like to go out to dinner tonight? Maybe catch a movie after?"

"Go out?" He gave her a deer-in-headlights look.

She sucked in a heavy breath and glanced away. She'd read too much into their conversation. "Forget I said anything." Brushing past him, she rushed to her apartment.

"No, wait." He caught up to her, placing his palm over the lock as she tried to stick the key in. "I think you misinterpreted what I meant."

Spinning, she stared at his chest. His arms encircled her, yet made no contact. She glanced up at him, struggling to catch her breath.

He set a hand on her shoulder then ran his thumb along her jaw line. "It's been a long few days and I don't feel like going out anywhere."

She had another idea, but wasn't sure she could speak. His simple touch had left her tongue numb. "Come over to my place later then. I'll make dinner, and we can watch a movie here. If you fall asleep on the couch, I'll drape a blanket over you. You won't have far to go when you do wake up." Gods, could she sound more desperate?

His lips curved into a wry smile. "I thought you already had plans tonight. Isn't that what you told the other guy?"

"I, um...."

"Kidding." His smile widened. "That sounds nice. What time would you like me to come over?"

"Around six?" Plenty of time to clean up and get to the grocery store, if she could think of something to make. At that moment, she focused on nothing but Chal's gaze, his proximity to her, and his fingers working their way across her shoulder and along her spine.

"Sounds good." He kissed the corner of her mouth then backed away as if he hadn't set her soul on fire. "I'll see you then." Grabbing his suitcase, he hauled it behind him. At his own door, he unlocked it then gave her a quick wave before disappearing into his apartment.

Tongue still paralyzed, Angela touched her face where Chal's lips had been. A friendly gesture? Or, a promise of more to come when he returned? If he returned. He'd promised to meet her in the mornings, yet failed to show. Would he do the same in the evening? Time would tell.

Chal stood naked in front of his closet. Learning the languages of Earth had been easier than deciding what to wear for his appointment with Angela. A date. He'd searched online to learn what constituted proper attire for his evening, only to learn he'd agreed to a possible romantic rendezvous next door. Against his brother's wishes.

Chal's family issues involved meeting Slade back on the ship to be reminded of the rules of human interaction. Or lack thereof on his part, especially after he'd trusted the wrong people in Moscow.

Yet, regardless of Slade's warnings, Chal refused to say no to his neighbor. Not after the gleeful energy she'd radiated upon seeing him that morning, and the spark of bliss that had embraced his soul with her gentle touch. Slade had yet to set foot on the planet, giving him no right to make assumptions about the people who lived there. Chal admitted his naivety upon his first landing on Earth, the mistakes he'd made. But Angela was nothing like Veronika. If he'd trusted his instincts with the woman in the first place, he never would have ended up close to dissection. He shivered, running a finger along the scar below his naval. A definite close call. Thank goodness Slade had found his location, otherwise he might not have transported him away in time. Though his brother vowed never to transfer him from the city again. Not with the noticeable tang it left in the air. Hence, why he had to give the impression of departing on a trip when summoned by Slade.

Deciding on a pair of jeans and a plain gray sweater, Chal dressed, driving Slade's warnings to the back of his mind. Angela had lived next door for over a year and could not have been involved in his near-death experience. After locking his apartment, he shoved his keys in his pocket with five minutes to spare. Hard to believe he'd traveled millions of miles that morning only to end up a matter of feet down the hall for his evening.

He knocked, far more anxious to see Angela than a week ago. When the door opened, she nearly stole his breath. With her hair tied loosely behind her neck, she wore a patterned-flower dress cinched in the middle to accentuate her sexy curves. The dress ended at the tops of her thighs, exposing some skin between the material and her matching knee-high socks.

Chal gulped, not wanting to appear a fool for drooling. Yet, he could think of nothing other than peeling her clothes off and savoring her delectable human body.

"Hi." A smile lit her face. "Come on in."

The emotions she threw off revealed nothing but joy and perhaps a bit of nervousness. Nothing fake or false in her reaction. Yet, upon her turning away, he adjusted himself, recalling the evening not so long ago when Veronika had welcomed him into her home. He'd fallen victim to the seductive sway of her hips, all the things she'd promised to do to him. And he'd been more than willing to let her strap him to her bed.

"Sit down." Angela snapped him back to the present, pulling out a chair at her two-person table. "I made balsamic-glazed steak rolls. I hope you like them." She brought the plates over to the table, and the tempting scent of the food filled his nostrils.

"It looks and smells delicious." The replicated meals of the ship all tasted the same and the scents all blended together with the recycled air. One whiff of whatever she had made, and he never wanted imitation cuisine again.

"Just something new I tried." She poured a red liquid into two upside-down bell-shaped glasses then set them on the table. "And a cabernet sauvignon to go with it."

He smiled and nodded, unaware of what that even meant. Not a term he'd learned when studying the languages of Earth. When she sat across from him, she placed her napkin over her lap. Chal did the same, ready to enjoy the meal in front of him. And the woman who'd made it, he'd enjoy after.

"Before we eat...." She lifted the odd-shaped glass delicately between her fingers. "Let's toast to new neighbors and new relationships."

A toast. He remembered those from Moscow. Only Russians preferred vodka and beer over the red liquid. "To new neighbors and new relationships." He tapped his glass to hers then took a small sip. His first toast on Earth had sent his head spinning and made moments of time disappear from his memory. Not a mistake he planned to make again.

He set the glass down then began to eat, savoring each delectable bite. Red meat and vegetables cooked together in some kind of sauce sent his taste buds zinging.

"So, where are you from?" Angela dabbed her napkin to the corner of her mouth. "I've tried to place your accent, but I can't."

He mimicked her use of the napkin to hide the dread twisting in his stomach. "I, um, travel a lot. So, I pick up a bit of an accent from everywhere I go."

"You travel?" She leaned forward, her eyes wide. "What do you do?"

Telling her a transporter divided his body into millions of pieces before piecing them back together again wasn't going to go over well. He didn't want to end up on a dissection table after one week in the new city. "Um, I'm sorry, I don't understand."

She narrowed her eyes as if she'd asked the most obvious question. "What is your occupation? What do you do for a living that allows you to travel so much?"

"Oh, I'm an anthropologist." An answer he'd prepared before returning to the planet.

"Really?" She tilted her head to the side. "I never would have guessed. So, what brings you to Alerto?"

Desperate for an answer, Chal forked a piece of steak into his mouth, chewing while thinking. Why did anthropologists move to the city? *Oh yeah.* He swallowed. "I'm actually tired of never having a permanent place to call home. Looking for a corporate position here." His other option was with the government, but he couldn't risk a background check.

With a brief smile, she nodded. "So, where was your last position? Any place interesting?"

"Moscow." He grimaced, remembering the sting of the knife across his stomach, of his narrow escape. "Russian mafia. Not an experience I ever want to go through again."

"I can imagine."

"So, what do you do?" He had to change the topic before she asked him something he hadn't prepared for.

"I'm an intern at a property management firm."

The lack of enthusiasm in her voice surprised him. Didn't people in America get to choose their career? "You don't like your job?"

"I do." She scooped some vegetables onto her fork. "The work is great. It's the place, the people I work with."

"The people?"

"Yeah, I feel like I don't fit in there. Even after a year, no one remembers who I am. Probably should have studied to be a teacher instead."

Chal failed to understand. He'd met Angela only recently, but could never forget her kind smile, the wide array of emotions she experienced yet hid from her features, and the delicate curves of her toned body. His cock stirred. In the future, he hoped for a more intimate view, a hands-on lesson in making love to a female from Earth. One that didn't turn into a class on Memonon anatomy.

Somehow, he made it through dinner without getting his background story mixed up. And she never questioned his responses. When the time came to clean up, he jumped right in to help. He'd read on the Web that women appreciated a man who helped with domestic chores.

She took the dishes from him with a smile before stacking them in a rack and closing them into a box. "No need to worry about them now. I'll run the dishwasher later tonight."

He stared at the box in the counter. A machine that helped with daily chores? Interesting.

Fascinated by the technology, he nearly missed the sudden change in her emotions. Nervous, with a hint of guilt. As if she expected something bad to happen. Had she been contacted by the thugs? Arranged for them to take him away?

He eyed the door and windows. All locked. Maybe she hadn't turned him in. Yet, he couldn't ignore the emotions plaguing her. "Is everything okay?"

"Yeah." She grabbed a sweater from the arm of the couch and pulled it on, hiding her bare skin from view. "I was wondering what movie you wanted to watch."

No, it was something more. A deeper worry. "I'll let you pick. I trust you." To be in her apartment took confidence she didn't suspect he was anything other than human. And he hoped she trusted him, too. Besides, he had no clue as to what movie titles he would enjoy. He'd only learned what they were earlier that day.

"Um, okay...."

While she stood in front of the television, scrolling through a list of titles, Chal sat on the couch. He took the corner position, allowing her to sit as close or far away as she desired. Though, he hoped to have her in his arms, or if he was lucky, writhing underneath him by the end of the night.

A burst of sound filled the room, like the crescendo of a musical motor starting. Thank the gods Angela missed his startled gasp. When the noise faded, she sat beside him, her side pressed against him. Much closer than he'd expected.

As if remembering they'd known each other for a week, she jumped away from him, staring with wide eyes. "I'm sorry."

"Don't be." He draped an arm across her shoulders and guided her back to his side. "I like it when you're close to me."

She stiffened, radiating the same nervous anticipation she had earlier. "Really?"

He stroked the side of her face. "If I didn't, I wouldn't be here."

Her fear spiked, but quickly ebbed away as she nestled up to his side, her head resting on his chest. Was she afraid of him? Why? Did she know he wasn't from Earth? But how would she have found out?

With her relaxed, Chal brushed the thoughts aside. He became engrossed in the movie, a story about a man from Earth falling in love with a woman from another planet. It had to be some kind of sign. "Hmmm."

Angela glanced up at him, her fingers splayed absently across his stomach. "What?"

"Do you think that's possible? For someone from Earth to fall in love with a being from another planet?"

"Yeah, of course." Her words came out so nonchalantly, as if relationships with aliens happened all the time.

"Seriously?"

Her body tensed. "I mean, why not? Interracial relationships are much more common. A relationship with an intelligent being from another planet is the next step, right?"

He sure hoped so. Resting his palm on her hip bone, he resisted the urge to scoop her up in his arms and take her to the bedroom. Could living in this part of the world be so easy for his kind? "What about you? Could you fall in love with an alien?"

She smiled, her body relaxing again. "I am absolutely sure I could."

"What about a regular human being?" Slowly gathering her skirt up her legs, he waited for her answer. Would she reject him?

"Could I fall in love with someone from Earth? Sure." She moved her hand down and began to rub his inner thigh. "If that someone is you."

Lust oozed out of her pores, accelerating his desire. He sat up, anxious to kiss her sweet lips. So soft and tender. She wrapped her arms around his neck and leaned back, pulling him on top of her. Chal plunged his tongue into her mouth the way he wanted to experience other parts of her.

Angela held the hem of his sweater, drawing the material up until he was forced to draw back for a moment to get the dang thing off. As she trailed her palms up and down his back, Chal slipped his hands under the skirt of her dress. He yearned for more. All of her. No internal warnings with his neighbor. Every inch of his being encouraged him on, to make the ultimate connection with the woman who said she could love an alien.

Clasping her waist, he ran his thumbs along the edge of her undergarments. With a throaty moan, she thrust toward him. Encouragement?

He lifted his head and gazed into her honey-colored eyes. "Do you want this?"

She nodded and pulled him back down, claiming his mouth the way he yearned to claim her. When she elevated her hips, he slid his fingers beneath her undergarments and shimmied them down her thighs.

A piercing alarm filled the room, as if her panties were fitted with a siren. Bolting upright, he closed his eyes and slammed his palms over his ears.

When he peeked for a glance of Angela's reaction to the noise, he saw tears trailing down her cheeks, her face illuminated by red and blue lights.

"No," she cried. "Not now. Not with him."

He followed her line of sight, spotting a round object on the floor at the foot of the couch, the source of the light and most likely the noise. *A Lisivian predictor!* Flashing red and blue, warning of the worst kind of danger.

Chal scrambled to his feet, grabbing his sweater from the floor on the way out of the apartment. The woman he thought he might be able to have a future with possessed an extraterrestrial artifact, one of a race dead before he was born. She had no reason to have it in her possession unless she hunted aliens. Hunted him. He'd failed to detect Terran deceit once again. And he had to get out before he ended up tied to her table with a knife to his throat.

Her sobs did nothing to change his mind. Perhaps Earth wasn't the best place to settle. His kind was destined to meet an end like the Lisivian. Though, a better way to die than being tortured and experimented on. Fighting the urge to glance back, Chal fled from Angela's apartment. He had to pack. Take the bad news back to his brother, and leave the planet forever.

CHAPTER FOUR

"Take it." Angela shoved the orb into her brother's arms. After the extraterrestrial object had interrupted her evening and sent Chal fleeing her apartment, she'd driven the four-hour trip home. No way did she want the stupid sphere any longer. "The thing is broken. It keeps me up at night and chases away my dates."

"When it's flashing red, it means the guy isn't meant for you." Adam, must have heard her drive up the gravel driveway to her parents, having walked over from his house to meet her. "Dad and I told you many times."

If only her problem was that simple. She yanked an overnight bag from the back of her car and slammed the trunk shut. "And what does it mean when it flashes blue and red, hotshot? Or when it somehow manages to get free of the box you put it in to roll from your bedroom and out to your living room?"

"It moves?" Adam raced to catch up with her as she traipsed up the walkway to her parents' front door.

"Yep." She turned the handle, the house never locked so long as someone remained home. "And if you stick it in the oven, it will bang around trying to escape."

"No shit. You're kidding, right?"

Once inside, she tossed her luggage in the corner of the kitchen and plopped onto a chair. "Unfortunately no."

"You must have done something to it then." Spinning the chair across from her, he straddled the seat and faced her. "It's never acted like that before."

With a huff, she rolled her eyes. Maybe coming home was a bad idea. Tossing the orb in the trash bin behind her apartment building would have caused less frustration. "You are not blaming this on me. It sat in my bedroom for a year, not a single flash. Definitely didn't help with the asshole I dated when I first moved in and another dickhead three months later."

"Whoa! So, you've dated three guys since you moved to the city?"

She glared at Adam. "Don't you say a word. Before Sera, you had plenty of dates, most of the girls a one-time thing."

"That's because they weren't the one. Red light, remember?"

"And what about the ones you didn't bring home?" Adam could act innocent all he wanted, but she wasn't naive enough to believe him.

"Still, you have to be careful."

"Okay, Dad."

"Did someone mention my name?" Their father appeared from the hallway, wearing his robe and his hair a mess.

"Sorry for waking you." She stood and gave him a hug.

"Sure." He wrapped his arms around her. "With all the arguing, I thought I'd gone back in time to when you both still lived at home."

"Me, too," her mom said, joining them in the kitchen.

"Sorry." Angela hugged her as well then sat back at the table. "I came to return the orb. It's malfunctioning and waking me in the middle of the night."

"And stopping you from getting laid." Adam mumbled the words, but judging by the clench of her father's jaw and the way her mom's cheeks flushed, they'd heard.

"Shut up." She kicked him under the table. Even as an adult, he still irritated her. "Don't you have your own family to take care of?"

"They're all sleeping." He stood anyway and put the chair back. "But since you managed to wake Mom and Dad, I'll head back to my house and crawl into my warm bed with my wife."

She scowled at him. "You mean Sera's house."

"Hey, I pay—"

"Adam, go." Their mother pointed to the door.

When he left, she shook her head. "It never ends."

"I'm sorry, Mom. I didn't mean to wake either of you when I came in." She eyed the crystal sphere Adam had abandoned on the table across from her. "But, I can't have the orb anymore. I'm returning it so I can get a full night of sleep."

Her dad put his hand on hers. "Tell me what it's doing."

She recounted the events of the past week, from the orb flashing when she first met Chal to it rolling out of her room during her date. Though, she omitted what they had been doing when the sphere chased him away.

Her father rubbed his chin. "You said it flashed red *and* blue every time this Chal fellow came over?"

"Yes, and even when he wasn't there. He'd left on a business trip during the week, and it still flashed in the middle of the night." She rested her head on her folded arms, the late night catching up with her.

Her dad pursed his lips together in thought. "Interesting."

Nope, not even close to any word she'd thought of to describe the situation.

"There's only one time I remember the orb flashing both colors." He grabbed the crystal and rolled it from hand to hand. "Heck, I'm not even sure whether what I remember was a dream or reality."

"Tell us, Luke." Her mom yawned. "Whatever it is could help Angela figure out what's going on."

"Fine." He held the orb out. "When I was really young, about four Earth years, I was confined to my quarters again. My parents, as part of the council, were meeting with another nomadic race, the Memonons. I never did meet them, so I have no idea what they look like. But, I do remember my orb flashing red and blue the entire time they were on the ship. A few hours after as well. Later, my mother told me they had to go to the other ship for the next meeting because the orbs emitted a high pitch tone only the Memonons could hear."

Angela sat up. "Oh my gosh! Chal covered his ears at the same time I noticed the orb rolling across the floor. I couldn't hear anything, but from the pained expression on his face, he sure did."

"That's it then." Her mother nodded. "Your neighbor Chal is a Memonon. You're both aliens, a perfect match."

Yes, because it's completely normal to run into other alien species on Earth. "Um, Mom?"

"They're good people," her dad interrupted. "At least, they were many years ago. I'd love to talk to him, learn more about his kind, and what he knows of my own."

"But, how Daddy? When he ran out, he didn't seem like he'd ever come back." No matter how much she willed the whole thing a terrible dream.

"If they're on this planet, they're not going to be running around telling everyone what they are." He tapped the orb. "Imagine if you saw one of these in someone else's home."

"I'd assume they broke into my place and stole it. Then I'd be worried what else they knew about me."

"Exactly." He stood and pushed his chair in before seeing the orb in the sink. "Shouldn't roll out of there. Anyway, if you want to see him again, you're going to have to tell him what you are. It's the only way he's going to trust you."

"It's nice to finally get permission to tell someone." All her life she'd been forbidden to reveal her family's secret to anyone. Their lives depended on it. Though, she never did inherit the abilities her father and Adam had. Her eyes never turned all black, and if she wanted to know how someone felt, she had to pay attention to their body language, or ask them.

"Tread carefully though, my angel. You don't want to tell him when you have an audience. If you can't get him alone, you might want to forget about him."

She didn't think she could. After a week, Chal had engraved himself into her heart. Was it because he had alien ancestors, too? Or was she simply desperate to find a soul mate?

Her mother moved beside her and ran a palm over her head. "Go to bed, sweetie. You look exhausted."

Yes, it could all wait until the morning. She headed upstairs to her old bedroom. Exactly the way she'd left it. Or maybe a little cleaner. Not bothering to change out of her clothes, she flopped onto the bed and closed her eyes.

"It was smart of you to put a tracker on her car, but I don't think these people are like the Terrans you dealt with before."

Chal hovered his chair over to sit beside Slade. Letting him rest, his brother had focused the ship's satellites on Angela and the people she'd run to. "So, what do you think they are?" He hadn't risked being caught for nothing. Remaining on Earth to place a beacon on her car cost him extra minutes and after teleporting away, he'd left an energy residue behind. Easy to trace if one knew what they were looking for.

"To be honest, a family. If you take a closer look at Angela and this guy here." Slade pointed to the man who had met her the night before. "They look alike. Plus, they resemble this older couple here. Could be her brother and parents."

Slade's attention to detail amazed Chal. He'd only really observed Angela, her frustration and sadness. Emotions he'd caused and could feel even when light years away. As if they'd already formed a bond after such a short time.

No way! She was from Earth. They had no connection, should have never spent any time together. Why did his sexual desires block his common sense with his life and that of his people on the line?

Slade flicked Chal's ear. "And this female here with the two kids is expecting again."

"So?" He yearned to escape the observation room, forget her as Slade had insisted when he'd arrived the night before.

"They're not alien hunters." Slade zoomed the view even closer. "But, why would they have a Lisivian predictor?"

"The million-dollar question."

"Huh?" The line of spikes on Slade's scalp flared.

"A saying I picked up on Earth." From whom, he couldn't remember.

Slade chewed on a sprig of some plant grown in the ship's greenhouse. "There's got to be something I'm missing."

Chal took another look, watching Angela hug those around her. When she reached the older male, she paused a little longer before he passed the indicator to her. She seemed reluctant to accept it from him. But when she did, she tossed it in the trunk of her vehicle.

Slade jumped off his seat, flinging the hover chair across the room. "That's it! The eyes."

"What do you mean?" He leaned in closer. "Her eyes look the same as any Terran."

"Not hers, dumbass. Her father's."

Switching his focus didn't help. Chal couldn't understand what the man's eyes revealed. "I still don't see."

"Gods, with how observant you are, maybe I should have been the one to go to Earth." Slade pointed to the older man's eyes. "Watch closely. Don't blink or you'll miss it."

Chal stared, waiting for some revelation. And then he saw it. "They're black. That means.... No way. They all died."

"Obviously not." Slade slapped him on the back. "Guessing that man's age, I would say he was a young child when his kind perished. Somehow, he got off the ship before the illness spread through."

"And Angela...." His mind fumbled over itself trying to process the news.

"Your girlfriend is a Lisivian, or at least half. And that means you're going back to Earth."

Chal's heart raced. "But you said—"

"I know, but that was before I realized who we were dealing with." Slade guided him to the single-person transporter in the corner. "You need to learn more. Get close to her and her family. Find out how he's survived among the Terrans for so long. And if he can help us. That information will surely convince Gille and the council to move ahead in our plans to migrate to Earth."

If what Slade believed was true, sure. But that meant returning to Angela, experiencing their strange bond, then leaving her again to help his people.

CHAPTER FIVE

Angela leaned her laundry basket against the wall while she locked her apartment. Thirty minutes had passed and if her clothes weren't already dry, they would be soon. Best to get down there early than to find her clothes thrown haphazardly on the table. Or worse, gone.

Passing by Chal's apartment, she purposely avoided glancing at his door while the butterflies in her stomach took flight. A week had passed since their date, and she hadn't seen him. No chance to ask him if he was indeed a Memonon, and therefore, no information to pass along to her father, who called every other night to find out what she'd learned. Forget a face-to-face encounter to ask. If he was avoiding her, she didn't need another confrontation to make the situation worse.

Turning the corner into the laundry room, she stopped dead. Grant's friend from the exercise room stood in front of one of the washing machines, shoving his clothes inside. Since when did he live on the same floor? As she stepped back to avoid an encounter with him, he spun toward the entrance and smiled at her. Crap!

Caught, she headed inside, intent to grab her laundry and get out.

"It's Angela, isn't it?"

Great! The one person she didn't want to remember her name did. "Yep, I'm collecting my laundry here."

"I'm Jason." He held out his hand, but she ignored it."I guess we did get off on the wrong foot." He leaned against the washer, his feet blocking her way through the narrow room. "I assure you, I'm not like Grant."

"And that would mean?" Gods, why couldn't he stop talking and let her do what she'd intended? Why couldn't it be so easy?

"Yes, I know he can be an asshole, but I promise you, I don't use women the way he does."

He stepped toward her, and she immediately wedged the basket between them. The term *guilt by association* had been coined for a reason. "So, what? Your relationships last one month instead of one week?"

Enjoying the drop of his jaw, Angela jostled past him to the dryer containing her clothes. She set the basket on the floor, opened the dryer then emptied the tumbler.

"C'mon, Angela, give me a chance." He stood across the aisle, blocking her exit. "Have dinner with me tonight. Then we'll go dancing. That's it. No pressure. Just fun."

"She can't." Chal stood behind Jason, arms crossed and lips pursed.

A sudden burst of rage flashed through her. Chal had no right to say what she could and couldn't do, even if she didn't plan on dating Jason. Ever. He'd ruined her fun at rejecting the guy.

"Call me and let me know." Jason slipped a piece of paper on top of her laundry, as if he hadn't heard Chal.

Moving aside, he allowed her to pass without another word, only to have Chal reach for the paper as she slipped by him. She lifted her elbow, blocking him and nearly tossing the laundry at the same time. No way in hell would she call Jason, but that piece of paper was hers to throw in the trash. Besides, where had Chal been all week? Did he only show up when other guys hit on her?

"Angela, wait."

She refused to turn around for him, storming all the way down the hall to her apartment. But by the time she'd dug to the bottom of the basket to retrieve her key and unlocked the door, he leaned against the wall beside her.

"We need to talk."

Tossing the clothes and keys inside, she stood in the entrance, blocking his view of her home. "No, we needed to talk last Saturday, last Sunday, or Monday even. Not today. It's too late. I get the message. You've avoided me all week, because you weren't away on business. I heard you enough times slamming cupboards, drawers, and arguing with the voices in your head."

"With my brother."

"Whatever. Plenty of time to come over and talk."

She ducked inside and shut him out, but couldn't quite latch the door, Chal obviously pushing on it from the other side.

"I know what you are." The words came out in barely a whisper, but loud enough for her to quit fighting him. "I know what that thing is on the floor behind you, and even though it's giving me a killer headache, I'm still here because, as I said, we need to talk."

Grabbing the front of his shirt, Angela yanked him inside, and locked the world out. "Fine, what do you know?"

Chal squeezed his eyes shut and rubbed his temples. "Can you put that thing away first? I won't last much longer if it keeps going off."

"I've tried, but it keeps getting out of my closet." She'd even tied the handles on the closet shut with an old wire clothes hanger, but the orb still managed to escape.

"Put it in the tub, close the bathroom, and then the bedroom. It will at least give us some time."

She did as he'd said, only because she wished she'd thought of that days ago. Returning to her living room, she found him sitting on her couch, the same spot he'd occupied a week earlier. She sat on the chair, needing distance from him and her ill-timed desires. The material of his shirt clung to his skin, outlining the toned chest of the man she'd yearned for. Still did. His hair tied in a bun served to accentuate his strong jaw, his emerald green eyes, and his lips. Lips that had sent sparks dancing through her. Her pulse raced and she glanced away. "So, what do you know?"

"I know you're Lisivian."

"Lisivian. Interesting." She'd never learned the name of her race, her father too young to remember when he'd arrived on Earth.

"Yes, and the sphere is a Lisivian predictor, used by your kind to make decisions." He settled into the corner of the couch, making himself comfortable as if he would be there for a while. "It flashes blue to predict a good outcome, red for a bad one, and both colors when it senses danger."

"So, that makes you the cause of the danger, since it's flashed both colors since you arrived." And she could attest to how dangerous he had already proved to her heart.

"Normally, I would say yes, but not this time." He leaned forward, resting his elbows on his knees. "I think the warning is for me, not you, but I'm still trying to figure out why."

"Because you're Memonon." Had she pronounced it correctly?

He furrowed his brows then shook his head. "So, how long have you been on Earth?"

"I was born here. My father...." Wait, she refused to give Chal any more information before he told her about himself.

"What were you saying about your father?"

"No way, not until you tell me what you are." Information sharing went both ways. He already knew more about her kind than she knew of his.

He stood and headed for the door. "When you're ready to talk, let me know."

"This isn't all about me." Angela launched off her chair, racing to block his exit. "I know you're an alien, too."

Chal beat her to the door, closing it behind him. Fuming, she dashed into her room and the bathroom, nearly tripping over the orb on her bathmat. She picked up the crystal ball and carried it through her apartment. Stepping into the hall, she whipped it at him, aiming for the back of his head. With any luck, it would knock him out.

"Take it, since you want to know what it means so bad. The orb has never been of any use to me anyway."

No matter what Slade forbade him to say, Chal could no longer walk away from Angela. Her anger and hurt he could handle, but not the fear. Gods, he'd been stupid to think he could get information from her without revealing his own secrets. Slade, too. She'd grown up hiding her identity from the world, and he'd thrown information in her face that would get her killed. Or worse, tortured.

A foot from his door, he spun. The predictor flew at him, and blinded by the flashing lights, he jerked his hand in front of his face to avoid contact.

The orb smacked his palm. He didn't grab it fast enough, and it hit the ground with a smack. Did not shatter though, thankfully.

Sure, he'd be upset, too, but he would never throw the indicator at someone, especially their head. Or maybe he would if he believed his life in danger.

After picking up the sphere, Chal rushed back to her. Looking at her face, he froze at the color of her eyes. *Shit*. Didn't she know not to do that in big cities? Or anywhere! How had she not been caught?

He shoved her inside and locked her apartment. "You can't do that. You'll end up in a lab somewhere, dissected into tiny pieces."

"Well, you're the only one who knows what I am, so does that mean you're turning me over to the authorities?"

"No!" Setting his hand on her shoulder, he cringed at the wave of revulsion exploding from her. "Angela, I would never do anything to put you at risk. But, you can't go throwing alien technology around in public, or transforming your eyes like that. Someone's going to notice."

"My eyes?" She covered them with her hands.

"Yes, the all-black thing you Lisivians can do. I thought you did it back in the laundry room, but I know you for sure did it seconds ago. I thought you'd have better control of them by now."

"No." She shook her head. "I'm half-Lisivian, and I don't take after that side of my gene pool. My eyes have never turned black. Never. If they had, I *would* be in a lab, not here, talking to you."

"I know what I saw." He brushed the hair away from her face. "What I see now."

She turned to the mirror in her foyer and gasped. "No way." With the tips of her fingers, she examined the skin around her eyes. "For as long as I can remember, I always wanted this ability. But now that I have it, I don't know how to control the change." A tear trickled down her cheek, but she swiped it away, chewing on her lips. "Why do you care?"

"Because I want to know more about you, about your family. Because I care about you." Standing behind her at the mirror, he let his own controls go. "But, I guess I should also tell you what I am."

The reaction he'd expected didn't happen. Instead, she pivoted to face him, smiling. Rising to the tips of her toes, she ran a hand over his row of spikes. "Wow."

"I am Memonon." He set the predictor on a side table then clasped her hips, pulling her closer. "A race that had many dealings with your own far away from this planet."

"I know, my dad told me." She glanced over at the sphere. "But what about your reaction to the orb?"

Yeah, what about that? He hadn't noticed the piercing shrill or the blinding flashes since he'd picked it up in the hallway. Instead, the crystal pulsed a faint blue with no detectable sound. "It changed its mind about us?"

She punched his shoulder. "More likely about you, since it never came to life for me before you knocked on my door all grumpy with my mail. Even Grant couldn't make the thing flash. Though, I should have seen red the entire time I was with him."

Not a name Chal wanted to hear mentioned again. But why the delay in the orb working for her? Maybe the same reason for the delay in her abilities—she was a late bloomer. Regardless, he yearned to know more about her life on Earth, and continue what they'd started the last time he'd been in her apartment. "If you're up for it, why don't we sit and talk some more?"

CHAPTER SIX

A cool tingle washed over Angela's eyes, the first time, she'd felt the transition. Anyone looking at her would see the inky color and run the other direction, praying to their god to banish the demon from her soul. Though, not Chal. She'd longed to have an alien ability all her life, living as a regular human to an extraterrestrial father. But now she had one.

Taking another peek at the orb, she smiled. It finally worked, too, approving of Chal and what she intended to do with him. Because talking remained the last thing she craved.

Clasping his shoulders, she rose to her toes and kissed him. He pulled her closer, capturing her bottom lip between his, amplifying her desire. Nothing beat a hot guy who knew her secrets and still wanted her.

Slipping her hands into his back pockets, Angela edged them toward her room. She refused to let go of him for a second, her head tipsy with lust. If the orb hadn't interrupted them the last time, she would already know how wonderful it could be with him. One red flash from the crystal and she'd smash it, watch it shatter into a million pieces then return her attention to the sexy alien she craved.

He leaned over her, grabbing her ass and lifting her up. As if by instinct, she wrapped her legs around his waist. Holding her bottom, he shuffled blindly through her apartment. Cock hard through his jeans, he ran his tongue along hers, ramping up her desire. How much farther until they reached her bed?

Her back collided with the wall. Not her room, but she couldn't wait much longer. Chal's weight sandwiched her between the plaster and his hard, muscular body. He kissed along her jawline and down her neck. Why couldn't their clothes vanish in a puff of smoke? Winding her fingers under the hem of his shirt, she lifted the cotton material, craving skin-to-skin contact. With a heavy breath, he straightened, giving her the chance to remove the clothing. Heart racing, she gazed into his hungry eyes, well aware of their shared need, but also of something deeper, a bond like no other. She thrust toward him. That connection could be explored later. Sex came first.

Flicking her tongue across his earlobe, she whispered, "Take me to my bed. Now."

In a matter of seconds, she lay on her sheets, her dress somewhere on the floor, and Chal between her legs, running his tongue along her inner thighs as he delicately plied her panties off. Lust sizzled through her veins. How much longer would he tease her? Any guy she'd been with before would have fucked her in the foyer with the amount of foreplay they'd experienced.

After removing her underwear from her foot, he tossed the material across the room and spread her legs open. Without warning, he darted his tongue along her clit.

Holy mother of the universe! She bucked as rapture raced straight to her brain.

Placing his palms under her ass, he lifted her hips and continued the pleasure-laced torture. Angela gripped the bed sheets, and swayed toward him, heat balling low in her belly.

He ran a finger along her entrance. "I love how wet you are for me."

Not just wet. Desperate. She rocked harder, longing to feel him inside her.

First, a knuckle, but not even close to enough. A full digit. Then two. He drove deep inside her, continuing to tease her clit with his tongue. Divine!

Like an avalanche, the crescendo hit her hard, sweeping her breath away. Through the orgasm, he continued to tease and torment her, her body twitching with every thrust and flick. Another release tore through her, leaving her clinging to the edge of sanity.

"So responsive to my touch." Getting to his feet, he unbuckled his belt then removed his jeans, baring the rest of his sculpted body to her.

She took him all in, from the passion in his emerald eyes, the intricate patterns of ink across his shoulders and upper body, to his rigid cock, her pussy pulsating. Growing up, if she'd known he was her future, she would have been more patient in waiting for her soul mate. And their connection would only grow stronger with the ultimate bond.

Rolling over to her nightstand, she yanked open the drawer and grabbed a condom. Regardless of their connection, she wasn't ready for a baby and had no knowledge of his past. Cupping his balls in her palm, Angela sat on the edge of the bed in front of him. He had markings on his shaft, too. The same complex design as on his upper body. Had he gotten his cock tattooed as well? Or were they not tattoos at all, but the natural markings of his race?

Plucking the condom from her hand, Chal tore open the package and rolled the latex over his shaft. He crawled over her, his weight pushing her back on the bed. She had no time for curiosity, her need chased away all other thoughts.

He rained kisses across her shoulders and her neck, her mind delirious with his assault on her sensitive flesh. Grasping his waist, she pulled him nearer, craving more, willing him inside her.

"I've never wanted anyone the way I want you." His warm breath sent sparks of pleasure dashing from her brain to her toes.

"Take me." If he didn't soon, she'd implode, raw need consuming every inch of her body. The tip of his cock brushed across her folds. She moaned, shifting closer, demanding more.

He drove into her. Angela sucked in a sharp breath, lights flashing behind her eyes. A wave of emotion rippled through her. Not her own, but Chal's. After all this time, she found her abilities with him, drawn into his mind. Contentment, lust, and an overwhelming hunger. Plus, something else, something beyond her reach.

He rotated his hips, sank in and out, over and over, drawing her from her thoughts and his. Gripping his biceps, she engaged him thrust for thrust, meeting his desperate gaze. His desire mixed with her own, intense and exhilarating, carrying her toward release. He lifted her leg, slamming harder, plunging so much deeper. She clung to the edge of sanity. Then he slowed, licking his thumb before he swept it across her hypersensitive clit. Digging her fingers into the sheets, she burst in an explosion of ecstasy, jerking and twitching, all control of her body passed on to Chal and the pleasure he brought.

Without giving her any chance to recover, he flipped her over, positioning her over his hard body. Holding her waist, he swirled his tongue around her nipple, feeding her excitement and lust. How did he know her body so well? Any other guy she'd been with took a couple tries to figure out what she liked. If at all.

He sucked and nibbled, alternating from one breast to the other, leaving her desperate to be filled again. Sliding back, she tried to reestablish their connection, but his bent legs kept her from her goal, a tease along her wet heat. "Please, I need you inside me."

With a sparkle in his eye and the corner of his mouth upturned, he straightened his legs. As he held the base of his cock, she lowered onto him, enjoying the sweet bliss of his length. Hands on his chest, she rocked, each movement amplifying her pleasure.

"Gods, you are amazing." He clung to her sides, helping to quicken her movements. His muscles tensed and his face contorted into a pained expression, the soles of his feet set on the bed to pound into her from underneath.

Throwing her head back, Angela chewed her bottom lip, surprised by another impending orgasm. With an ever-increasing growl, Chal fucked her hard, his cock swelling inside her and the tip ramming her G-spot.

With a roar, he climaxed, holding her tight on him. His body shuddered, seizing her in a rush of intense pleasure, a molten burst of total release. She collapsed and screamed against his throat. Never had anyone been able to satisfy her mind, body, and soul.

Clenching his shoulders, she remained on his chest, struggling to catch her breath. She refused to move, never wanting to break their bond, for if it did break, her heart would shatter.

Chal woke with the most painful hard on ever. His dick nestled nicely between the crack of Angela's ass, and he fought between the need to take a piss and the urge to make love to the one woman he could have a future with. A short future, once he was called back to his ship, but a sweet one nonetheless.

Moving his hand up her firm body, he brushed a thumb across her pebbled nipple. With a quiet moan, she rolled back, her butt putting pressure on his bladder. That need won. He slipped from her bed and headed for the bathroom.

When he returned, he found her sitting up in bed, the blankets covering her bottom half. "Good morning, gorgeous," he said.

A slight smile appeared, barely reaching her tired eyes. "Hi there, sexy."

His heart swelled. He couldn't ask for a better bond partner. He crawled onto the bed, ready for another round. Until his stomach rumbled.

She laughed. "I guess the pizza wasn't enough to satisfy your hunger."

Wrapping his arms around her, he pulled her onto his lap and kissed the side of her face. "Not when I couldn't get enough of you." His cock hardened, slipping between her legs, as if searching for her slit. "Still can't."

She moved to straddle him, but his belly growled again, and she fell back on the bed. "I'd better get you fed."

As much as he adored her cooking, even the homemade pizza she'd whipped up in between moments of passion, he wanted to make breakfast for her. He'd studied hard and rarely burned anything now. Squeezing her thigh, he said, "Come over to my place and I'll make you breakfast. Bring a change of clothes as well. We'll shower and then.... Better bring a change of clothes for tomorrow, too."

A grin lit her face from ear to ear. "You sure you want to be around me that long?"

"Every minute of every day, if possible." Until he was forced to say good-bye to her. He had so much to ask her, so much to learn. Yet, he had no immediate reason to rush, preferring to savor her body as much as possible before he had to say good-bye.

By the time Chal finished eating, he desperately needed a shower, the scents of body odor, sex, and the food he'd cooked mixed together into a pungent aroma. Angela didn't seem to mind, staring at him from across the table, a lazy smile playing across her lips. Just the sight of her stirred his desires, but seeing her in nothing but his shirt, only a few buttons done up, the barely visible curves of her breasts teased him beyond belief. And her long, creamy bare legs filled his mind with visions of when they'd been wrapped around him as he'd pounded into her. His dick throbbed, longing to plunge deep inside her again. Thank goodness he'd worn sleep pants instead of a restricting pair of jeans.

"That was a wonderful breakfast. I'm impressed, considering you'd never cooked before you moved here." She sipped her coffee then swallowed. "So, what do you feel like doing now?"

"You." He stood and reached out to her. "Let's go have a shower." He'd waited long enough. Her hand in his, he hurried to the bathroom, not bothering to shut the door behind them.

Spinning to face her, he backed her to the wall and clasped her wrists, lifting her arms above her head. His body pressed to hers, he claimed her lips, feeding his desires. She drove him mad with lust, a feeling that consumed him to his core.

He blindly unbuttoned her shirt then ran his palms over her breasts, his mind delirious with want. Cupping her ass, he yanked her closer. No way would he make it to the shower. Heart thundering, he reached down, spreading open her hot thighs. Slipping two fingers through her slick folds, he circled her core. "I'm sorry, but I can't wait."

She slid her hands under his waistband and shifted his pants off his hips. Encircling his straining cock, she ran her thumb across the swollen tip. Stars above and below, she had the magic touch. He lost control with her and had no will to gain it back. Disoriented, he failed to catch her as she slid down the wall to her knees. But when she gazed up at him and grasped his dick, it seemed as if she'd planned the move. Stroking his shaft, she leaned closer and ran her tongue across the head.

He cursed, electric heat barreling straight to his brain. Where had she learned to do that?

Gods, he didn't care, only yearned for her to do it again. Her tiny hand moving in long, slow strokes, she engulfed the entire tip, her warm mouth and busy tongue torture to the fire building inside him. Gripping her shoulders, he rammed into her, his primal urges taking over. In an instant, his muscles tightened. He jerked out of her mouth, shuddering waves of orgasm threatening to knock him to the floor. He placed his palms on the wall for support, his head spinning.

Angela continued to stroke him, her grip loose, but enough to keep his body in spasms. Struggling to catch his breath, he glanced down at her and jumped back. His release coated her breasts in a shiny, sticky mess. He helped her to her feet. "I'm so sorry. I didn't mean to—"

She touched a finger to his lips, her eyes twinkling. "Don't worry about it. I'll wash up in the shower. Go find a condom in my bag and then come join me."

He'd never moved so fast in his life. If the square packages hadn't been at the top of her bag, he would have dumped everything out to find them. In the morning, when Angela left for work, he'd have to purchase more. He only hoped she'd packed enough to last the rest of the day.

Condom in hand, he opened the shower. She was already wet, soap suds through her hair and running across her provocative body. Beautiful no matter whether in the shower, waking up with messy hair, or in the throes of an orgasm. He couldn't get enough of her.

Grasping her waist, he slipped in behind her, careful not to shove her to the opposite wall. So close to her naked body, his dick responded right away. No downtime with her, as if they truly were made for each other. He palmed her slippery stomach up to her soft breasts. A perfect handful. But her quiet moans from his gentle caresses proved even better. Cock hard and seeking entrance, he walked his fingers along her belly to her feminine folds.

He didn't get far before she spun and moved him into the spray of the shower. "Time to get you washed up, sexy." She lathered him from head to toe, leaving only his hair untouched.

He couldn't stop touching her, but every time he reached between her legs, she slapped him.

"Stop it. Let's get this done first. On your knees." She pushed on his shoulders until he kneeled in front of her. After the distinct click of his shampoo bottle, she ran her fingers through his hair, twisting, scrubbing, massaging. Absolutely divine. And at the perfect height, too.

He pulled her closer, sucking her pert nipple into his mouth, rolling his tongue around until she lost concentration and thrust toward him. Exactly how he wanted her.

Rising, he moved her under the spray with him to wash away the suds. He stifled a groan, his senses clouded, feeling nothing but lust. But she reached for the condom first. Guiding him to the bench, she tore open the package and rolled the latex over his erect shaft. With her hand on his shoulders, she climbed on, settling over him. Jolts of pleasure raced through him, and he took everything she offered, their bond like no other.

Through the driving hunger, he managed to get to his feet, lifting Angela with him. He held her against the wall, and with new purpose, fucked her hard.

"Oh gods!" She clawed at his back, her foot on the opposite wall. "I'm...I can't...oh shit."

Her body spasmed, the hardest he'd ever experienced with her. She clung to him, her breath escaping in ragged gasps.

Turning off the shower, Chal carried her out of the stall and to his bed, grabbing a towel on the way. Laying her on the thick cotton, he dried her the best he could.

She swatted at him. "I'm fine. Fine. Just intense. Gods, that was amazing."

Ego soothed, he relaxed and his worry dissipated. "So, what do you—"

"Keep going." She spread her legs. "Take me. I want you to feel what I felt."

He didn't need any more encouragement. Reaching over for a new condom, the other having fallen off somewhere in the bathroom, he put it on and plunged inside her. After a slight adjustment, he found the perfect angle, drawing moans of pleasure from her, the pulsing of her core like oxygen to his anxious fire. He slammed hard, desperate for release. A heartbeat later, his mind filled with something else. No, someone else. He could not only feel his own desperation, but Angela's energy as well, their souls coming together in a gigantic mesh of passion. The damn burst, and he exploded in wave after immense wave of release. He groaned at the shock of rapture pulsing through to his core. Struggling to hold himself up, he gazed at Angela. But, he didn't have to see her to know what she felt. She was in his mind, and he was in hers. Impossible, yet they'd done it. The beginning and the end. He'd known nothing before then.

CHAPTER SEVEN

Angela shoved open the office door and strode outside, thankful to be finished with another anonymous day at work. Two more weeks until her contract expired, and no one had met with her to offer a renewal. Her rent contract expired in a month, which meant locating another job in Alerto quick, or moving back home. If she was lucky, she could move in with Chal. A bit rushed, but not when neither could deny their bond.

After a whirlwind weekend of sex, delving deep into each other's minds, and even going out for dinner, Chal had wanted to walk her home from work. But, a text message ten minutes earlier said he'd left late and would meet up with her along the way.

She'd changed from a skirt and heals to shorts and runners, more appropriate for the hike home. On a normal day, she would take the subway three stops over, but walking hand-in-hand with Chal held far more appeal, something a normal couple on Earth would do.

The crowd of people finishing work bustled along with her, but beyond the stairs leading to the subway station, it thinned out. She no longer had to fight for space on the sidewalk, and could set her own pace. The sun shone on her, a couple hours of light still left in the day, but not a blasting heat as it would be in the coming summer. A few restaurants even had outdoor-seating sections already. Birds chirped and flew between the few trees lining the street, a far cry from the wildlife and woods surrounding her childhood home. Gods, she missed the place. And what was with the smell of the city? Back home, the scent of trees and open water greeted her every day. But here, the streets often reeked of something sweetly curdled. An odor the rain managed to wash away for only a few hours.

Yet, she wouldn't wish away her time in Alerto. She'd required the space away from her family, a chance to grow on her own. Plus, she never would have met Chal. Would he consider living away from the city? Not where her parents and brother had settled, but some place nearby? Smaller than the metropolis they lived in?

Angela smacked into a solid object. A car? Shit, she hadn't been paying attention to the path in front of her. How many streets had she crossed lost in her thoughts? Putting her hands out, she felt not a steel frame, but a body. She stared up at the monster of a man she'd run into. Not very tall herself, she shrank beside the guy, well over six feet, the defensive tackle one didn't dare cross.

"I'm so sorry." She stepped to his side and tried to pass him, but he moved to block her path. Massive arms crossed, he glared at her.

Her heart raced. The last thing she needed was a confrontation with the giant. "Listen, I'm sorry for running into you. I wasn't paying attention. I know it's no excuse, but I really feel bad."

The guy reached into his pocket. For what? Not a gun, but something else that would harm her? Angela sighed with relief when she saw a picture instead of a gun. He shoved it in front of her.

"Do you know where this man is?" he asked with a thick accent. Russian, maybe?

She stepped back to focus on the picture. Chal. *Shit.* "Why? What did he do?"

The man's arms twitched a split second before he grabbed for her, giving her a chance to spin away and make a run for it, only to trip over what felt like a foot. She caught a glimpse of the woman it belonged to on her way to the ground. Her palms hit the concrete first, splitting open across the rough surface. Then her chin, the impact slamming her tongue between her teeth. She groaned in pain as tears rushed to the corners of her eyes and blood filled her mouth. A knee pressed on her back, knocking the air from her lungs. Then her arms were wrenched behind her back and wrists shackled in cuffs.

As someone yanked her to her feet, she sucked in a deep breath. "Help!"

The woman darted in front of her, opening the rear door of a black sedan.

Angela glanced around for someone to help her. Anyone. But the streets were suddenly empty. She raised her foot then slammed her heal on her captor's instep. He gripped her tighter. Closing her hands into fists, she aimed for his nuts, but missed. When he nudged her forward, toward the car, she ducked, letting herself fall to the ground. Anything to get out of the man's grasp. A few seconds and someone might arrive to help her. "Fire!" Her throat burned from yelling so loud, but all she wanted was someone to poke their head out and see her, call 9-1-1 if they refused to intervene.

The giant lifted her from the ground, holding her under his arm. She kicked and wiggled to no avail. "Help me, please!"

Her cries went unanswered. The man tossed her into the back seat and shut her in. Facedown across the seat, she kicked the door at her feet. It refused to budge.

Her stomach lurched as the car sped off. She was trapped. Her two captors, whoever they were, took her because of Chal. What had he done? Her mind spun and sweat beaded across her skin. What did they want with her? Oh gods, did Chal tell them what she was?

Blinding pain burst in Chal's head. He pressed the tips of his fingers to his scalp, trying to massage away the throbbing. He was already late to meet Angela and couldn't afford any more time. If not for a call from Slade, he would have arrived at her office long ago, be hand-in-hand with her and ask her how her day went, maybe stop at a bistro for dinner.

The torment came again, like a knife stabbed into his brain. He stumbled sideways, arms out, searching for something to hold onto until the sensation passed.

"Sir, are you okay?"

The question came from somewhere around him, and the person wasn't screaming or calling him a monster. His spikes hadn't flared; he still had some control.

Another voice. A cry for help. Not close by, but an echo of a time already passed. Something had happened to her.

He squeezed his eyes shut, wishing the pain away. He had to find her, and couldn't do so in his current state. Opening his eyelids, he glanced around for someone to help.

A crowd of women sat on the steps of a house across the street, knitting needles still as they stared at him. "You okay, boy. Been drinking too much?"

"No." He stepped away from the wall, willing the agony to hold off until he learned what happened to her. "I'm looking for my girlfriend. She was supposed to meet me around here."

"You sure about that? Maybe you imagined the whole thing."

"Her name is Angela. She's just over five feet tall with long blonde hair. Very fit." An image of her flashed through is mind, cuffed and shoved into a small space.

One of the ladies across the street stood. "Only young girl fitting that description around here got arrested the next block up."

"Arrested? What for?" His stomach churned as dread chilled his blood.

"Yeah, by two undercover officers." The woman nodded. "Sure fought them, too. I was hoping she'd get away. Make things more interesting around here."

Shit! "Why didn't you help her?" Horrible ideas of what could have happened to her flipped through his mind.

"Around here, one doesn't interfere in police business."

Great! Nobody even questioned her getting taken off the street. "These officers, what did they look like?"

Another woman stood and hobbled across the street to him. Too slow compared to his racing heart. But if he wanted to locate her, he needed information.

"First was a big guy with a bald head. Wore a black suit. Looked more like a hit man from a movie than the police."

"And the other?" His stomach twisted. Had his worst fears happened to his bond mate?

"A woman. Long, dark brown hair. Skinny little thing with too much makeup. Never could have handled the woman they arrested, but hey, that's what she has a partner for."

Pride and fear battled within him. Angela was tough for her size, but no match for those who had captured him when he'd first arrived, including Veronika. He had to find her before she ended up on their dissection table. "Which way did they go?"

The second woman pointed up the street. "East. Then they turned north after a few blocks. Not the direction of the station, but who knows?"

"Thanks." He couldn't get away fast enough. Veronika and Pato had Angela, and nothing good would come of it. He ran in the direction the woman had pointed then dashed into the first alley he came upon. Glancing around to ensure no one saw, he pressed the lone button on his watch—not a watch at all.

"Chal, how convenient. We were just talking about you."

His blood froze. "Zeru, what are you doing in the observation room? Where's Slade?" He didn't have time to deal with the guy who had hated him since childhood. He needed Slade's help. Now.

"I would ask you what you're doing on Earth, but Slade already filled us in." Chal cringed at the sneer in his voice. "But, it's time to come back home."

The familiar tingle of the transporter spread through his body. He had no time to object before his body dematerialized into energy and flew across the solar system. Arriving on the ship, he came face-to-face with Zeru holding Slade in cuffs.

Chal's sister, Gille, stepped forward with a pair of electrified restraints. "Seems you've been leaving the ship without permission, scouting Earth all on your own."

He stepped back on the platform. "Wait. I know what we did was wrong, what I did. But, I have to save Angela. The thugs who tortured me have her."

"And why should we care?" Zeru glared at him, his spikes standing up straight along his misshapen head.

"Because she's half-Lisivian and her father survived on Earth for years."

"Impossible," Zeru spat. "They died out years ago."

"It's true." Slade turned to Gille. "I saw the family myself. Somehow the father escaped before the virus wiped them out. I should have told you sooner, but I hoped Chal would get more information."

He nodded, confirming Slade's story. "But, she won't be alive for long if we don't get her away from the thugs. They'll dissect her then go after her family."

Gille shrugged. "I don't care. You both went against direct orders, undermined my authority. If I didn't have other issues to deal with, I'd flog you both." His sister stepped onto the platform, holding out the restraints. "You will be confined to the brig until the other issues are dealt with."

"No." He sidestepped her and barreled toward the console. If no one would help him, he'd find Angela himself, but he refused to wait around while she was cut into pieces.

A jolt pierced his spine. Before he reached the console, he fell forward, rocketing toward the floor. Try as he might, he couldn't reach out to brace for impact. His head hit the ground and he heard the crack of his skull a split second before fire lit through his brain. His stomach heaved, the agony overwhelming. He tried to move, escape the pain, but nothing cooperated. And then everything disappeared.

CHAPTER EIGHT

"Where is he?"

The same question over and over.

"I don't know," Angela replied. After kidnapping her off the street, her captors had thrown her onto a cot in a barred cell, the woman remaining behind with her.

Pinching Angela's nasal septum, she twisted. "Tell me."

Tears raced down her cheeks. "I already told you. He was supposed to meet me after work, but he didn't show."

"Bullshit." The interrogator let go of her nose then slapped her cheek, the impact jarring Angela's neck. "We searched the streets already. He's not there."

Closing her eyes, she sucked in a deep breath. Maybe he didn't plan to meet her. Maybe he stayed at home and wanted her to walk for some strange reason. But she refused to give him up. Even if he had reported her to the authorities, she wouldn't do the same to him. She wasn't like that. "Then I have no idea where he could be."

"But you do." The crazy bitch grabbed a scalpel from a nearby table and held it in front of her. "You know where the alien is, and you're going to tell me. We followed you back to your apartment building last night. What happened after?"

"I had dinner with the guy, yes. We went back to my place, yes. But when I woke up in the morning, he was gone. Sent a text this afternoon saying he would meet me after work, but as you know, he didn't show." And the reason for his absence worried her more than the blade resting against her face. She'd felt his presence for a few minutes after she'd arrived in this hell, experienced his panic and concern. Then it all vanished, like someone had reached in and ripped him right from her soul. Had the assholes already caught him and were now toying with her?

The woman brushed the flat side of the blade along her cheek. "Was he a good fuck? Is that why you're protecting him? Because, honestly, I've had better."

Her face heated. No way could this wench have slept with Chal. Not with that reaction. Even so, she didn't want to think about him with anyone else.

"Oh, he didn't tell you about me?" She moved the blade under Angela's chin and around to the other cheek. "When you finally do give him up, you'll have to ask him about me. Name's Veronika. Ask him about all the kinky stuff we did. Did you know he likes hot wax poured on his body during sex? Or that he enjoys being tied up and flogged?"

"No." Angela clenched her fists behind her. Bile burned its way up her throat.

"Yes."

A sting sliced across her cheek. She winced as drops of liquid trailed along the side of her face and pooled along her jawline. Blood? The bitch had cut her. Anger surged though her. Her eyes tingled and she quickly closed them. These people had given no indication they knew she was an alien, and she had no plans to tell them. Breathing deep, she willed her eyes to appear Terran again.

"He likes to be cut, too." Veronika sliced her other cheek, quicker and deeper than the other side.

Blood flowed faster, streaming along her skin. She glanced down. Crimson puddled on her shirt. Her head spun and her ears filled with a piercing buzz.

"Did you see the scar on his stomach?" Veronika traced a finger along her second cut. "That was from me."

"You're sick." The room shifted in front of her. She clenched the cot to aid in staying upright. Who knew what the woman would do if she passed out?

"No, you're sick." Veronika bent and stared in her face. "You fucked an alien. I can forgive that because he is hot, and hey, I fell for him, too. But, I can't understand why you're protecting him. There's more of his kind waiting to take over the planet. And by protecting him, you're aiding in their future invasion."

"That's not true." She hadn't talked much with Chal about his people, but she'd been in his mind, seen his thoughts. They only wanted a safe place to live, a chance to leave their ship and survive, nothing even close to overpowering the people of Earth.

"Bullshit," Veronika said again and yanked Angela's arm but couldn't bring it forward with her wrists still cuffed. She grabbed her hair instead, slicing off Angela's locks and piercing the back of her neck. "If you're not with us, you're with them, responsible for the incursion."

She winced. The room spun double-time and the ringing in her ears grew louder. Her head hit the cot before she realized she was falling. She held in a whimper. Her skin burned where Veronika had sliced her open, but she refused to give her the satisfaction of a sound. She'd rather bleed to death than give her any information about Chal.

A loud boom echoed around her, the shockwave lifting her off the mattress for a moment. All sound disappeared as if sucked into a vacuum then smoke filled the cell, and Veronika dropped to the floor in front of her. Beams of light danced before Angela's eyes and dark figures darted back and forth. Real or a figment of her delirious mind? Then one of the forms dashed toward her and picked her up into its arms. Her savior or another captor? She had no idea, only that it wasn't Chal.

She flailed and kicked. "Leave me alone! I'll never tell you anything." Wrenching free, she surged forward with no idea how to get out, but she had to escape. And get the cuffs off. The loss of blood sent her equilibrium cartwheeling. Her knees gave out and before she could stop, she collapsed to the cold cement floor.

An arm reached behind her shoulders and heaved her upper body off the ground. "Angela, stop fighting. You're safe with me. I'm Chal's brother and I'm going to take you to him."

Chal had mentioned a brother. But, she had no push left in her. Letting her head fall back, she succumbed to the darkness dragging her under.

Bright lights pierced Angela's eyelids. With a groan, she covered them with one arm while she gained her bearings. Her muscles ached in varying degrees and her head throbbed. She wouldn't be the least bit surprised to learn she'd been run over by a tank.

A familiar scent tingled her nasal receptors. Disinfectant. Nothing like the rotten stench of the cell she'd been in moments ago. Moments ago? Had she been there a short time ago, or had hours passed? Maybe days? One way to find out.

She squinted her eyes open, drawing in the brightness a little bit at a time. Moving nothing more than her head, she glanced around. Not one light shone on her, but several. They hung inside the opaque tent surrounding her bed. A contamination unit? Oh gods, was she in some kind of laboratory? Someone had learned she was an alien, too.

Figures bustled around on the other side. Her heart raced and her breathing became ragged. They were going to experiment on her then cut her into pieces, put her parts in glass jars to examine for years to come. And they'd do the same to her family.

No! Sitting up, she searched her surroundings for a weapon, something to defend herself, end her life if need be. She refused to be part of someone's science project. If she couldn't escape, she'd make it very difficult for them to work with a nice, clean alien body. Because they'd make what Veronica did to her face and neck seem like child's play.

Angela touched her cheeks, the back of her neck. Smooth, but did she have scars?

A zipping sound came from the end of the tent near her feet. She gasped. The enclosure parted and a figure stepped through. Definitely not human. A female figure though, with piercing emerald eyes, and long brown wavy hair. Five inch spikes stuck up from her scalp and disappeared behind her. Webbing joined each spike together, plum-colored with black veins, reminding Angela of butterfly wings. She wore a white pantsuit with a plunging neck line, revealing the tattoos covering her chest and up her neck to just below her ears, the same intricate pattern as Chal.

"Are...are you Memonon?" Angela's throat burned, the question sounding more like the croak of a frog than her voice.

"Lights thirty percent. A glass of grots." The woman stepped closer and reached into a recess in the wall Angela hadn't yet noticed. She handed her a cup, clear liquid inside. "Yes, I am Memonon. You're on our ship. Now, drink up."

Their ship? She'd traveled across the solar system while unconscious? How? And by whom? She still felt no connection with Chal, no presence in her soul, no one else's emotions in her mind except her own.

Raising the cup to her lips, she took a quick sniff of the liquid inside. Nothing. Could be water or poison, but she couldn't resist. She took a sip, enjoying the way the concoction coated her throat and relieved the rawness. A liquid medicine of some sort.

After clearing her throat, she attempted to speak again. "Who are you? Why am I here?"

The woman pressed several buttons on the bed's console, sending the head upright before guiding Angela against it. "I am Vega, the threa for the ship, what you would call the head doctor. Now, lie back so I may examine you and answer your questions." She waved some kind of device in front of Angela, staring at the readings showing up on the screen next to the bed.

She took another sip. "Once again, why am I here? I appreciate you saving me and treating my cuts, but I don't understand why you brought me here."

"My cousin, Chal, insisted."

Angela swallowed a shout of glee. "He's here? Can I see him?"

Vega touched her shoulder. "I'm sorry, but—"

"Oh gods, he's dead." A flash of heat washed over her and the room began to spin. "I should have known when I felt him fade away, but I didn't want to believe it."

"No, he's not dead." Vega touched her forehead and raised the foot of the bed. "He experienced head trauma shortly after he arrived. Has been unconscious ever since. But, I'm curious as to what you meant when you said you felt him fade away."

Angela concentrated on her breathing, attempting to slow her racing heart. Chal was still alive. Not dead. "He's my soul mate, according to the orb. And we have what he called a soul bond. After I was captured, I could sense him, knew he looked for me, but then that feeling disappeared." A tear slipped down her cheek. "I thought he'd died."

"Faculae." Vega pressed the back of her arm to her forehead. "I wish I would have known you two had soul bonded."

With the touch of a few buttons, she had the tent sucked into the wall, exposing Angela to the entire room and other Memonons scurrying between various stations, the women with the most beautiful row of spikes all the way down their backs in varying colors. Though very few of the men had theirs displayed at all.

"If you're up for it, I'd like to move you to Chal's room." Vega pressed another button and kicked the platform supporting her cot. The bed lifted with a jerk.

"Yes." Though she guessed the doctor had already decided for her.

Vega headed out of the room, Angela's cot floating along behind her. Floating, as in no wheels, nothing underneath except air. She gripped the sides in fear her bed might tip over and deposit her on the floor.

Without any effort, she followed along behind the doctor, trying to take in as much of the ship as possible. But the plain white walls couldn't keep her mind off Chal, like what condition she'd find him in when they reached his room. Though her worst imaginings didn't prepare her for when she finally saw him.

The back of his head wrapped in several layers of gauze-like bandages, he laid on his bed, absolutely still. Tubes of varying thickness and with a variety of colored liquids running through them, connected to a thick cuff wrapped around Chal's wrist. The part of his face she did see was swollen and blue, a darker shade indicating bruising, and a lighter hue showing how close he was to death. Her throat constricted. Oh gods, how had he managed to stay alive? If not for the occasional blip on a screen over his bed, she would assume him already deceased.

"I don't know what else to do for him." Vega positioned her bed next to Chal's. "You're our last hope. If your soul bond can't bring him back, nothing will."

Fear clenched her heart in a vice. She sensed nothing from him. The spark that had warmed her soul back on Earth, gone, replaced by a cold chill.

She reached for his unrestrained hand and clasped his fingers. Freezing to the touch. A corpse.

Her eyes burned with the onset of more tears. "What...what happened to him?"

Vega growled. "A member of our crew stunned him and he fell with no way to catch himself, to break his fall. I managed to mend his skull fracture and other broken bones, examined him for clots, and other issues, but I cannot understand why he is still unconscious."

Angela reached for his wrist. A faint pulse beat under her fingers, his heart likely the only thing keeping him alive. He could very well be brain dead.

Shit! She wiped away an escaped tear. Not even a month had passed since she'd finally met her soul mate. And he was going to die. Rip her heart out when he did.

Vega touched her shoulder. "I'm going to go get his brother and sister. I'll be right back."

She nodded. The doctor could likely call them with the technology she'd seen on the ship. But the doctor was giving her a chance to be alone with him. To say good-bye.

CHAPTER NINE

"Angela, you need to eat. Starving yourself won't help either of you." Slade set a plate of bland, colorless food on the table beside her. It held no appeal like every other meal he'd begged her to eat.

She'd spent a week at Chal's side, praying to all the gods in the universe to bring him back to her. Yet, his condition hadn't changed, his body cold like it had been kept refrigerated, his life spark lost. Maybe his soul had already moved on to a new life, leaving her behind. Unfair how little time they'd had together.

"Angela, please." Slade held a fork in front of her the way one would feed a child.

Obligingly, she opened her mouth. Her stomach rumbled as she chewed the tasteless mixture. Nothing she would ever eat back on Earth, but she had little choice so far from home. And she refused to leave Chal's side until he either improved or succumbed.

"And another one."

She turned away from the fork, from Slade's pleading eyes. Another mouthful and she'd gag. No way she wanted to puke all over him. He'd been nothing but kind to her, checking in often. Though his concern could be more for his brother than her.

Gille proved the opposite, insisting Vega fit her with an IV line after the first meal she'd refused to eat. And as first-in-command, she seemed to have little time for Angela or Chal, like they were a nuisance to her.

Grasping Chal's hand, she hoped for some warmth, a spark of recognition, something to indicate he had improved. But he was colder than ever, his soul lost to her. Gods, how much longer would his body hold on like this?

The door whooshed open. She didn't have to turn around to know who'd entered. She couldn't help but feel the woman's animosity. But deep down, her deep-seated fear and concern for her people remained the only reason she excused Gille's attitude.

"Angela, I request you join Slade and I in conference room two." She tapped her foot on the floor. "I've been patient long enough, but there are some questions I need you to answer."

Slade stood, positioning himself between her and his sister. "Can't we do it here?"

"You know we can't. Chal will be fine without her for a short time. And to be honest, she could use a trip to the wash tubes first. Her stench is making my eyes water."

Struggling to her feet, Angela gave in to the request. She'd only left Chal's side over the past seven days to use the waste disposal unit, a fancy toilet. Her muscles ached, and a shower, even if waterless, might renew her hope, give her new inspiration to locate Chal's spirit and bring him back to his body.

Vega arrived to help her from her clothes and into the tube. Having remained stationary for so long, Angela's muscles ached with the slightest movement. Thank goodness for the handholds in the shower, or she never would have stayed on her feet for the five minutes of cleansing.

A new set of clothing waited for her upon her exit. Vega had disappeared, replaced by Gille with her hands on her hips, and lips pursed, obviously not willing to help her dress.

If not for the steam in the tube, her muscles would have been more uncooperative, but she managed to dress fast and followed Chal's sister down the hall to a private room where Slade already waited. He gave her a halfhearted smile as if he understood how cold Gille could be.

Sitting in the first chair she came across—the one next to Slade—Angela leaned back. From the moment she'd met Gille, she'd expected a ton of questions from her, all with the intention of interrogation rather than getting to know her. Best to get comfortable.

"So, when did you arrive on Earth?"

Right out of the starting gate. Not even a *how are you feeling*. But the Memonon had her information wrong. "I was conceived and born on Earth. Coming here is the first time I've ever left the planet."

Gille wrinkled her forehead. "But, I thought you are Lisivian. That's what my brothers tell me."

"I am only half." She covered her mouth to stifle a yawn, her lack of sleep and proper food catching up with her. "My mother is from Earth, but my father is Lisivian. He arrived on our planet as a child."

"How is that possible? The Lisivian perished before I was born."

"No." She gripped the arms of the chair. "You lie."

"It's true. A virus wiped them all out." Slade rested a hand on her shoulder. "Your father is the last of his kind, but we're not sure how he survived."

An enormous pressure bore down on her chest. Her heart raced. She struggled to breath, to figure out where this sensation came from. Yes, it was sad to learn her ancestors had perished, but the sensations came from somewhere else.

Oh gods. Chal! He'd returned and she wasn't there.

Fighting the burning in her legs, she hobbled out of the room toward the one where he lay.

"Angela, wait! We're not done."

Gille's crisp tone wouldn't stop her. "Later. I have to get to Chal. He's back. I can feel him again."

Chal had finally escaped the void, the dark, never-ending space he'd been trapped in for what felt like an eternity. The entire time, Angela had called to him, begged him to return. And he'd fought, for her, for the bond. When he'd first seen the light, it came as only a sliver, perhaps his imagination, wishful thinking. But he'd searched for the source anyway, found her voice became louder as the beacon grew in intensity. She had helped guide him home.

When he opened his eyes, he found himself alone in a medical room on the Memonon ship. Far from Earth and Angela. Yet, he could swear he felt the tingle of her touch on his palm. Was she already dead, dissected by her captors and her spirit now haunting him?

A cry escaped from deep inside. In the void, he'd held onto the hope of seeing her again, but now he didn't even have that. The only sound in the room remained the beep of the equipment attached to him. He'd lost his bond mate, and a piece of his soul along with her.

Chal started at a sudden commotion outside. Footfalls and voices yelling. His brother and sister. And another woman. He gasped. Could it be?

Something slapped on the door as if urging it to slide open faster. Angela fell through the entrance, Slade catching her under her arms before she hit the ground.

She was alive. On the ship. In front of him. Chal's heart leapt. He reached out to her, but his hand only shook in place. No matter how much he willed it, he couldn't move his arm. What in the universe? He bent his knee. Or thought he did. But the sheet over him didn't lift up. Same with the other leg. He couldn't move anything. Nothing but his eyes. His chest tightened. This had to be a dream. A nightmare. He couldn't find Angela again only to be bedridden for the rest of his life, unable to have sex with his bond mate, or even hold her in his arms.

He closed his eyes, willing the horror to end. When he opened them again, she stood beside him. She clasped his hand, her touch soft, her skin warm. But he could not squeeze in return.

"Aahhh!" Even his scream didn't work as intended, coming out as a low groan instead.

He yearned to sit up, move around to relieve his aching muscles. If only they worked properly.

"Okay, time to leave." Vega burst into the room, clapping her hands. "Gille and Slade, I'm sure your time is better spent elsewhere."

Angela released Chal, following his brother and sister out. Vega grabbed her wrist, halting her retreat. "No, I need you to stay here. Chal requires therapy to get his motion back, and I believe you're the perfect motivation for him."

She planted her feet. "How long is it going to take?"

Shit, she didn't plan on sticking around with him immobile. Though, he couldn't blame her. She was young and they hadn't known each other very long.

"Hours, days, weeks." Vega shrugged. "Maybe longer. I don't know."

Angela returned to his side and brushed stray strands of hair from his face then cupped his cheek. "Okay. I'll be here as long as it takes. Because when he's better, he is going to meet my parents."

He stopped trying to move and let the relief sink in. Laying on his back would not be a permanent position. And she didn't plan on leaving while it was. Thank the gods. For her sake, he would try with all his might to gain movement again. Even if it meant meeting the parents of the woman he loved.

"He smiled." A tear slipped down her cheek as she ran her fingers along the side of his face. "You smiled."

And he planned to do so much more so long as his body cooperated.

CHAPTER TEN

Angela focused on the road and the other drivers around her as she traveled the highway to her childhood home. Though she couldn't help an occasional glance over to her passenger and the gorgeous ring he'd slipped on her finger the day before.

Upon her return to Earth, she'd learned she'd been fired for not showing up to work, had a notice taped to her apartment door granting her two days to move out, and listened to multiple messages from her family wondering where she'd disappeared to. When she'd finally talked to her father on the phone, he'd insisted she come home at once.

Fortunately, she managed to weasel a night with Chal before making the four-hour drive. And that's when he had proposed. She had no idea when he'd had time to get a ring, especially since he still had problems walking and hadn't left his apartment after he'd returned to Earth with her and Slade. But, after all they'd experienced over the past few weeks, she didn't want to be anywhere but by his side.

Signaling right, she glided onto the off ramp. Only twenty minutes from home. Would her parents approve of Chal? Would they be upset she'd accepted his proposal without meeting him first? A wave of nausea rolled through her and she gripped the steering wheel.

No, she was an adult now. And while she respected her parents' opinion, she'd already made decisions affecting the rest of her life. Decisions that would expose her to a world she'd never known.

Chal stared at the scenery they passed like a puppy experiencing snow for the first time, anxious to get out and play, his eyes wide and mouth hanging open. Slade had offered the use of the transporter, but she'd refused, needing time to rehearse what to say to her parents. Besides, Slade had two apartments worth of belongings to transport, enough to keep the equipment occupied for the rest of the day.

When Angela pulled into the driveway, her father's truck was missing, a good indication he and Adam weren't yet home to interrogate Chal. She had time to get the rest of the family on his side before they showed up.

After putting her car in park and turning off the ignition, she raced around to the trunk to grab the wheelchair.

Chal stood on one foot, leaning on the open passenger door by the time she reached him. "I told you I could walk on my own. I don't know why you had to bring that contraption along."

"Okay, hotshot. Give it a try." She wheeled the chair away, giving him room to walk. A week of therapy had allowed him to stand on his feet again, but not without assistance and definitely not for long periods of time. Vega had insisted he used a wheelchair after Angela had told her a hover chair wouldn't work on Earth. But her boyfriend remained stubborn, unable to admit his limitations.

Chal let go of the car and two steps later, his knees began to shake. Not good. Angela wheeled the chair toward him, catching him as he fell. Though part of her wanted to say *I told you so*, she held it in. His still posture and clenched fists further evidence of the frustration rolling off him.

Hands on his shoulders, she massaged his tight muscles. "Don't beat yourself up. You've come so far already."

"I know, but I'm not used to this." He pounded the arms of the chair. "I hate being confined to this thing."

"Yes, I know." She remembered how hard it was for Adam after he'd been run over. Hopefully, he could help Chal out. So long as he didn't pull the big-brother routine again.

"Auntie Angie! You're here!" Two kids burst from the house next door and raced along the path toward them. Their very pregnant mother waddled behind.

Zach, the younger of the two, halted in front of Chal and stared at him. "Who are you? Are you our aunt's bo-oyfriend?"

Melody shoved him out of the way and stuck her hand out for Chal. "I'm Melody. You must be Chal. Grandma Rachel told us you'd be coming. Though Adam's not too happy."

Angela rolled her eyes while Chal shook the little girl's hand. She should have known it would be Adam who wouldn't let his own sister grow up rather than her parents.

When Sera made it to the end of the path, she gave Angela a hug. "It's good to see you. And you leave your brother to me."

She laughed. Sera and her children had felt like part of the family when they'd moved in, long before she'd dated Adam. "Sera, this is Chal, my fiancé. Chal, this is—"

"Wait! Did you say fiancé?" She grabbed Angela's left hand. "Let me see. Let me see." After a quick glance at the ring on her finger, Sera hugged her again. "Congratulations. He's really the one?"

She nodded, smiling. Sera knew all about the Lisivian need to be with their soul mate and how she'd never expected to find hers.

Leaning over, Sera hugged Chal as well. "It's good to finally meet you. I'm so happy for you both."

As soon as she straightened, Zach hopped onto Chal's lap. "Will you take me for a ride?"

Sera yanked him off. "I'm so sorry if he hurt you."

"No, no." He attempted to lift himself out of the chair. "Actually, if you and Angela will help me up to the porch, the kids can take turns pushing each other around in this thing."

"Are you sure?" Angela didn't know whether him asking for help or letting the kids play with his chair shocked her more. She hadn't run into any young children on the Memonon ship, so she didn't know if there were any, or how he'd take to her niece and nephew.

"Yes." He slung one arm over her shoulder and the other over Sera's.

They helped him up the stairs to a patio lounger where he could stretch out his legs.

The door to the house opened and her mom came out with a tray full of glasses of lemonade. "I thought I heard you all out here."

More hugs were exchanged as Sera passed around the drinks. The kids even abandoned the wheelchair to sit with the adults.

Zach took a sip of his lemonade then put it back on the table. "Auntie Angie, I can't believe you're going to marry the doofus."

Melody smacked Zach across the head. "You're not supposed to say that."

When Sera finished glaring at her son, she turned to Chal. "I'm very sorry. He's been listening to Adam too much."

Chal smiled, his grin bringing a sparkle to his eyes. "It's okay, I understand. Slade and I don't much care for our sister's husband. But we tolerate him because she loves him."

Angela remained surprised Chal tolerated the guy at all since he was the one who'd shot him, the reason he ended up in the wheelchair.

"I'm very happy you're getting married." Her mother rubbed her arm. "I know your father will be, too."

Sure, she said that now, but would her mother still be as happy when she learned of their plans for the future?

Chal grasped Angela's hips and pulled her onto his lap. He hadn't had a moment alone with her since they'd arrived at her parents. It took him needing help in the washroom to get five minutes without her nephew begging to go for another ride, or Adam trying to intimidate him across the table.

She turned, straddling his thighs and setting her arms on his shoulders. "Well, we made it through dinner."

He rested his forehead on hers. "Yes, but now the kids are gone, so it's time to tell them where we'll be going. Your brother will hate me even more when he finds out. Maybe your entire family."

"No." She kissed his nose as if she wasn't about to break her parents' hearts. "I've moved away before. And it's not as if I'll never see them again."

No matter how much she reassured him her parents would accept her decision, he couldn't ignore the gnawing in his gut, or her own anxiousness. He had to go, but she didn't. As much as he would miss her, he'd offered to go alone, give her a year to figure out if she really wanted to be a part of his life and his Memonon family. Yet, she'd refused, willing to give up everything she knew to be with him and help his people.

Slipping off his lap, she stood and walked out of the bathroom. "Best to get out before they think we're doing something inappropriate in here."

Adam grunted in agreement as Chal wheeled out in the hall toward the kitchen. Why did Adam dislike him so much? He couldn't figure it out. Did he already know his sister's plans? Or was his reaction some kind of sibling backlash, the same Angela had experienced from Gille?

She sat beside him at the table and held his hand. "Besides being engaged to Chal, I have another announcement to make."

Adam sneered. "Don't you dare tell me you're pregnant. You barely know the guy. And in the short amount of time you have, you were abducted, tortured, and then abducted again. Imagine what could happen to your child."

"Would you shut up!" Angela stared across at him, the tension in the room growing thicker by the second. "None of those things were Chal's fault. Why can't you be happy for me?"

"Because I'm your brother, and it's my right to be an asshole to your boyfriend, especially since those scars on your cheeks and the back of your neck are from knowing him."

"No, it's not your right." Her nostrils flared as she pointed a finger at him. "If you don't have anything nice to say, you can leave. I've had enough of your bullshit disguised as concern."

"Fine." Adam leaned back in his chair and huffed out a breath. "I'm sorry, Chal. Welcome to the family. But, if you ever—"

"Shut up," she repeated.

Chal barely had time to digest Adam's partial apology before the excited question came from his mom. "So, you are pregnant?"

"No. No way." Angela waved her hands in front of her. "That's not at all what I planned to say."

"Thank the stars," her father mumbled.

What a tough family. Chal clasped her thigh and shook his head.

Probably best she didn't tell them now.

"Yes." Angela stood and planted her palms on the table. "I'm going to be leaving Earth for a while, and none of you can stop me. I'll be teaching the Memonons about living here, and when they all come down to this planet, I'll be helping them to adjust."

Not exactly how he'd hoped to tell them, but her family knew now and Chal braced for their objections.

Immediate silence followed, the tension like a balloon about to burst. They were thinking of a way to keep her from going with him, breaking them apart.

Her father finally furrowed his brows. "I think...I think that is very commendable. Similar to what your mother did for me, only on a much larger scale."

Her mother nodded at Chal. "Yes, she told us what happened to the Lisivians. We wouldn't want that to happen to your people. If there is anything we can do to help, too, let us know."

"I, uh...." Not the reaction he'd expected at all. Had he suddenly shifted dimensions? "Thank you."

"I'm sure Dad and I could hire on a couple of guys. Or women," Adam quickly added in. "To work for us. Help them get their feet on the ground."

"Wow." Her family had completely surprised him. Maybe their problem was with him, not his people. "Thank you."

"We all know what it's like to be outsiders on this planet." Adam nodded to Angela, smiling for the first time since Chal had met him. "We want your kind to feel as welcome here as we do now."

She sat and squeezed his hand under the table, her eyes glassy as if she might cry.

"Of course, we're going to miss you like crazy," her mom said. "So, you have to visit as often as possible, call even more."

"And no getting married without inviting us," her father added, glancing over to Chal. "That I will not approve of."

"I would never do that, Dad." A tear escaped. "I need you to be there to walk me down the aisle."

They spend the rest of the evening sharing stories of times when they'd almost revealed their alien secret to the wrong people. And Chal told them about the first time Angela's eyes had changed, an occasion he'd been lucky enough to witness. Their uncertain evening had turned into a joyous one. He could only hope the rest of the planet welcomed his people as easily as her family had welcomed him, even with a few bumps—or brothers—along the way.

Angela unclenched her fists, the now familiar tingle of regeneration leaving her body. Beside her, Chal sat in his chair, more anxious than ever to walk on his own again. The next time they left the ship, along with every other Memonon still on board, he should be on his feet.

Without informing her brothers, Gille had sent small teams of Memonons to Earth to explore, and if all went well, settle. One group had located an abandoned town, which they'd managed to get permission to occupy and restore. They'd studied the local culture, and succeeded in fitting in. But, it was those who knew nothing of Earth she had to educate.

A hover chair darted toward Chal, coming to rest beside him. She moved forward to help him switch from one chair to the other, but he shook his head. "I think I've got this."

And he did, his legs supporting him during the transfer. No wobbling or buckling of his knees, he was determined to get out of the chair and back on his feet for good.

"Welcome back!" Vega sat at the console of the transporter room, her head wrapped in thick bandages from her recent surgery. "So, how did your family take the news?"

Angela stepped from the platform. "Better than expected. How about your procedure?"

Glancing up, Vega patted her head wrap. "I must have taught Thun well by example, because I'm still alive." She faced Chal. "So's your sister."

Angela sucked in a deep breath, letting go of her animosity toward Gille with the exhale. She'd be working side by side with the First-in-Command, getting all the Memonons prepared to live on Earth. Adapting to a new culture wasn't the only challenge—they had to look Terran, too. Gille and the doctor had already started by having their flares removed. Where the males could control the protraction of their flare, the women couldn't, the webbed spikes on display at all times.

"Good to hear." She hugged the doctor before reaching for Chal's hand. "I'll need a couple of days to get some lessons together, but in the meantime, is our room ready?"

"Yes, it is." Vega gave a knowing smile. "You're in the family quarters on deck four. Room nineteen. Think you can get there on your own?"

"I'm sure of it." Chal squeezed her hand, his chair taking him toward the exit before her feet got the message to move.

She rushed to keep up, anxious to get to their first apartment together.

Not his place where she'd had to stay at because she'd been kicked out of hers. And definitely not her childhood bedroom where she'd refused to do anything but kiss him out of fear her parents might hear. It would be their home, at least until they left for Earth, where they would live in a place all their own.

Entering the family quarters, she jumped as a little Memonon girl with her head bandaged darted past her, chasing a younger boy, possibly her brother. The children had been on the ship all along, just not in the medical wing she'd been cooped up in. Many adults gathered in the common area, conversing and lounging on sofas set into the floor. Kids played all around, some of them intent on winning a game on a holoscreen, and others, a bit older than the rest, tucked into a corner for a private conversation.

Chal stopped in the middle of the hall. "What is it? Why are you so happy all of a sudden?"

"This." She stuck her arms out and spun in a circle. "It's so normal. They're all going to fit in just fine on Earth." If she didn't know better, she might believe they were all from her home planet.

"I hope so." He rotated his chair around, somehow managing to scoop her into his arms. "But, right now, it's time for you and me."

Zooming along the perimeter of the room, he found the entrance labeled nineteen and touched his thumb to the lock pad. The door slid open and he carried her inside, over the threshold. "Welcome home, gorgeous."

She didn't have time to take in their new apartment, with Chal racing to the bed and depositing her onto it. Heaving himself from the hover chair, he rolled onto the bed and sidled up to her. He leaned forward to kiss the corner of her lips, running his hand along her side. "I can't believe you're here. When I first met you, I never expected you to be my bond mate. And even after we got together, I didn't think you'd want to come here, to help my people learn to live on Earth."

Angela chuckled. "When I first met you, I thought you were an asshole. I never suspected you to be alien, and definitely didn't expect to be sharing a bed with you."

He rolled on top of her, propping himself up on his elbows. "But then you saw my charming side."

"No, I was tired and delirious. And you were a better option than Jason."

Chal winced. "Please don't mention him again."

"Why? You jealous?" She lifted his shirt at the hem, running her palms across his back, drawing him closer. "Because I never wanted him. You're far hotter with your man bun and all." Reaching up, she tugged out the elastic, letting his hair fall around his face.

He groaned, rocking against her. "I want you."

"I know, it's been awhile." She stuck her thumbs under the waist band of his shorts. "But we need to remove our clothes before—"

He sat up, straddling her waist, and ripped her shirt open before she had the chance to finish her sentence. Snapping open the front of her bra, he palmed her breasts, eliciting a heavy sigh from her. She hadn't realized how much she craved his touch until that moment.

Raising her hips, she shimmied out of the rest of her clothing before helping Chal out of his, seeing him in all his naked glory. His native markings turned her on beyond belief, no matter how many time she saw them, traced the patterns across his skin.

Condoms! "Where are the condoms?" She didn't want to be in the middle of a moment only for it to disappear while they searched for protection.

"We have something better." He reached for a bottle on the nightstand. After flipping off the lid, he spritzed a clear liquid onto his cock. In an instant, the stuff formed into a thin cover from his tip down to the base of his shaft. "All set."

She straddled his waist, anxious to take the lead. Chal had regained control over his muscles, but she didn't want him to tire too fast. Grasping his shoulders to anchor herself, she slid over his shaft and leaned forward to kiss her man. Her soul mate. She'd finally located him after several years believing he didn't exist. But he did, and they were together, making love in their new home. Whether by fate, or simple alien attraction, she'd found the man she would spend the rest of her life with. No matter where it may take them.

TAKEN BY THE BILLIONAIRE
ALIEN NEXT DOOR
A BONUS STORY

Moving into a new home always proves stressful, but moving into a mansion bigger than all the houses I've ever lived in combined left my head spinning. Growing up, I had daydreamed with my mother about her marrying a billionaire, but I'd never expected it to happen. And I didn't reckon she would meet him while working at a museum of used props and costumes from old sci-fi television shows and movies. I mean, the geeks who filled the place failed to notice the cleavage showing in her low-cut tops. But, she did meet her billionaire, and I'd just unpacked the last box of the day of my belongings in my new bedroom in his house, a space with a closet and bathroom each larger than the last room I'd called my own. The best birthday present ever. As of today, I was legal to drink, vote, and everything in between in every state.

I didn't plan to live in Stephan's house for long, especially since my mother didn't need me to help her pay rent any longer. But Stephan had insisted I stay, at least until I finished community college, since continuing my education hadn't been an option before Mom met him.

Breaking down all the empty boxes, I groaned at the thought of having to interact with my new stepbrother, thirty-year-old Barron, a six-foot-two douche bag who still lived at home. Sure, he worked for his father's investment firm, but he had more than enough money to live on his own, a fact he rubbed in my face the few times we'd met. Otherwise, he'd never said much else, giving me the evil eye over dinner, as if I tried to take his fortune away. Hardly! I wanted my mom to be happy, and Stephan Gaskill managed to do that.

Though, I wouldn't experience their joy for the next month, since Barron happened to be my only company while the happy couple toured Europe on their honeymoon. Sure, the house had a staff of twenty, but they all had their own duties excluding keeping me company.

I gathered the flattened boxes and headed out of my room, to put them in the trunk of my car. But I needed to park the convertible Stephan had given me—a welcome-to-the-family gift—in the garage at the far end of the property. And I didn't have a remote—the one my new stepfather ordered had not arrived yet. Which meant hunting down my stepbrother for his. After sending him a quick text, I waited for his answer. The house had an intercom system, but it didn't reach every room. I figured a direct text would be the fastest and easiest way to get in contact with him. Five minutes passed and no answer came. He either didn't have his phone on him or was ignoring me. I assumed the second option, given how welcoming he had been when I'd pulled up earlier in the day with my belongings. The simple text he'd sent then had said, *Door is open. Your room is at the top of the stairs.* Nice. Great company for the next thirty days.

Not wanting to leave the car outside with dark clouds looming, I shoved the boxes back in my room and headed out in search of Barron. I walked the east and west wings of the house, peeking inside open doors and putting my ear to the closed ones. Nothing. Returning to my room, I caught the scent of something delicious wafting up from the main floor. It reminded me of my grandmother's house, where fresh-baked food had never been in short supply. If she hadn't passed away before I'd turned eight, I would weigh three times what I did. Following my nose to the kitchen, I found one of the house staff busy cooking, I guessed our dinner, a meal Stephan insisted be eaten in the formal dining room.

I didn't know the cook's name, but he nodded and smiled. "Can I help you, Miss Erika?"

"Yes, I um.... Do you happen to know where Barron is?"

"Probably next door with Master Laken." He shook his head. "He spends most of his time over there. I'm not sure he even sleeps here anymore."

"What does he do next door?" And why did rich kids stay at home so long? If I hadn't felt obligated to help my mom, I would have moved out at eighteen. Maybe Barron and his friend still liked to geek out on video games, or maybe they were secret lovers?

"Heavens if I know. Though, while I feel sorry for the staff at the Montgomery's, I enjoy the hours when Master Barron is not around."

Interesting. I wasn't the only one who'd clashed with Barron. "Am I allowed over there? I have something quick to ask him and he's not answering his phone."

"Is there anything I can help you with?"

"Um, I need a key to the garage." I shrugged. "I don't suppose you have one."

"No, but I can call over to Bianca, the Montgomery's chef. She can let you in and point you in the right direction."

I clasped my hands together. "That would be great."

Staring out the kitchen window over to the Montgomery's, I tried not to eavesdrop on the man's conversation. The monstrous house appeared the same size as Stephan's, too big for only four people. Did all rich people live the same, with so much space they didn't have to interact with each other? And meeting Barron's friends held little appeal, not if they acted anything like him.

"Okay, you're good to go." The man tucked away his cell phone. "Head out the back door and follow the garden path over to the Montgomery's."

"Thank you." I exited the house, determined to find my stepbrother, bug him the way any sister should her brother. I had so many years to make up for.

"Be sure to tell Master Barron dinner will be served in an hour. It would be nice if you were both at the table this evening."

"Okay," I called over my shoulder. I hurried along the garden path, wanting to get the car parked indoors before the first raindrop fell. Though I doubted Barron would join me for the meal.

A pretty woman about the same age as our cook met me at the Montgomery's back door. Bianca? If so, I'm sure she traded more than recipes with our cook. "Miss Erika, it's great to meet you. I hope you are adjusting to your new home."

"Thank you." I curtsied, not sure where the instinct came from. "I just have a question for Barron if you can help me track him down."

"Sure." She led me to a set of stairs. "Down there to Master Laken's private area, where he likes to entertain friends."

"Thank you." I nodded this time and followed the steps down. Find Barron and go. I didn't want to be in anyone's *private area*, especially when I didn't know them.

In the first room on the lower level, what I assumed to be the den, not a single soul existed. If he spent all his time in the lower level, it wasn't in this room. Turned off, the flat-screen television sported a thin layer of dust, with a giant family portrait hanging on an angle above it. The picture must have been taken years ago, when the children had been in their early teens, not adults as I assumed they would be.

A faint hum came from my left, a noise reminding me of the constantly running factory a block away from where I used to live. Maybe it would lead me in the right direction.

As I traipsed down the hall past a multitude of closed white doors, the sound grew louder. But unlike the noise from the factory, this was a higher-pitched sound, almost like a song. I followed the hall as it veered to the right, a steel door at the end. Not inconspicuous at all. It had a simple lock on it, no keypad or anything complicated. So, what lay behind it couldn't be very valuable. Probably a maintenance room containing the furnace and other equipment to run the monstrous house. Since the latch hadn't caught and the door stood open a crack, I pushed it wider and peeked inside.

I spotted a guy who could be my stepbrother. Except he had dark hair and stood naked, save for a pair of tight silver shorts. Skin the color of golden honey covered wave upon wave of tight muscle. A flash of warmth washed over me as I imagined licking him all over, going down on my knees in front of him to find out if he tasted as sweet as he appeared.

Sure, I shouldn't fantasize about a stranger, but I couldn't help myself. Barron wasn't around, and this guy exuded sex appeal. A god compared to the strung-out sleazebags I'd had to choose from in high school. Maybe I craved some attention since I only had seven more hours before my birthday ended. A day I'd spent by myself, while my friends worked or took care of their brand-new babies.

But, I wouldn't have to be alone if I approached the eye candy in front of me and ripped off his tight shorts and discovered what hid underneath. Touch and taste and.... Oh, God! I crossed my legs, trying to ignore the throbbing of my pussy.

I sucked in a deep breath in an effort to gain control over my body. Could the hottie in front of me be Laken? And if so, where had Barron disappeared to? Changing my focus, I glanced beyond the guy's luscious body to see what captivated his attention.

With delicate movements, he traced his finger across intricate black patterns on the large, round steel object in front of him, part of a...a....

I stared, unable to move. I think my heart paused for a beat or two while my mind tried to digest the bulky mass in the center of the room.

A spaceship. An honest-to-goodness flying saucer. I gasped. If a model, its creator had designed a damn realistic one with perfect angles and the occasional dent. Maybe from impact with space debris. On the other side of the room, sliding metal doors, heavy chains keeping them closed.

The guy studying the craft spun around, rigid, as if in shock.

I jumped back, not only at being caught, but because of his eyes. They were black. All black. No white, no irises, just a glossy black.

I spun to leave, but the guy moved faster than any human should be able to, appearing in front of me before I made it out the door.

"Who are you? What are you doing here? And why...?" He sounded normal though, seemed like any other hot, red-blooded American.

"Erika." As I glanced down to avoid his creepy stare, a war broke out inside me. I couldn't help but notice his washboard abs and the large bulge in the front of his shorts. If not for the inhuman eyes and crazy-ass speed, I would jump him right there, no questions asked. "I'm Barron's stepsister. Is he here?"

"No, who told you he would be?"

"Bianca?" My voice came out in a squeaky whisper.

"Of course." He sighed. Actually sighed.

I dared a peek at his face again. His eyes looked normal this time, or mostly. His irises were a light blue, almost white, a color I had never seen before in humans, and they stood out even more in contrast to his wavy, dark-brown hair. But they weren't black, which made me wonder if I'd imagined the whole thing. Maybe a trick of the light? But nothing explained his speed, or the spaceship. I glanced over my shoulder to ensure it still sat there. Yep. One flying saucer in the basement of a billionaire's house.

"Your brother's not here."

"Stepbrother," I said automatically, returning my attention to Mr. Sexy. "Now, tell me, who are you?" I wanted to add *what are you*, but thought better of it.

"I am Laken."

"Then where is Barron?" For a brief moment, I worried about my new stepbrother. "What have you done with him?"

The sigh again, as if I'd asked the dumbest question.

Laken shook his head. "He's with my sister." Placing his palm on the wall, he leaned against it and crossed his ankles. "Always says he's coming over here to hang out with me then takes off with her. I only cover for him because I'd rather have both of them out of my hair. I prefer to be alone."

"So you can study the spaceship?" If not for the strange abnormalities, I'd assume him a science geek who'd built a giant model of some ship from a sci-fi show. But, no.

"Spaceship?"

"Yes, the one behind me." I crossed my arms. He couldn't pretend it didn't exist. The thing occupied half the room, at least fifteen feet in diameter, the space obviously designed to hold the craft.

"I, uh.... You don't...?"

Confused? Cute, but it didn't work on me. "Your sister, is she like you?" And did Barron know? Because I couldn't imagine him seeing anyone who wasn't rich, beautiful, *and* human.

He frowned. "Like me? You mean—"

God, I hated the playing-stupid routine. "Yeah, with the all black eyes, speediness, and such."

"What exactly do you think I am, Miss Erika?"

"An alien." There, I'd said it, and I expected him to laugh in my face and deny it.

Instead, he placed his hands behind his back and stepped nearer. "And what if I am?"

My breath caught. "I...." I should have kept my mouth shut. No, I should have waited for Barron to text a reply, never come over to the neighbor's house. Now, I was stuck in a basement hangar with a flying saucer and a guy who could be from another planet.

Laken inched closer, and closer still. I moved along with him until my back hit a wall on the other side of the room. Trapped. Trying to duck away wouldn't do me any good. He'd only race around and block my way again. My heart beat so hard, I expected it to thump right out of my chest. Would he let me go, or did he have other plans? If I screamed loud enough, would someone come to my rescue?

Leaning forward, he placed his palm on the wall behind me. "What if I told you I knew the instant you came into this room?" He ran his other hand along my cheekbone, tucking my hair behind an ear. "What if I told you I could feel your attraction, smell your sex?"

A shiver raced down my spine. Sure, I wanted to jump his bones before I'd seen his eyes. Now, I yearned for a way out, a clear path to escape from Mr. Sex-on-a-stick who may or may not be an extraterrestrial.

He dipped his head so close to mine, his warm breath brushed my neck. A flash of heat washed over me. Fuck, it had been so long since I'd been with any guy. Did it really matter where he came from?

"What if, Erika? If I am an alien? Would you still find me attractive? Would you still want to lick me from head to toe? Suck my cock? Would you want me to fuck you against this wall, in my spaceship, and on every single surface of this room?"

If not for him sliding his knee between my thighs, I would have melted into a puddle of lust at that moment. Who was I trying to kid? I had the hots for an extraterrestrial. I wanted to do everything he said, craved to feel his alien cock thrusting in and out of my pussy. Running away wouldn't work, and wouldn't satisfy my aching need.

I cupped the bulge in his pants. "Yes, I want all of that." I'd never had the opportunity to be fucked by a man of his caliber. Whether he came from Earth or beyond, I wanted to experience him.

Laken grasped my wrists, raising my hands above my head. Pressing his groin against me, he kissed along my jawline until his lips met mine. Hard, demanding, he plunged his tongue in my mouth, claiming it the way I wanted him to claim the rest of my body.

Releasing my wrists, he slid his hands down my arms, my sides, resting them on my hips. Synapses fired under my skin, demanding more from him. I pulled him even closer and wrapped a leg around his thigh. All worries about where he came from fled, lust remaining the only thing on my mind.

After cinching the skirt of my dress up, he leaned down and gripped the cheeks of my ass. His lips separated from mine for an instant, but enough to draw in a deep breath. God, I'd never expected to get fucked against the wall by a stranger when I'd walked into the Montgomery home, but now I didn't want to leave before it happened.

He lifted me, pinning me even tighter to the wall. I wrapped my legs around his waist, craving him closer, wishing the clothes between us would disappear so he could ram right into me.

Reaching between my legs from behind, he yanked my thong to the side, exposing my throbbing pussy. So close. I wanted to shake him, make him drop me so I could yank off his tiny shorts before hopping onto his glorious cock and going for a ride. But when he drew his finger across my clit, I shuddered.

Yes! Bright lights danced behind my closed eyes. I rocked across his finger, savoring what he offered.

"Hold onto me."

I snapped to attention, surprised by his sexy baritone voice. I'd forgotten what he sounded like. Clutching my wrists behind his neck, I did as he'd asked. Then he released me. If I hadn't had a tight hold, I would have crashed to the ground.

Hard lines of determination formed on his forehead as he worked around me to remove his shorts. I had to cross my ankles behind his back, losing my grip when he wiggled to get free from his clothing. After kicking the material across the room, he pinned me to the wall again. He kissed along my neck, down my chin, reigniting the rush of desire. The tip of his cock brushed along my labia. So close. Dangerously close. Fuck, what was I thinking?

"Laken, stop."

He rested his forehead on mine and stared into my eyes. Black again, but I refused to run. "What do you mean? You want to leave?"

I gripped the back of his head. "No! God, no. Maybe pause is a better word."

His cock flexed, and I jumped as it pushed through my entrance. Way too close.

I shimmied my hands between us and shoved his shoulder. "Condom." Lowering my feet to the ground, I planted my hands on his chest and pushed him back. "This isn't going any further until you put a condom on. I don't care who or what you are."

Sure, I used birth control pills to prevent pregnancy, but I didn't want some freaky disease from the alien next door.

He squeezed his eyes shut then opened them wide, as if hoping to make them look human again. But they remained a glossy black.

"Listen." I stepped closer and gripped his balls, rubbing the heel of my hand along the base of his cock. "I think you're hot, regardless of what you are. I want you to fuck me, but we need to use some form of protection."

"Okay." He nodded and placed a hand on my shoulder, squeezing gently.

A tingle spread through my body, beginning where his palm rested on my skin. Nothing like our desperate passion. Something different. More like frigid water rushing through my veins. When the sensation reached the tips of my fingers and toes, I disappeared. No other way to describe it. I stood there with Laken, and then I was gone, floating in nothingness. But, only for a few seconds. When I returned, I'd left the hangar.

Giant pillows covered in black satin cradled my naked body, my dress and undergarments having been left behind somewhere. Laken lay to my right, propping his head in one hand and brushing hair from my face with the other.

I pushed up onto my elbows. "Where are we?"

The circular room smelled of steel, but I couldn't see beyond the dark plush curtains hanging around the large...bed?

"In my room. I had to bring you here for protection."

"Yes, but how?" I drew in a sharp breath as he circled a finger around my nipple. It took every ounce of concentration to focus on my thoughts rather than his ministrations. "We were in that hangar room one second, and the next we were here. And I'm naked."

"Because I am what you believe me to be." He rolled onto me, pressing me deeper into the soft pillows. His knee between my thighs, he captured my lips in a hard kiss, sucking, plunging his tongue into my mouth, like our session in the hangar had never ended.

Yearning to clear some things up before I got it on with an

extraterrestrial, I turned my head to the side. "Hold up." I stared into his black eyes, examining them for the first time, knowing what I saw wasn't my imagination playing tricks on me. "You really are an alien? Like, from outer space?" I had to be sure, not feel like a fool when I learned my assumptions were incorrect.

He rolled back to my side. "Yes."

The curtain surrounding us parted, and with a whoosh, a panel folded out, opening to another room. No, not another room. We were still inside the hangar, but inside the spaceship. I was in a flying saucer.

Laken gestured toward the opening. "You can leave if you wish."

An invisible weight pushed on my chest. "You want me to leave?" Sure, I barely knew him, but in no way did I have any urge to leave. And it hurt to think he might wish me gone.

"No." He rolled onto his back, resting his hands behind his head. "But if you can't handle what I am, you're more than welcome to go back home."

I glanced out the door then back at him. He'd known my thoughts when I'd first noticed him, so he should have known what I hoped for then. Closing my eyes, I visualized what I yearned to do to him, what I craved for him to do to me.

He groaned, and I opened my eyes when his fingers dug into my hip bone. The ship's door had already closed, and the curtains swung shut. Laken's mouth hung open and his cock jutted straight up, ready for what I'd pictured.

Crawling between his spread legs, I grasped its base. So freakin' hard, I couldn't wait to feel him inside me. But first, I wanted a taste.

With gentle pressure, I eased the foreskin down to expose the swollen head. Bending over him, I ran my tongue over the tip. Spicy, like nutmeg and cinnamon. At his quiet moan, I grinned. So empowering to have an extraterrestrial from some unknown planet at my mercy.

Staring up at the enigma he was, I engulfed the entire tip.

He bucked his hips. "Sweet heavens," he hissed through his teeth.

When I took his whole cock in my mouth, he growled, the noise echoing around the spacecraft.

As I bobbed up and down, he thrust to meet me, never afraid to vocalize his pleasure. I'd never been with a noisy lover. But then, we weren't trying to hide what we were doing from parents or roommates.

The muscles in his legs tightened. His cock swelled even more, nearly doubling in thickness. Ready to blow, and he hadn't even fucked me yet. He'd be asleep in a matter of minutes. Oh well. I could only hope for an invitation to return. I clutched his slippery shaft in my hand and stroked, jerking him off until he released.

As the dark, sticky liquid shot across his chest, Laken jerked and twitched with an eerie silence. Had I done something wrong? Hurt him somehow?

I ran a hand over his thigh. "Are you okay?"

His eyelids flicked open, one eye black and the other human looking, with that piercing clear-blue color. One or the other I could handle, but not one of each. I crawled backward until I hit the curtain.

"Wait!" He sat up, his body clean, as if his skin had absorbed his release. "It's your turn."

He grabbed my ankles and yanked me across the pillows toward him. My feet were in the air and his tongue buried in my pussy before I had any chance to speak—though I had no objections. He hadn't fallen asleep after his release and seemed anxious to pleasure me, so I didn't dare say a word. I gripped the black satin, reveling in each swirl of his tongue, the way the muscle seemed to fold over itself, flicking my clit at the same time he thrust inside. The perks of being an alien? Or was he just plain gifted? I had no time to consider, desire pooling low in my belly. Heat flared across my skin. I erupted in a flash of euphoria, synapses firing from head to toe.

Reaching up my body, he pinched my nipples, sending another wave of rapture through me. I tilted my head back, longing for a deep breath and for my heart to stop pounding.

At the sound of crinkling plastic, I glanced around for him. It took me a few seconds to focus, but I found him to my left, tearing open a condom package. Pinching the tip, he rolled the thin latex over his shaft, obviously not a stranger to how they worked. Had he been with a lot of women from Earth? Did they all know his secret, too? Oh God, what if he fucked them then killed them to keep anyone else from finding out?

A gust of wind blew across my face. Laken kneeled between my legs, and used his strength to hold my arms above my head. "Jealousy and fear are very unbecoming for you."

Shit. He couldn't read my thoughts, but he'd come pretty damn close to sensing my emotions. I used to dream my boyfriends had such an ability. Now, I wasn't so sure I liked the invasion into my mind. "But, how many—"

"One." He ran his tongue along my jawline before nibbling the skin below my ear. My worries disappeared. My thoughts vanished. Delirium set in.

"I've only had one lover," he whispered in between his sensual assault on my neck. "We parted ways a few months back. She signed a contract to keep my secret, and I signed one to keep the secrets of her family."

His mouth left my skin, and he stared down at me, the tip of his cock resting outside my entrance. "The same way I will keep yours."

Mine? I didn't have any secrets. At least none he would know after meeting me less than an hour earlier. "But—"

He plunged, stealing away the rest of my words. *So thick.* I didn't think he'd have room to move. Full, I felt unbelievably full. Yet, I experienced no pain. Only a heightened sensitivity to his every motion.

"You're like me, Erika." He managed gentle strokes, pushing deeper with each one. "I knew from the moment you stepped into my hangar."

"No." The word came out in a whimper, not because of what he'd said, but I didn't think I could handle any more of his cock inside of me, my head ready to explode from the buildup of energy. I couldn't concentrate on his words, what he had told me, only the fullness immersed in my core. The urge to push him out battled with the desire for more. I held on tight to his biceps, unable to control the increasing pressure.

Laken grabbed my hips and thrust harder. Faster, burying himself until he could go no farther. He lifted my legs onto his shoulders and pounded my pussy. The tension never let up. I yearned for release, my body ready to burst into flames.

"C'mon, baby. It's time to come for me." Switching to long, slow strokes, he brushed his thumb over my clit—the spark I needed.

I cried out as the waves of ecstasy took hold. Gripping the cushions around me, I writhed under him. He never let up, continued to grind in and out, keeping me in a state of bliss. I'd never come down from such a high before, yet still couldn't find the ground. I abandoned the search, heading for another release.

He held my thighs against his chest and drove his cock. Jolts of pleasure raced through me as I detonated for a second time. Electric tension like no other.

Laken groaned with his own release, his magnificent body shuddering. "Oh, Er-i-ka."

When he stopped convulsing, he lowered my legs and leaned down to kiss me. The urgency and lust were gone, his lips filled with passion, as if we weren't strangers. Like we'd made love hundreds of time before.

Made love? No. I barely knew him. He was an alien. A billionaire alien, for fuck's sake. And me, a poor girl who had a new, rich stepfather. But, I could never change where I came from.

Laken kissed my nose, my forehead, my cheeks, slipping out of me. "Gods, that felt so good, to be with someone of my kind."

I missed the pressure of him inside me. Shaking my head, I pushed the emptiness aside and focused on what he had said. "Your kind?" He'd admitted being from another planet. But, I wasn't. Nope, born and raised in a public housing development. Not Tent City, but nothing like the gated community we lived in now. And definitely not another planet.

"Yes, your father—"

"Was never around." I tried to push Laken off, but he held tight. "He fucked my mom and left the next morning, said he'd grab them some breakfast but never returned."

"His name was Andreas." He brushed a piece of hair from my forehead, ignoring my objections. "He came to Earth with my family. But the government discovered him. Probably the morning after you were conceived."

Impossible. My father was a good-for-nothing asshole who'd used my mother and tossed her away when he'd gotten what he wanted, not some space traveler stolen away before he knew he would be a father.

Laken said, "My parents tried to locate him, rescue their friend from the compound where the government held him. But, by the time they found him, he was dead."

A lump formed in my throat. "No."

"He would have made a wonderful father. And, you kind of look like him."

My heart slammed against my ribs, trying to escape. Tears burned the corners of my eyes. "Then why didn't—"

"Shh." He wiped my cheeks. "No one knew he'd conceived a child. Otherwise, my parents would have brought your mother here to live with us, help raise you. But, I recognized your soul the moment I turned around. It's the reason I can read you so well."

"You're making this up." Somehow, he'd tapped into my psyche, feeding me what I'd wanted to hear my entire life. Or something like it. A story that made my father out to be a hero rather than a piece of dog shit.

"Can't you sense it?" Still keeping his weight on me, he reached over for another condom, taking the old one off and replacing it with a new one. He licked the skin between my breasts then ran his tongue up my boob to circle my nipple. "Can't you feel our connection?"

When he slid back inside, I felt whole again, but not because my father came from another planet. I simply enjoyed sex. With Laken.

"You don't need to make shit up to fuck me." I wrapped my leg around his, knocking him off balance and onto his back. Bracing my hands on his shoulders, I eased back onto his cock. "Please don't feed me any more lies."

He was the best fuck I'd ever had, but it would never happen again. This would be my last orgasm with him and I planned to make it the best one yet. I rocked my hips, focusing on nothing but my driving hunger, the bottomless ache for another release. My mind whirled each time his dick hammered my G-spot.

Heaven! The electric tension barreled through me, a spiraling end to our time together. His cock swelled right before he crested. He pulled me down to his chest, holding me tight as he emptied his seed. Thank goodness I'd insisted on a condom. Who knew what the crazy alien might have spread to me if I hadn't? Or maybe he wasn't an alien at all, just skilled at creating illusions.

I struggled free from his arms, ready to find my clothes and head home. Never would I take the path through the garden to the Montgomery's again.

Laken didn't stir, didn't say a word. But, burning tingles ran up and down my spine as he watched my every movement.

Crawling to the edge of the array of pillows, I brushed the curtains aside. The door remained closed. I rose to my feet and palmed the cold, gray steel, hoping to push it ajar.

A white light flashed in front of me. Temporarily blinded, I blinked hard, trying to regain my vision. Instead of the wall of the spaceship, long, brown grass blew across an open field. Far in the distance, the sun glinted off a large object partly embedded in the ground. Seven black inky figures sauntered toward me, their forms becoming clearer with each step. Two were smaller—children hanging onto the hand of an adult. One of the tall figures limped behind, struggling to keep up with the others. Who were they and what did they have to do with me? Cold steel met my palm, making the vision just that—a vision. A gift from Laken or the ship itself?

I focused on the children, curious to understand who they were, why they existed in my delusion. A boy and a girl, both around eight or nine, they had dark, wavy hair, the boy's much shorter, feathered around his forehead and ears. Familiar. I'd seen them both not long ago. Yes! In the den on the way to the hangar. The family from the portrait. Laken and his sister, their parents holding their hands.

Then I noticed their eyes. All black. All seven pairs. Alien. They wore silver jumpsuits, the material dirty and ripped in places. Was this the day they had arrived on Earth? The day they'd crash landed? The Montgomerys and...?

I didn't recognize the woman or the man beside the family. But they vanished, everyone from the vision except the man limping. My stomach twisted. I hadn't seen him clearly before, blocked by the others, but now I could not mistake his identity.

Oh God, Laken hadn't lied. A tear trickled down my cheek. I'd always thought I looked like my mother. Not anymore. I was built like my father, compact up top, with long legs. We shared the same nose and chin, the same straight, walnut-colored hair.

The man had a large gash covering his right thigh, his injury slowing him down. My mom had mentioned playing nurse to my father the night she'd met him. I'd tuned out, not wanting to hear about their kinky sex. Yet, she hadn't meant it that way at all.

I reached out to him, yearning to help him, talk to the man I'd never known. But I couldn't push past the edge of the ship. The vision faded and I fell back on my ass, my head spinning from the revelation about my father. About myself and what I was.

Strong arms surrounded me, pulled me against a warm chest. Laken kissed the top of my head. He never said a word, simply held me as I shook and sobbed, my heart breaking. My father, stolen away from my mom and me.

When the tears subsided, I crawled off his lap, embarrassed by my blubbering outburst. Like he wanted to be a part of that.

Feather-soft kisses danced across my shoulders. He rubbed my arms from behind. "I'm so sorry."

I spun. "Don't be. I'm glad I finally know the truth. My dad wasn't a deadbeat." Just dead.

Laken traced his finger along the back of my hand. "No, he was a well-respected member of our crew."

Gazing into his dark eyes, I let the last of my sorrow wash away. "Will you tell me about him tomorrow?"

"What I remember, sure, but why not right now?"

I checked my watch. "Because I have about five minutes before I'm expected back home for dinner." Leaning forward, I pushed on his chest, knocking him back on the pillows. "But first—"

Laken yanked me down on top of him before flipping me onto my back. "I'm going to fuck my alien girlfriend."

"Girlfriend?" I'd only met him, but after the recent revelation, I couldn't imagine being with anyone else.

"Yep." He reached for another condom then rolled it over his cock. "We might as well have some fun while I teach you all the things you can do."

I didn't care what I could do at that moment. I wanted him inside me, craved the connection. One person to another. One alien to another. Spreading my legs, I grasped his hips and tugged him toward me. As his cock slid into me, I sighed. Pure bliss.

I'd begun the day a stranger in a new neighborhood, a new life. But, by the end, I'd found myself, and a hot, alien boyfriend.

Laken held me tight, gently rocking his hips. And we kissed. No desperation. Only passion. A deeper bond than I'd ever imagined possible in such a short time. Our bodies moved in sync and I reveled in the intoxicating rapture before surrendering to divine ecstasy.

ABOUT THE AUTHOR

Jessica E. Subject is the author of science fiction romance, mostly alien romances, ranging from sweet to super hot. Sometimes she dabbles in paranormal and contemporary as well, bringing to life a wide variety of characters. In her stories, you could not only meet a sexy alien or two, but also clones and androids. You may be transported to a dystopian world where rebels are fighting to live and love, or to another planet for a romantic rendezvous.

When Jessica is not reading, writing, or doing dreaded housework, she likes to get out and walk with her giant, hairy dog her family adopted from the local animal shelter.

Jessica lives in Ontario, Canada with her husband and two energetic children. And she loves to hear from her readers. You can find her at http://jessicasubject.com and on twitter @jsubject. You can also subscribe to her electronic newsletter at http://eepurl.com/eX1Zw.

www.ingramcontent.com/pod-product-compliance
Lightning Source LLC
Chambersburg PA
CBHW061202170626
46809CB00003B/1203